Praise for DEA

'A very funny and sparkling début from a writer who is here to stay' Joseph O'Connor

'It's hilarious ... everything from existentialist nuns to hard ass girls. Every single man should read it to affirm how sad we really are' Dermot O'Leary

'An insightful, very funny novel about the confusions of growing up, at whatever age. A fresh and absorbing peek into the mind of a bloke who's never quite got around to facing up to life' *Heat*

'If you really want to know how men behave when they're behaving really badly, read this. This is very funny' *Company*

About the Author

Damien Owens was born in Monaghan in 1971 and studied English at Queen's University, Belfast. He has worked as a copywriter and a technical writer, and has contributed to a number of magazines. He now lives in Dublin. *Dead Cat Bounce* is his first novel.

DEAD CAT BOUNCE

Damien Owens

FLAME
Hodder & Stoughton

Copyright © 2001 by Damien Owens

First published in Great Britain in 2001 by Hodder and Stoughton
A division of Hodder Headline

The right of Damien Owens to be identified as the Author of the Work has been
asserted by him in accordance with the Copyright, Designs and Patents Act 1988.

A Flame paperback

2 4 6 8 10 9 7 5 3 1

A CIP catalogue record for this title is available from the British Library

ISBN 0 340 79283 3

Typeset in Fournier by Palimpsest Book Production Limited,
Polmont, Stirlingshire
Printed and bound in Great Britain by
Clays Ltd, St Ives plc

Hodder and Stoughton
A division of Hodder Headline
338 Euston Road
London NW1 3BH

This is for Eileen and Marie and Eithne.

ACKNOWLEDGEMENTS

Special thanks are due to my agent, Faith O'Grady at the Lisa Richards Agency in Dublin, and to my editor, Angela Herlihy, at Hodder and Stoughton in London. Stars, both.

I also want to acknowledge the support and help of all those friends who had to put up with a lot of whining about how this book would a) never be finished and b) never be published. Although all of my friends (and several strangers in the street) had to hear about it ad nauseam, chief among the whinees were John Bond, Trish Byrne and Christine Doran. Thanks for not punching me.

1

As a place to meet your friends for a drink, Jolly's had only one thing going for it – it served drink.

There was no Jolly, of course. The place was run by a huge Corkman called Leonard, who was anything but. It might, with greater accuracy, have been called 'Miserable's' or simply 'Bastard's'. It was dark, shabby, and always smelled vaguely of burnt toast. We could be found there two or three times a week, muttering sincere complaints and not moving. That's the Irish for you.

It was a Friday night and it was the usual crowd – Stevie, Go-go, Norm, and me – talking the usual load of complete toss. I had begun to tune out, staring blankly at what later turned out to be Catherine's ass. Well, I mean it later turned out that her name was Catherine. I recognised it as an ass straightaway, and a bloody good one. She was standing nearby with two other girls and a bloke, probably moaning about Leonard's almost comic prices, or his gracious serving style ('You. What?') I idly assumed that the bloke was her boyfriend. She looked like the got-a-boyfriend type. And I hadn't even seen her face properly yet.

'You're a jammy bastard,' I remember Stevie saying, as I dragged my eyes away. 'Jammy, jammy . . . *bastard*.'

'Who is?' I asked, although I could have guessed he was talking about Norm. If I passed a stranger on the street and they were talking about some jammy bastard, I would have assumed they were talking about Norm.

'This gobshite,' Stevie said, pointing his thumb in the predicted direction.

'You've either got it or you haven't,' Norm said, smug as you like.

Go-go hooted and rolled his eyes. 'If what you've got is it, then I'm glad I haven't got it, and I hope I never get it,' he said.

I had completely missed the start of this. 'Remind me again what you're on about?' I asked.

'Wednesday night,' Stevie said, patiently. 'I met Jammy here for a quick pint in town, and he fecked off with some nurse.'

'She was a doctor,' Norm interrupted. 'Not a nurse.'

'What was her name?' Go-go asked.

'Doctor something,' Norm replied, not even trying to be funny. 'Anyway, you should've seen this one. Stevie, what was she like?'

Stevie shrugged. 'She was . . . very . . . attractive.'

There was a pause as we waited for him to elaborate. He didn't, so Norm forged ahead.

'Anyway, the interesting part of this story is not that I caught the eye of some stunning beauty in a pub and she felt drawn to me – you have to expect that. No, the interesting thing here is the way matters proceeded. Now. We're getting on grand – do you come here often, I like your watch, I hate this song . . .'

'Where were you at this stage?' I asked Stevie.

'I'd fucked off home,' he said. 'No point in hanging around.'

Norm nodded. 'Once I get 'em talking, boys, I'm not coming back. You might as well get your coat and go.'

'Well, it's either that or you come back in such a stink that you're not worth talking to. Either way, there's no point staying.'

Norm ignored the slight and went on with the story. 'So. We wind up back in her place – cup of coffee, I like your plants, where'd you get the beanbag, you know how it goes. Before long, we're climbing all over each other. Things are progressing well, and then she starts to get all serious, you know, *talking*.'

'Uggggh,' mocked Go-go. '*Talking*.'

'All about herself, of course, how men treat her like shit, how nobody can see past her looks, how they're all after one thing. I told her it wasn't true, we were after *one of two* things, but she never even laughed.'

The three of us tried to suppress smiles but couldn't.

'Yeah, I know, a fucking great line. She never even smiled. So on she goes about her intelligence, her sensitivity, her love of the outdoors, etc, etc, etc. I was getting really bored, and I still had one hand up the back of her shirt, which was starting to look a bit stupid, what with all the bloody talking going on. So I thought I better declare my intentions.'

'And?' I said.

He cleared his throat. 'I told her that was all well and good, but personally speaking, and I was only speaking for myself here – I fancied the hole off her.'

We shook our heads in disdain.

'Next thing you know,' he continued, 'she's leading me by

the hand off into her bedroom. Not a word out of her. Big smile, though. All pleased.'

'I don't get it,' Go-go said.

'Me neither,' I added.

'Well, *listen*, I'm not done yet. Later on, we're lying there, and it's driving me mad, I have to know. So I ask her. Why the big change of heart? One minute it's all men are horny scum, then wham! – *Basic Instinct*. Just like that. And you know what she says?'

Shakes of the head all round.

'She says she was "touched" when I told her I could see "beyond her body" to "the whole woman".'

'When did you say that?' Stevie asked.

'I *didn't*. It turns out, right, it turns out when I said "I fancy the hole off you", she thought I said "I fancy the whole of you".'

He made a sweeping gesture to suggest wholeness. Our jaws dropped. There was a moment's quiet as we all struggled to find the words. That was when a pale hand patted Norm on the shoulder. It was Catherine, or The Girl With The Ass, as I knew her then.

'I couldn't help but overhear your . . . conversation,' she said in measured tones, 'and I just wanted to let you know that you are the most pathetic bunch of wankers I have ever come across in my whole life.'

I know – I *know* – that Norm was going to make some joke about her 'coming across' him any time she liked, darlin', but he didn't get to speak. She was off on one.

'Is this really how you talk about women? Buncha schoolboys. Buncha children. Your type makes me sick. Jesus Christ. What's the matter with you? Frigging *Loaded* readers.'

Christ, was she mad. And heart-stoppingly pretty. Brilliant

blue eyes and high cheekbones. Pale as a stone. Petite, but athletic-looking. It was like Claire Danes and Winona Ryder had a baby.

'How do you think it makes a woman feel, having to listen to this sort of shite in a public place? You go out for a quiet drink, talk to your friends, have a laugh, and you get *this*.'

She was wearing a crisp white shirt, black trousers, and sturdy black boots. She looked . . . tough. She made her girlfriends, who were watching this exchange with puzzled faces, look frilly and semi-transparent.

'It makes me want to puke. *Wankers*.'

Did I fall in love with her at first sight? Absolutely. But then she was the third girl I'd fallen in love with that day. Number two had been walking out of Jolly's as we walked in.

'Jesus. The nerve of you. The *cheek*. What, are you retarded or something? A wee bit special, are yiz?'

She blanched suddenly then and put her hand to her mouth. It had obviously just occurred to her that one or all of us might indeed be 'special'. We were probably staring at her with dopey expressions, in all fairness, and Norm's story hadn't been a particularly edifying one. But even by our standards, this was not a proud moment. She backed away slightly, and for one brief second looked ready to cry. If we'd all kept quiet, just shut it for ten seconds, she might have turned, grabbed her mates, and left. We would have become a terrible memory for her, the unfortunate simpletons she insulted one night in a horrible pub. 'I didn't know!' she would have told her friends, in tears of shame. 'I thought they were normal! I DIDN'T KNOW!'

That might have happened, but it didn't. Instead, Norm fixed her with a beady eye and declared, at considerable volume, 'Lesbians! You're all the bloody same.'

Well, she broke his nose. She threw herself across the table, spilling pints everywhere, and introduced her tiny fist to Norm's substantial nose with a gut-skewering sound that I can only describe as a 'crick'. One day someone is going to ask me if I know what nose cartilage sounds like when it suddenly leaves its natural home in the centre of a person's face for a new life underneath their right eye. 'Why, yes,' I will say. 'It goes *crick*.' Norm went spinning off his chair, blood and snot already gushing, as the rest of us jumped to our feet and . . . well, and nothing actually. We just jumped to our feet. Any kind of fighting would have been pretty much virgin territory to us. Fighting with a girl was brand-new material. Catherine – or The Girl With The Ass Who Broke Norm's Nose, as I now knew her – appeared quite stunned. Looking at her with something approaching awe, I mistook this for remorse. When she clapped her hands together and squealed with delight, I realised that it was in fact pride. Her friends had crowded around now, patting her on the shoulders and eyeing us with contempt. The solitary bloke among them marched up to me, presumably because I was the smallest, and poked me in the chest with his index finger.

'What the hell's going on?' he demanded, spraying me with saliva. 'What did you do to her?'

He was of average build, not much bigger than me in fact, but there's no doubt that he could have beaten me senseless if he'd wanted. I can say that with confidence because just about anyone can beat me senseless. The Girl With The Ass Who Broke Norm's Nose could have killed me stone dead.

'I didn't do anything to her!' I protested, adopting the classic arms-spread 'Who? Me?' pose that professional footballers often assume after they've kicked someone's kneecap off. 'We were having a quiet chat and she attacked us!'

This was foolish, on mature reflection, as it opened the door for her side of the story.

'Talking!' she howled, in mock horror, or maybe even real horror. 'Is that what you call it? Tricking poor defenceless women into bed with lies and then laughing about it behind their backs? You call that *talking*?'

Her friends, who clearly hadn't overheard us themselves, gasped and looked faint.

'It wasn't a lie!' cried Stevie, as if that helped. 'He did fancy the hole off her!'

Leonard appeared among us then, muttering long-suffering Break-it-ups. There was nothing to break up really, but everyone took a symbolic step backwards to form a small circle. Norm had made it back up onto his chair by now and was staring at the ceiling moaning almost inaudibly about assault charges.

'Out, all of you,' Leonard said, in a muted tone that suggested we could buy a drink first if we wanted to.

Since all any of us wanted was a swift end to the whole incident, there were no dissenting voices. The girl and her entourage sloped away quietly, still giving us the evil eye, and headed for the main door. They resisted the temptation to hurl further abuse as they left, which was something, I suppose. There were only a dozen or so other people in the place, and up until that point, they'd been holding their collective breath. Now that it was clear that there wasn't going to be real trouble, they seized the opportunity to laugh their arses off. Snatching ruefully at our jackets and staring hard at the floor, we made our way to the side exit.

Once outside, we stood around conducting a brief post-mortem. Though none of us would admit it, the real purpose of this pause was to avoid bumping into the other lot on the street. Looking at our feet, with an occasional nervous glance down the alley, we agreed that we had been treated harshly, not least by Leonard, who surely knew us by now. It would be a long time before we set foot in Jolly's again, we vowed. The viciousness of the actual blow was also discussed. Worthy of a man, Stevie observed – a man who had really practised his punching-people-on-the-nose technique. There was wincing and some sympathetic murmuring as we took turns to examine Norm's ruined hooter. When a few minutes had passed, and we were sure the coast was clear, we sloped out of the alley onto the street and split up, Go-go gamely offering to accompany Norm to casualty. As I turned to go, I distinctly heard Norm remarking that his attacker had at least one redeeming feature.

'Some ass on her though, eh?' he said.

2

Looking for a flat in Dublin is a scarring experience, like attending a war, or a Christian Brothers school. I had five different places in my first eighteen months here, each one like something out of Hieronymus Bosch, only colder and damper, with less pleasant characters.

And the landlords ... oh, the landlords. After a few days of it, you start to hate yourself because you own a perfectly good kitchen knife, yet still you let them live. 'Compact,' they nod, spreading their arms in some shit-brown little box and almost touching opposing walls. 'Convenient,' they wink, as the roar of passing traffic shakes the stolen Jameson ashtray from the three-and-a-half-legged coffee table. 'Furnished,' they boast, patting the ripped cushion on the ripped couch, shiny with age and lumpen with use. 'Frank and Benny are very happy here,' they conclude, gesturing to the dribbling middle-aged civil servants who could be your new flatmates. Frank and Benny invariably look like famous serial killers. They'd be happy anywhere without bars. (True story: when Fred West was arrested I sat bolt upright in my armchair and told the TV, 'Christ! I nearly moved into a flat in Ranelagh with that bastard!') You look at the landlord despairingly and think, I'm going to have to murder you now. But you don't say that. You say: 'I'm going to have to think about it.' Because, God help you, this might be the best place you see.

These are my excuses, anyway, for how I came to live at 23C Grosvenor Gardens. I had just been through three weeks of flat-hunting hell, enduring the wind and the rain, the barefaced lies told in the evening paper, the tedious trudging around, the absurd asking prices, the endless queues of Goths and hippies that somehow always got there before me (they have a network of some kind, I'm convinced). I had flicked fizzing light-switches, turned rusty taps, and patted profoundly springless beds until I could flick, turn, and pat no more. My feet felt like raw mince. My brain felt like cooked mince. I was vulnerable, and could smell defeat in the air.

The ad in the paper cheerily described 23C as a 'Neat flatlet with all cons'. Praying that the word 'mod' had been left out accidentally, I dragged myself through the drizzle one more time. It turned out, surprise, surprise, to be a badly furnished bedsit that received almost no natural light and was apparently decorated in some sort of belated tribute to nineteenth-century Poland. Still, it was actually quite a large room and was 'self-contained', a misleadingly upbeat phrase meaning that it had a shower and a loo of its own in a sort of alcove. What's more, the balding, sweating figure who showed me round (by spinning three hundred and sixty degrees on the ball of one foot and saying, 'Well, lad, here she is') didn't seem too objectionable. That is, he didn't appear to be actively evil, although he was a landlord and so had only a nodding relationship with the concepts of honesty and fairness. He was called Mal and I was given to understand that he had at least a dozen or so houses in his grimy empire, each divided into God knew how many flatlets. Best of all, there were no Franks and Bennys to contend with. As my search had gone on – and on and on – I had come around to the idea of living alone, even though this would mean the shame and ignominy of bedsitterdom. (A one-bedroom flat? Very funny. Not without a kidney sale – in a good market.) Twenty-three C was the third one I had seen and, though it still amazes me to this day, easily the best of them. Both of the others had smelled of things long dead, and the shared bathroom facilities were to be found a long way down draughty halls. One of them didn't even have a sink of its own. Still, the idea persisted, and even began to sound appealing. Living alone, I would at least be in sole control of my domestic affairs, and could work harder than ever on the screenplay which would soon propel me to fortune and/or fame. Anyway, when 23C proved itself to be habitable, if not ideal, I gave in.

The best thing about living alone, to my mind, is the sense of sanctuary. In times of crisis, you know you've got somewhere where you can have total peace to lick your wounds (or plot bloody revenge, as appropriate), without constant interruption from annoying housemates arguing about toilet roll or some such. The night of Norm's nasal misfortune should have been a case in point. I should have been able to go home, switch on the box, crack open a beer, and relax, safe in the knowledge that I was out of everyone's reach. But I had reckoned without the telephone, an invention I'm still not completely sold on. There was a Post-it note clinging precariously to ours.

JOE, it shouted. YOU'RE MOTHER PHONED. SHE WANT'S YOU TO CALL HOME URGENTLEY!!!!

Jesus H. Tapdancing Christ, I thought. What now? The note

had obviously been written by my downstairs neighbour Julie, who lived in the flat beside the communal payphone, and was its slave. I padded over to hers and knocked on the door. Moving with her customary speed, she struggled over to the door and cracked it open before barely two minutes had elapsed. As ever, the woody smell of hash accompanied her appearance between door and frame.

'It's yourself,' she pointed out, with a small smile. Julie liked me, I knew, probably because I could be relied on for Jaffa Cakes when the munchies struck. And the munchies struck Julie *a lot*. She was about thirty-five, I guessed, but it was hard to tell. Permanently dressed in leggings and a baggy jumper, Julie was not altogether unattractive, but so shockingly unhealthy-looking that all you could think of was getting her to sit down and take some soup or something. She looked a lot like how I imagine Celine Dion might look if she spent most of her time watching TV in the dark completely off her gourd. When I first moved in I had spent some time in her tiny flat – which although small was an actual flat, with no '-let' suffix – smoking and drinking and generally chewing whatever fat there was to be chewed. I gathered that Julie had been a teacher at one point, but she was so offhand about it that I thought it unwise to press the issue. There had evidently been a falling-out between herself and the Department of Education. Although we never argued and actually got on very well, I eventually stopped calling, mainly out of a vague sense of guilt. Julie was bright and sharp, when she wanted to be, and I somehow felt that my visits were contributing to her ongoing effort to simply sit out her life, as if it was a dance she couldn't do.

'Yup, it's me,' I confirmed, as she peered at me with bleary eyes. 'I saw your note.'

Julie blinked at me.

'Phone call?' I ventured. 'My mother?'

She snapped her fingers, or rather tried to and missed. 'Right, right. Yeah. That's right. You had a phone call.'

'I know. The note said it was urgent. Did it sound serious?'

She chewed on a fingernail and tried to dredge up some memory of this distant event. 'Yes,' she eventually said, with disturbing confidence. 'It sounded serious.'

I was shocked. The word 'urgentley' hadn't really impressed me all that much.

'Jesus,' I said. 'Actual serious, or, y'know, mother serious?'

This was asking a lot of Julie. She was really baked, even by her own very high standards (pun intended), and I was secretly impressed that she'd been able to write a note at all, never mind spell a good proportion of the words correctly. It would be an impressive achievement if she was able to distinguish between my mother's many phone voices.

'Mmmm. Uh. Mother serious, I would have to conclude.'

I relaxed slightly. The Dog was probably dead again. That is, our latest dog was probably dead. We went through dogs like nobody's business. 'OK. I'll give them a call. Thanks, Julie.'

'Nooooo problem.' She attempted a wink, not once but twice, and eventually had to settle for a simple blink.

As always, I felt a sudden urge to ask her if she was eating any actual food these days. Just as predictably, I also wanted to ask her how the hell she could afford all the drink and drugs on no obvious income whatsoever. Both urges passed in an instant, and I turned away.

I've probably been overly harsh about my flatlet. It did have one good point, in that it made me feel like an accomplished interior decorator. All I had to do was throw out Mal's shockingly ugly purple and black stripy curtains and hey presto, *Homes and Gardens*. Well, not quite, but the improvement was immediate and dramatic. The main problem, naturally, was space. When I first moved in, I spent a couple of happy days arranging and rearranging the few bits of furniture so that, finally, the table where I ate my baked bean sandwiches was as far away as possible from the two-ring mini-cooker where I fashioned them. Similarly, the narrow single bed was pushed to the diagonally opposite corner, remote from both cooker and table. The few clothes I possessed were crammed into a highly unstable wardrobe which, I was certain, would one day topple over and kill me as I tried to find a shirt. I also had a tiny portable TV perched on a stool by the 'bathroom'. A two-seater couch sat awkwardly against the back wall in a manner that reminded me uncomfortably of a dentist's waiting room. The most important item of furniture, a modest desk, was placed below the only window, whose sill was home to a crap portable stereo. The desk strained and creaked under an ancient Apple Mac and a ridiculously noisy printer, both of which wobbled precariously when I moved about. My plan had been to create a sense of space where there was none. In reality, it looked as if the room had been spun around so violently that centrifugal force had stuck everything to the walls, leaving a central plain of threadbare orange carpet upon which I paced endlessly.

Dropping my bag and coat, I went over to the kitchen – that is, the bit of the room that had horrible lino instead of horrible carpet – and raided the jam jar where I kept phone change. Frowning and sighing, I grabbed two fifty-pence pieces and a few twenties. But then a little voice in my head said 'urgentley' and I fished out the same amount again.

Although it was nearly eleven o'clock when I dialled my

mother's number, the phone was snatched up on the second ring.

'Joseph?' she said by way of greeting.

'Mum,' I smiled, or rather grimaced. 'What's up?'

'Joseph, I thought you'd never call. I've been waiting by the phone since six o'clock. If it's not one thing, it's another. Trouble, trouble, trouble, that's all I get.'

I waited for her to get to the point.

'Trouble, trouble, trouble,' she said again.

'What is it?'

'It's your sister. I don't know where to put myself. Merciful Jesus, your father would turn in his grave.'

She's pregnant, I thought.

'She's pregnant,' said my mother.

There was a pause as I considered a reply. Despite my good guess, this was quite a shock. 'Fuck me,' I said eventually.

Brief silence on the line.

'Well, thank God I was able to reach you,' she sniffed. 'Where would we all be without you? I was at sixes and sevens to know what to do. But you've cleared it all up for me. "Eff you." Never a truer word spoken. Thank you, Joseph, for those wise words.'

My mother, I should mention, is given to sarcasm in moments of stress. I struggled to think of a better line.

'When is it due?' I tried. The practical approach.

'End of May,' she replied. 'Just in time for your father's anniversary mass.'

I could hear a rustle as she made the sign of the cross. 'Is she upset?'

'That one! Upset? Are you joking? Do you know how she broke the news to me? "Mum," she says, and not a bother on her, "Mum, I'm going to have a baby in May."'

To my ears, that sounded like a perfectly reasonable statement of fact.

'Mmmm,' I said, trying to sound sympathetic, but unable to come up with a sympathetic sentence.

'Well, Holy God but you're a cool customer, Joseph. "Eff you" and "Mmmm". Is that all you have to say? Do you not even care who the father is?'

In fact, it hadn't even occurred to me to wonder.

'Who?' I whispered, suddenly concerned.

'Brendan Feeny,' she announced with as much scorn as she could muster. Which was a lot.

'Don't know him,' I muttered.

'Well, how would you? You're never here. I'll tell you this much – he hasn't even had the manners to come and introduce himself to me. Look at us, Joseph. Shamed before the whole town. Your father would tu—'

'Is Deirdre there?' I interrupted. 'Maybe I should have a word.'

'Huh! She's asleep. Sleeping like a lamb. And her poor mother down here on her own, worried sick, with no one to turn to . . .'

At last, she started to cry. I burped a quiet Guinness burp and looked solemnly at my feet. What a sensational start to the weekend. Viciously attacked in the pub, and now this, a fresh domestic catastrophe in a family that had recently cornered the market in calamity. As the sobs reached a crescendo, I grimly concluded that there was nothing for it. I would have to Go Home.

3

Going Home was something I tried to avoid in the normal course of events. Quite apart from anything else, it involved a three-hour bus journey along roads that, in places, appeared to have been recently carpet bombed. It also meant spending time in the waking nightmare that is Busáras, Dublin's eye-poppingly ugly central bus station which, to the virgin eye, resembles nothing so much as the set of *Taxi Driver*.

Busáras reaches a peak of unpleasantness every Friday evening when it seems that everyone in Dublin tries to leave at the same time through the same orifice. At least I was spared that extra misery on this occasion, opting for the eleven thirty Saturday morning service. Or rather, I opted for the bus that went at eleven thirty on average, but actually left any time between eleven fifteen and eleven forty-five, depending on the whim of the bus gods (to whom, of course, we are but playthings). There was an earlier departure, but I was trying to minimise my time at home — within reason. Arriving any later than early afternoon would send all the wrong signals. You had to watch your signals in my house.

There were quite a few people around that morning, squinting at the departures board with expressions of doubt, or sprinting frantically across the sticky floor when – a Busáras favourite, this – some bloke in an official-looking cap announced that their bus would now be leaving from a completely different gate to the one he had directed them to ten minutes earlier. I bought a ticket and sat down in the least grimy chair I could find close to my gate (or what was currently being called my gate). Assuming that those around me were going my way, I began to worry about which one of them I would end up sitting beside. Of all the many, many things that annoyed me about Going Home on the bus, the one that really got my dogs yapping was the sheer inevitability of my getting saddled with the least desirable seat-mate available. Over time, I had tried any number of strategies to avoid this difficulty, but to no avail. My first idea had been to jockey for position with an enthusiasm that bordered on violence, in the hopes of being on board first and getting a seat all to myself. There were a number of problems with this theory. For one thing, buses are a favourite mode of transport for the elderly and it just *looks bad* when you elbow one of them in the face as she shuffles gamely towards the door. More than once, I had to suffer filthy stares the whole way home, having neatly shunted some pensioner aside when the bus pulled in. And it plain old didn't work in any case. Even if I did get on early and nab a seat to myself, there were always too many passengers to allow me to keep it. So not only did I mark myself out as a selfish thug, I still had to share with whatever societal reject came sloping down the aisle with his egg-and-onion sandwiches.

I soon gave up trying to get on first, and experimented with a different formula – hanging around until the bus was nearly full. The rationale was simple. When the bus was nearly full,

I certainly wouldn't get a seat to myself, but at least I'd get to pick my seat-mate. Again, the scheme was a dramatic failure. I had foolishly assumed that there would always be a reasonable pool to choose from. This wasn't true. It wasn't even nearly true. Time after time, I climbed on the bus with fingers crossed, hoping that the only reasonable-looking girl in the queue had intimidated everyone else and was, even now, hoping she wouldn't have to sit alone for the whole trip. In reality, the only free seats were invariably located next to bulbous dermatology cases who were distinguishable only inasmuch as some of them sweated more than others. Worse still, when I chose my seat-mate myself, I had only myself to blame. After two hours and four lengthy anecdotes about the peace a man feels while fishing, I'd be punching myself on the thigh, convinced that I had managed to choose the worst of a bad lot.

So it was with some dread that I surveyed the current crop, discarding couples from my calculations on the grounds that they would be sitting together and posed no threat to my happiness. To my relief, there were quite a few of them, cooing and feeding each other boiled sweets or staring morosely into space, depending on the state of their relationship. Among them was a pair of lanky teenagers, who were in some discomfort because they had each refused to remove their hand from the other's back pocket before sitting down. For maximum contrast, they were seated beside a middle-aged man and woman who had clearly spent too much time waiting in bus stations together. She had some shopping bags arranged around her feet and periodically rummaged through them, apparently looking for nothing in particular. Meanwhile, he stared at the back of his hands as though they were a strange new life form. With mounting optimism, I realised that almost everyone there was with someone or other. And, unless I was

19

mistaken, there weren't enough passengers to fill a whole bus. It was looking good, and when the bus finally pulled in (at 11.42 a.m., by the way) I held back, letting everyone else climb aboard first. I was almost last to get on and – what rapture! – found that I had several options. Foolishly thinking that this unpleasant trip had gotten off to a remarkably good start, I slid into a seat towards the back and tried to make myself comfortable. The driver was just giving the engine a final gunning in preparation for blast-off, when someone outside slapped the side of the bus vigorously. A late arrival. I tensed slightly, but reassured myself that there were still several free seats. The doors swished open and an elderly female voice came whistling down the aisle.

'Oh, thank you,' it said, 'I thought I'd missed you.'

The driver got out of his seat and offered a helping hand to the new passenger.

'Come on now, I'm not that old,' said the voice. 'I'm grand, sit yourself down.'

The driver did as he was told, and the new arrival hauled herself up and in. I froze. It was a nun. A withered, pocket-sized nun. My mortal enemy! The worst of all possible seat-mates! I glanced around like a trapped animal. She wouldn't, surely, come all the way down the bus past several seats that she could have all to herself, just to spite me? My eyes widened in horror as she hobbled along the aisle, saying hello to literally everyone, individually. She moved like Tarzan through the vines, her bony hands gripping one headrest after another. At every moment she looked certain to fall, but still she kept coming. My skin crawled as I saw her go past one free seat, then another, then another. Frantically, I started trying to give off nutter vibes, twitching and rolling my eyes. But it was hopeless. She continued her relentless progress, and when I accidentally caught her eye I knew the game was up.

'Are you keeping this for anyone?' she inquired, with a toothy smile.

I couldn't pretend that I was, but considered pointing out that she could have a whole seat to herself not six feet away. 'It . . . I . . .'

'Good,' she said, and lowered herself in. 'Me feet's killing me.'

To explain my panic at being cornered by a nun, I would have to describe the depth of my feelings about religion. And I find that I can't. It's a problem that has plagued me for some time. I used to try to engage God-fearing associates in debate on the topic, but eventually gave it up because I invariably lost. Again and again I found myself backing down against people who said shatteringly stupid things like 'Go on then, *prove* there's no God.' I would become so tongue-tied, so utterly dumbstruck with incredulity and indignation, that I lost by default. So I don't even try any more, even though I am home to a contempt that is essentially bottomless. And by extension, I find true believers . . . unpalatable. Nuns, especially, give me the shivers. Some people get all freaked out by clowns. With me, it's nuns. A nun, as far as I'm concerned, is a grown woman who not only believes in Santa Claus, but wants to be an elf. The prospect of a three-hour lecture from one of them filled me with a terrible creeping dread. I never even considered the possibility that she might not feel like lecturing. She was a nun, I figured, and could no more pass on the chance to lecture a 'young person' than, say, Norm could pass on free beer. As the bus pulled out of the station and immediately ground to a halt in the Saturday shopping traffic, I retreated as far as I could into the corner, squeezing myself up against the window. Cursing my lack of a Walkman, I took out a book and glared at it, hoping for the same sort of effect a cat produces when it arches its back. But she attacked before we were out of the city centre.

'Not a bad day, thank God,' she said.

I didn't look up, but managed a 'Hmmph'. She's going to tell me about how God made the sunbeams, I thought.

'Are you going far?'

'Yes.'

'Me too. All the way, in fact.'

I stiffened.

'Do you like travelling by bus?' she ventured.

'No.'

'Oh, I love it, you get to meet people, don't you?'

'Hmmph.'

'It's more social, isn't it?'

'Hmmph.'

'And it's not uncomfortable.' She bounced on her seat to confirm this. 'Why don't you like it?'

I sighed and turned to face her, radiating bad temper. 'It takes too long,' I hissed.

'But sure, what's the hurry? One day you'll be an old fogey like me and everything will take time. A *long* time, for some things.'

I made no reply and she seemed to get the hint. Exhaling softly, she folded her hands in front of her, closed her eyes, and fell asleep. And that was how we sat, for almost an hour. This ancient, fragile nun napping quietly while I periodically cast dagger looks in her direction, certain that she would begin speaking in tongues, or worse, at any moment. But she remained so still and silent that I actually began to forget about her, and started worrying in earnest about the scene awaiting me down the road. There would be tears for sure. And shouting. I had had enough tears and shouting in the past two years to last me a lifetime, yet here was a fresh batch. Stevie was fond of saying that the light at the end of the tunnel was usually an approaching train, and I knew what he meant. I was feeling profoundly sorry for myself – a familiar experience – and was having difficulty thinking of anything positive that I might be able to contribute. Then, apparently at some unseen signal, my companion sat up straight and rubbed her wrists vigorously. It was as if someone had suddenly flicked her switch to 'On'.

'I nearly fell asleep there,' she said, winking at me.

I raised an eyebrow. For the past few minutes she'd been making gentle snuffling noises that I feared might turn to fully fledged snores.

'Would you like a bit of Toblerone?' she inquired.

I shook my head. 'No thanks.'

She reached into her small bag and rummaged around. 'I think I will. I like a bit of chocolate.' Grunting with the effort, she broke a bit off and popped it in her mouth. 'Ik very tuk.'

'Sorry?'

She chewed for all she was worth and swallowed. 'I say, it's very tough, the old Toblerone.'

I really had nothing to say on the subject. 'Right.'

'You're having a bit of read, then?' she asked.

In fact, I wasn't. I'd been having a bit of a fret. But I thought it was my best chance of avoiding conversation and started studying the book again. 'That's correct,' I sniffed.

'I think I'll join you.'

For one horrible moment, I thought she meant she was going to start reading my book too, but she dived into her bag again and drew out a paperback.

At last, I thought. Peace. And that was when everything took a turn for the strange. Almost as soon as she had found her page, she began to giggle. Her shoulders bobbed up and down and the book wobbled in her hands.

'Hoo hoo,' she tittered. 'Heee. Heh heh.'

I shifted in my seat, and tried to ignore her.

'Ha,' she nodded to herself. 'Hoooo, dear me.'

I actually tutted. I'm not proud of it. I *tutted*.

'Oh, I'm sorry,' she said, resting a wrinkled hand on my forearm. 'Am I disturbing you? I'm sorry. But this is very funny. I can't help myself.'

She turned the book's cover towards me. It was *The Hitchhiker's Guide to the Galaxy*.

I looked at her, then at the book, then at her. A few seconds ticked by before I spoke. She looked me right in the eye, challenging me to say something.

'It's not a very . . . nun-like . . . choice,' I said.

She peered at the cover, clearly pleased with herself. 'Oh? What makes you say that?'

I was on uncertain ground here. It was as if a fundamental law of the universe had been repealed. I wouldn't have been any more shocked if gravity had suddenly been nullified and we were having this conversation in mid-air. 'Well . . . it's . . . it's . . .'

'Yes?'

'It's *funny*.'

She slapped her thigh and began another giggling fit. 'Are the poor nuns not allowed to have a laugh?' she asked me.

I was suddenly very embarrassed. What was my point? 'No, it's not that, it's just . . . it's just that I don't associate nuns with humour. At all. In any shape or form.'

She winked again and patted my arm again. 'You weren't educated in a convent were you?'

I had to smile. 'Close. I had the priests.'

'You "had the priests"? The way other people have lice?'

Another smile from me. What the hell was this? A funny nun? 'I think I'd have preferred lice, thanks.'

She executed a mock wince. 'How come?'

I was still sure that she was working up to some sort of lecture, but found myself starting to babble. 'Don't get me started. Look, no offence, but I'm not religious. Well, that's an understatement. I'm as far away from religious as you can get. I hate it. I absolutely hate it. It's pathetic, as far as I'm concerned, completely pathetic. It's beyond me how intelligent people can go along with it. Lies from top to bottom. Lies and scare-mongering. Stories for scaring children. There's more—'

'I get the picture,' she interrupted. I blushed, and felt foolish. '"No offence", you said. Why do you think I'd be offended?'

'Well, because . . . you obviously are religious. You're a nun. Last time I checked, they were only taking religious people.'

We were both giggling now.

'It doesn't mean I expect everybody else to be. I used to, of course. But now I really couldn't care less. So what do you call yourself?'

'Joe,' I said, wondering if this familiarity made me vulnerable in some way.

'Eh, right. My name's Frances, but that's not what I meant. Do you call yourself agnostic, or what?'

More blushing. 'Oh. No. Atheist. Well, pantheist, technically, but . . . never mind.'

Sister Frances held up the crucifix that she wore around her neck and pointed it towards me. 'Back! Back!' she cried.

I laughed, and seriously considered the possibility that she might be a normal old woman on her way to a fancy dress party. Feeling emboldened, I decided to set the record straight. 'Look, er, Sister Frances,' I said, 'I won't try to convert you if you don't try to convert me.'

She smiled and nodded. 'I'll just pray for you,' she said.

'And I'll think for both of us,' I replied, the standard put-down.

There was a moment's silence. I thought she had taken offence, but then she nodded and returned to her book. The giggling began again almost immediately.

Asking advice from strangers has always been a dangerous trait of mine. I gave up psychology at the end of my first year in college on the say-so of a taxi driver. So it isn't too strange that I pounced on Sister Frances. It was par for my particular course.

'Sister Frances?' I said in a voice not my own.

'Hmmm?'

'Can I ask you something?'

She closed her book and gave me her full attention immediately. 'The answer is "no",' she said. 'I don't miss sex. You can't miss what you never had.'

This time I blushed from the soles of my feet. 'No, no, it's not that,' I croaked. 'It's a . . . personal matter.'

'Oops,' she said, but didn't blush herself. 'I thought sex was all young people cared about. Especially *atheist* young people.'

I knew she was ribbing me, and let it slide.

'Well . . . eh, Sister Frances, it's—'

'Hold it,' she interrupted. 'You nearly choke every time you have to say "Sister". Call me Frances.'

'Well, Frances,' I went on, 'I'm going back to my mother's

house to . . . to what, I don't really know. I'm supposed to . . . help, I think. There's been a sort of a – a crisis.'

She nodded. 'Your father's dead, then?' she asked.

'What? I mean . . . *what?*'

'I'm not wrong, am I?'

On top of everything else, she was a closet Miss Marple, it seemed. 'Well, yeah, he is. How do you know?'

'You said you were going to your "mother's house". A peculiar phrase, that. And you're "supposed to help". You sound like someone with unwanted family responsibility to me.'

I nodded slowly.

'And people's fathers die all the time, you know,' she concluded. 'It's quite obvious, really.'

'Well . . . yes. He died about two years ago.'

'I'm sorry to hear that.'

I never knew what to say when people said that. What were they sorry about? It wasn't their fault, any more than it was mine. If it was anyone's fault, it was God's. And he didn't even have the decency to exist.

'Yeah. Cheers,' I muttered. 'The thing is, it hasn't been easy for my mother . . . it's been very difficult, in fact. For her. And now, there's something new for her to worry about.'

I paused, half expecting her to say, 'Your wee sister is pregnant, isn't she?' But she merely nodded for me to go on.

'I got a phone call last night. It turns out that my sister – younger sister – is . . . y'know . . . with child.'

What did I expect her to say, I wonder? She didn't know the real circumstances of my family life, and even if she did, how could she possibly help? More to the point, this was still a nun, after all, and Ireland was still Ireland. There was every chance,

I was suddenly aware, that she might disappoint me and launch into a sermon.

'Congratulations,' she said, smiling broadly.

'Excuse me?'

'Congratulations. You're going to be an uncle. Your sister is going to be a mother. Your mother is going to be a grandmother. There's going to be a whole new person running around.'

I frowned, unconvinced. She didn't seem to get it. 'That's all well and good,' I said, 'but the girl's only nineteen.'

'I'm not saying the situation is ideal,' Frances replied. 'But you can't turn back time. It's going to happen whether you like it or not, so you'd better look on the bright side. Will the father stick by her?'

'I haven't got a clue,' I told her. 'I've never met him. I know my mother doesn't like the sound of him.'

'She wouldn't though, would she?'

'No,' I conceded.

'Do you think your sister will want to get married?' Frances asked.

I hadn't even considered that. The idea of Deirdre being someone's mother seemed farcical. The idea of her being someone's wife wasn't far behind it. Every time I went home she had some new bloke in tow, it seemed. Even if this Feeny person wanted to marry her, I just couldn't picture it. She was practically a child herself, for God's sake.

'I don't know about that, either,' I admitted. 'I haven't even spoken to her. All I know is that she's up the . . . pregnant, and my mother is fit to be tied.'

Frances chewed her bottom lip, considering. 'You seem more worried about your mother than your sister,' she said eventually.

28

I nodded slowly and deliberately, hoping to communicate the real problem without having to go into detail.

'Is your mother still a bit . . . high-strung?' Frances guessed.

'You could say that,' I replied. 'Or you could say that she's lost the plot completely.'

'But you wouldn't say that, would you, not about your own grieving mother?'

I felt my old friend guilt creeping up my spine. 'I didn't mean that,' I said. 'But this is not what she needs. Or deserves.'

'Maybe it's exactly what she deserves,' Frances said. 'You're forgetting that children are one of God's blessings. Don't look at me like that. They are. It seems terrible now because it's a what-do-you-call-it, an abstract idea. When it's a real little person, it will become a joy. Tell your mother that. Is she religious?'

I cast my eyes upward. 'Is she ever.'

'Then tell her you got it from a nun.'

I grinned and promised that I would.

'Now,' Frances said, 'we'll say a few decades of the Rosary to ask the Blessed Virgin for strength.'

My mouth flapped open and shut and I felt my temper rise.

Frances wagged a spindly finger at me. 'Gotcha,' she said, and laughed like a drain.

By the time the bus finally pulled in at my destination, I felt a little better. It would never have occurred to me in a million years to try to put a positive spin on Deirdre's pregnancy. Left to my own devices, I would probably have launched into a damage limitation exercise and tried to convince my mother that it wasn't that big a deal. This was an interesting alternative. It wouldn't work, of course, but at least it was different.

'Well, this is me,' I told Frances.

She began the complicated task of getting out of her seat to let me past.

'Righto. Best of luck, then,' she grunted as she dragged herself up and out into the aisle. 'I'll be thinking about you.'

'Thanks, Frances,' I said as I slid past. I meant it too. She had really helped – or tried to anyway – and had wreaked havoc with my image of nuns.

'Don't forget, now. *The baby will be a joy.*'

I smiled at her and tried to imagine myself using those words. 'I'll tell her. Thanks again.'

'Bye.'

'Yeah. Bye.'

She offered me her hand and I shook it delicately.

'Don't worship anything I wouldn't worship,' I advised and took my leave. Even with a nun I actually liked, I couldn't resist. What a tool.

Outside, it was – naturally – piddling rain. I pulled my collar up and checked my watch. Five to three. I would be getting the six thirty bus back to Dublin the next day. That meant around twenty-seven hours at home. Not that I was counting. Feeling renewed self-pity wash over me, I grabbed my bag from the bowels of the bus and started for home. It was no more than a fifteen-minute walk and, realising this, I was suddenly gripped by fear. Fifteen minutes and I'd be going over the top into no-man's land. Fifteen minutes before the tears and raised voices. I could feel my feet getting heavier, each step harder to make than the last, and I wasn't even out of the bus station yet. Then a voice interrupted my gloom.

'Joe! Oi! Joe!'

I turned and squinted at a waving figure over in the car

park. It was a second before I recognised him. Darren Brady, a bloke I'd been at school with. He'd been known to us as One-shift Brady in those days, on account of his lack of romantic success. Originally, he'd been called No-shift Brady, but one fateful Saturday night towards the end of our school days, he copped off with some harpy in Cleopatra's, where we went to drink cider and act hard. The girl in question looked a lot like Denis Taylor, the snooker player. From then on, he was One-shift, and probably still was, for all I knew. As I walked over to say hello, I was suddenly struck by the cruelty of this. It wasn't like the rest of us were beating them off with a stick, but still he was picked on and ridiculed to within an inch of his life. People, eh?

'Hi, Darren,' I said. 'How are tricks?'

'Never better,' he assured me. 'Back from the big smoke, then?'

'Yeah, flying visit. Check on the old homestead, you know how it goes.'

Big talk.

'So what are you up to these days? You're not still a bloody student are you?' He spat the word 'student'.

'God, no,' I laughed as if the very idea was absurd. In reality, I considered going back to the sanctuary of pointless education almost every day. 'I'm working in PR.'

Darren looked at me blankly. 'Fuck. What the hell's that?'

'Well . . .' I began and then ground to a halt. 'It's . . . a bit like advertising. Only without ads.'

Darren nodded. No doubt this was just the sort of wanky, non-specific occupation he had envisaged me doing.

'What about you?' I asked.

'Chickens,' he beamed.

31

'Ah,' I said, wondering if I had misheard him.

'Me and the brother have a big chicken operation going this year or more. Great money in it.'

'Really?'

'I don't know what to do with it, half times, honest to God I don't. There's only so many holidays you can go on, you know?'

Chickens! Why hadn't I thought of that? In fact, I probably had thought of it, before laughing a derisory laugh and deciding on an arts degree.

'Are you going somewhere?' I asked, getting the subject off fowl-related wealth.

'Naw, picking the sister up,' Darren said. 'Another bloody student. Physics or philosophy or some bloody thing.'

I nodded and tried to think of something to add.

'Speaking of sisters,' Darren went on, 'I hear yours is going to be a mammy.'

'How the hell do you know that?' I snapped, sounding angrier than I intended.

'Calm down. It's no big secret. Our Amanda told me. Don't ask me how she knew. When's it due?'

'May,' I grumbled through gritted teeth. If my mother found out that it was common knowledge, things would be even worse.

'Well, tell her I was asking for her.'

'You don't even know her,' I snapped, unreasonably.

Darren nodded slowly. 'True,' he said. 'Don't tell her then. Whatever you like.'

A small hatted and scarfed girl appeared between us. Darren's student sister, evidently. I recognised her from the bus.

'Right,' she said, without even a hello. 'Come on, I'm fucking starving.'

Darren fished about in his pocket for keys. 'Do you want a lift?' he asked me, nodding in the direction of an expensive-looking car.

'No thanks,' I muttered, trying not to sound bitter and jealous, and failing. 'I'll see you around.'

'You might,' said One-shift, and turned away.

I began to plod home.

4

My mother's house – home – was a bungalow on the edge of town. It had always felt quite big, really, as there had only ever been four of us there. Now that it was just Mum and Deirdre, it struck me as being huge. The front garden was small and sported few flowers, but there was an absurdly big lawn at the back, which took practically a whole day to mow. When I was younger I used to charge my parents for performing that service. I think my dad admired my nerve, but Mum invariably treated me to a few bars of 'No Charge', delivered in a slow Texas drawl and accompanied by a withering look of disappointment. *For the naan months ah carried yew – no charge.*

It was a boring-looking building, unremarkable in every way. No curves or swellings, no verandas or porches. It had the shape and proportions of a house brick, dropped into a field. Ever since I can remember, it had been repainted every third June, and never the same colour twice. Mum and Dad chose their hues wisely, never doing anything too outlandish, going from pale yellow to white to pale fudge to mid-yellow to cream. Except for June 1992 to June 1995. During that awful period, our house was blue.

35

Not pale blue, or sky blue, or mid-blue, but fuck-off BLUE. People would stop outside and point, laughing and scratching their heads. 'Frigging menopause,' Deirdre concluded, kicking a wall. But we'd have done anything, Deirdre and I, to have those blue walls back. In a move so literal it was embarrassing, Mum had the place painted dull grey within a month of my father's death. Deirdre, who could have written a good hour's worth of stand-up material about the changing colours of our house, had me in hysterics on the phone one evening, doing a perfect impression of Mum scouring through a colour chart. '*Golden Sunset* . . . no . . . *Autumn Rapture* . . . hardly . . . *Ocean Spray* . . . no . . . Ah, here we are! *Painful Death.*'

As I stood before this greyness now, I was not even remotely surprised to see that all the blinds had been drawn. It was typical of her recent behaviour to worry that 'people' would discover our terrible secret, while at the same time telegraphing the fact that something was wrong. With the first of a long series of deep sighs, I swung the gate open and approached the door. I didn't even get my keys out before I saw a twitch at the window and heard footsteps inside. The door opened a couple of inches and my mother peered out, squinting at the daylight.

'Is that you, Joseph?' she croaked.

'Nope,' I said, 'Robert Redford. You wanna run away to Hollywood?'

She fancies Robert Redford something rotten, my mother. Most days.

'Funny,' she grimaced. 'No, really. That's very funny. At a time like this.'

She opened the door a little more and I stepped in.

'How are you?' I asked, giving her a peck on the cheek. She looked at me like I'd gobbed on her.

'How do you think I am?' she snapped, hugging herself. 'I didn't sleep a wink last night. I haven't eaten since I heard. I feel sick to my stomach. My head is swimming. My hands are shaking.'

Tiny pause.

'And nobody gives a damn,' she said.

I felt my throat constricting, and ground my teeth to stop myself from shouting. She never allowed me an opportunity to say something warm and supportive. She always got the cry for help in first, so any words of comfort were a response, rather than an offer. In the first six months after Dad died, Deirdre and I would watch her day after day, sitting by the fireside with her head in her hands, weeping soundlessly. 'Cup of tea, Mum?' we would chirp constantly. The Irish panacea. Fucking *tea*.

'Come on, Mum,' I said, rubbing her shoulder awkwardly. 'It isn't the end of the world. This happens every day. It's not like years ago, people don't—'

'SHUT UP!' she bellowed, suddenly in real tears, from absolutely nowhere. 'You haven't got a clue! You can just swan off on the bus again when it suits you. I have to live here, I have to listen to them!' She screwed up her face in a mockery of concern. '"Oh, Bernadette, I'm so sorry about your trouble. Young people these days. They don't think of the parents, do they? And so soon after Gerry. And tell me, who's the father? Is it a local boy? And what do his people do? And has he a job? And will he stick by her?"' She looked at me in the half-light of the hall. 'And then, behind your back: "Well, I could see that coming. She took no interest in the children after he went. You reap what you sow."'

We weren't even out of the hall yet. My bag was still hanging from my shoulder. Steam was rising almost audibly from my damp jacket. Feeling eight years old, and hopelessly out of my depth,

I searched my numbed brain for something clever to say about small-town hypocrisy.

It came out as 'Will we have a wee cup of tea?'

Open fires have been ruined for me. To everyone else, they mean warmth and comfort. And that's what they meant to me, once. But I've spent too many hours staring into one with my mother, trying to think of something to say that might help, knowing full well that nothing can help, least of all my juvenile mumblings. Even in other people's houses, when I see one, my neck stiffens and my toes curl up and I think of crushing, oppressive silence. What can you say to someone when their partner dies? Plenty. But what can you say that *helps*? In my experience, fuck all. It was perfectly obvious to me that Deirdre's pregnancy was hardly great news, but compared to its illustrious predecessor, it wasn't so bad. I should have been able to articulate this. Yet here we were again. Sitting in front of the fire, letting our tea go cold.

'Is she in?' I asked, very quietly. I was consciously trying to not even look at the flames, all too aware of their soporific effect.

'No,' Mum replied, just as quietly. Her tears had subsided almost immediately, as they often did. She had watched me make the tea in almost total silence. Waiting for my help, knowing – surely – that I was as helpless as she.

'Work?'

'No, not today. She gets every second Saturday off. I think she went to meet that Riley one for coffee.'

Deirdre worked in Clean Getaways, the larger and more successful of the two travel agents in town. She had started working there during her school holidays, filing and gophering. But when she showed ability, they offered to take her on full time, and at a reasonable wage, too. That was the end of her going to college, and the beginning of another row with Mum. The conflict was mercifully short-lived, though. Even Mum could see that for all Deirdre's intelligence and zest, she had exactly the sort of temperament that should avoid third-level education. Lazy isn't the word for it. Deirdre could have found time to doss as a Roman galley slave. After a few days of heated bickering and countless 'turn in his grave's, Mum relented and Deirdre joined the workforce. She had made progress fast, and was now – to judge from the way she talked, anyway – practically running the place.

'Well,' I said, 'it's good that she's still getting out and about. You know, not sulking in her room.'

That brought a contemptuous 'Ha!' from Mum, who then seized on a favourite topic. 'I was never sure about that Riley one, and I'm even less sure of her now. Maybe she's the one who's been leading Deirdre astray.'

I almost laughed. No one had been leading Deirdre astray, that was for sure. Deirdre had been born astray, and I mean that as a compliment. If anything, Yvonne Riley's mum had the greater cause for concern on that score. Yvonne herself wouldn't say boo to a goose. Mum didn't like her, I suspected, because she had big breasts. Always very wary of big breasts, my mum. ('No shame, that Riley one,' she had whispered to me at the fireside one Saturday night as the girls giggled in the kitchen. 'Bouncing all over the place.')

'Yvonne's all right, Mum,' I sighed. 'And Deirdre's going to need a friend.'

'She's going to need a lot more than friends. What about a father for the baby? What about money? What about—'

'Let's not worry about the details just yet,' I interrupted. 'The main thing is to calm Deirdre down, let her know it's not the end of the world.'

'She doesn't need calming down, Joseph!' Mum yelled, once again reaching hysterics in the blink of an eye. 'She's perfectly calm! Not a bother on her! I'm the one who needs calming down!'

What else is new, I was tempted to say, but didn't. Not everything is about you, I was tempted to say, but didn't. You're not the pregnant nineteen-year-old, I was tempted to say, but didn't. Instead, I closed my eyes and counted backwards from five to zero. Slowly.

'You'll survive,' I said. 'You've been through worse than this.'

Why I said that, I don't know. It was a mistake I often made, to think that any given problem would pale into insignificance when compared with the real problem, which was my father's absence. It never bloody worked. All it ever did was give Mum another excuse to pick at her wounds. Like she needed an excuse.

'He'd turn in his grave, Joseph. Pregnant, at nineteen. His wee girl. He worshipped the ground she walked on, he really did. And this is how she honours his memory. By sleeping around, and getting into trouble.'

Five . . . four . . . three . . . two . . . one . . . zero.

'It would have killed him to see it. *Killed* him. It's a betrayal, that's what it is, a betrayal. She might as well have walked out to the cemetery and desecrated the grave. How could she do it? Doesn't she think? I don't know . . . I don't know.'

Five . . . four . . . three . . . two . . . one . . . zero.

'He was a religious man. He taught her right from wrong, we both did. And this is the way she thanks us. By sleeping around the town, like a . . . like a . . .'

I caught my breath.

'. . . like that Riley one.'

'Oh, for Christ's sake,' I said. 'For a start, I'm sure she didn't do it deliberately. And for another thing, she doesn't sleep around. You can be unlucky, you know.'

She looked at me with an expression of shock and outrage, which she was affecting, I'm sure. Despite appearances to the contrary, Mum was no prude.

'*Bad luck* you call it? She goes to bed with some stranger and gets pregnant and shames us all in front of the whole world and you put it down to luck? God, you're something else.'

'Well, I don't think it's going to do any of us any good if we make her feel like some sort of slut.'

She made no response to this, but looked a little chastened. I swallowed, and pressed on.

'I mean, you must feel at least some sympathy for her . . . don't you?'

This was what I thought of as a Minefield Moment. Over the past couple of years, I had learned that you could sometimes get through to the old Mum, draw her out of the dull grey fog through which she had come to view the world, and make her see the truth – that the universe was not designed with the express purpose of bringing her misery. If you succeeded you were rewarded with the sight of her almost visibly *morphing*, losing her hard edges and becoming her real self once more. But if you had said the wrong thing, had stepped on one of the (forgive me) emotional mines she had strewn around herself, then you were in serious trouble.

'I know she's no slut, Joseph,' she said, clearly upset by the very thought. 'And I know she didn't do it deliberately. But I want to know . . . I want to know when things are going to turn around. Where's the good news? When are we going to be back to normal?'

These were the sort of questions my mother asked me. Not

'How's work?' or 'Any girlfriends on the go?' or 'Did you see that documentary about spiders?' but 'When are you going to make my life bearable again?' This was how it had been for two years, and I was starting to believe that this was how it would always be. Don't let anyone tell you grief is about sorrow. Grief is about anger and disappointment and fear. I wanted to explain, as gently as I could, that things would never be the same again, but that didn't mean we were doomed to eternal suffering. I couldn't, though. Because I wasn't sure myself.

'I don't know, Mum,' I said, and tired of trying to resist, started to stare at the fire.

Deirdre didn't return home until almost seven o'clock. Doing her best to brighten, Mum filled the time by briefing me on the local news. A plumber in the town was in trouble for kicking his neighbour's dog to death. The dog had been called – get this – Mr Woof, and had apparently sealed his fate by Mr Woofing his little heart out at 3 o'clock one Sunday morning. I noted that anyone willing to call a dog 'Mr Woof' shouldn't cast aspersions about animal cruelty. Fiercely unsentimental about animals, including the dogs she so obviously adored, Mum agreed. Our latest dog – the fifth in four years – didn't even have an official name. I called him 'The Dog', as in 'Where's The Dog?' Mum called him 'The Poor Dog', as in 'Did anyone feed The Poor Dog?' Deirdre was given to calling him 'Veronica', as in 'Ye gettin' any, Veronica?' She was obviously hoping to give him a complex, and I think it was working, too. Since I'd arrived home, and probably for hours before that, he'd been running from the back door down the entire length of our outsized garden, pausing, rolling over twice, licking himself, and then repeating the whole manoeuvre in the other direction.

As well as the latest dog-murdering headlines, I heard tales of traffic accidents, pub brawls, and illicit, but widely reported affairs. I began to hear a weird parody of 'The Twelve Days of Christmas' in my head: 'Four cars a-crashing, three thugs a-fighting, two wives a-shagging – one deeeaaaad doooggg!' Just as the conversation was easing into a pleasant, everyday rhythm, a key turned in the front door, and suddenly Deirdre and her foetus were in the room.

'Hi, hi. Hiyer. Hi,' I said, getting to my feet and smiling too hard. 'How are ye?'

'H'lo,' she scowled, fiddling with her keys, and pouting.

Christ, I thought, what's wrong with her? Apart from the obvious.

'How do you . . . feel?' I asked.

'Fine,' she said, and burst into tears. Apparently all I had to do was say hello to any given woman in my family and she would start to cry. I shot a glance at Mum, thinking of her assurances that Deirdre had 'not a bother on her'. But Mum looked as shocked at this as I was. Deirdre was tough, far tougher than me. I really wasn't prepared for her to be seriously upset. I had counted on trouble with Mum, not her.

'Come on,' I said stiffly, putting an arm around her shoulders with my customary lack of grace. 'It's not that bad. We'll look after you. Won't we, Mum?'

'Uh . . . yes,' Mum nodded, not as convincingly as she might have. 'It'll be fine.'

Deirdre's sobbing continued unabated. I gave her back a little pat and retreated, embarrassed, wishing she would at least sit down. We looked like some sort of weepy Mexican stand-off.

'I just met *him*,' she sniffed. 'Y'know . . . for a chat.'

I nodded.

'I thought you were with that Riley one,' said Mum, helping not at all.

'And then I met *him*,' Deirdre snapped. She looked around the room as if she'd never seen it before and shrugged her shoulders. 'He said . . . things.'

Mum looked at me and raised an eyebrow. Listen to this, she practically mimed. I told you he was no good.

'Go on,' I urged. 'What sort of things?'

Deirdre studied the carpet and said, 'He told me I was the town bike and the baby could be anyone's.'

Mum blessed herself and went pale. I wondered if I would ever have a normal conversation again.

'What did you say?' I asked, after a – ha ha – pregnant pause.

'I didn't say a thing,' Deirdre said, her voice cracking. 'I just got out of the car and left him there. Asshole.'

'Good,' I nodded.

With that, Mum crossed the room and thumped me on the shoulder with a force I wouldn't have credited her with. Then she returned to her original spot like a poor actress in a terrible play – which this was beginning to resemble.

'What the hell was that for?' I wailed.

'He called your sister a bike! I know what a bike is, you know! And all you can say is "Good"? What's the matter with you?'

'I mean it's good that she had the sense to get up and leave him there! What's the matter with you? What am I supposed to do?'

'By God, your father would never have put up with it, I can tell you that for nothing. He would not, now. He would have . . . he would have . . .'

'What? *What?* Do you think I should get a frigging shotgun

and make him marry her? Is that what Dad would have done? Don't make me laugh. He would have told her to forget the stupid bollocks and get on with it.'

'Don't swear at me, Joseph.'

'I'm *not*.'

'Yes you are.'

'No I'm not.'

'Yes you are.'

'No—'

Deirdre threw her hands in the air and, well, screamed, really. 'Shut up, the pair of you! For God's sake, shut up! I don't care about him, so why should you? I've forgotten about him already. OK? Forget I spoke.'

She left the room with a flourish and immediately began howling on the other side of the door.

'Now look what you did,' Mum said and went into the kitchen to bang some cupboard doors.

From bitter experience, I knew that my only real option was a tactical retreat. So I spent an hour or so in my room, staring at the ceiling and periodically emitting enormous sighs. Well, I say 'my room'. I mean the room that had been mine when I was a child and now functioned as a warehouse for all the crap that Mum and Deirdre couldn't find a sensible home for and yet didn't want to throw out. Among its dubious treasures were dozens of Mum's dusty old records (Willie Nelson, Edith Piaf), several spare duvets, a deflated beachball, a pile of empty photograph albums, two semi-stringed tennis raquets, a non-functioning portable TV, a typewriter, an oar, a car roof-rack, and at least twenty pairs of beaten-up shoes and boots that no one would ever, ever wear again, even as a joke. It also housed some of my old stuff, of course, including a small, rickety bookshelf for the books that I had liked when I was younger and stupider. I wouldn't have had these in my Dublin flatlet for love nor money, yet I kept them here, out of sight, but not quite out of mind. Ah, simpler times, I told myself, running a critical and quite frankly snobby eye over their battered spines. *Kane and Abel*. *The Amityville Horror*. *Firefox*. *The Eagle has Landed*. What kind of a teenager takes solace in Jeffrey Archer, I wondered idly. I had – naturally – been a sullen and uncommunicative teen but, to my eternal relief, not the sort who wrote poetry about how no one understood except the flowers. And I never painted my room black or shaved my head or complained about 'The Man', either. Instead, I contented myself with shouting at anyone who dared to speak to me and, when cornered, threatened to have my ear pierced. Nothing scared my parents like the prospect of a punctured lobe.

'I'll do it, I swear!' I would howl, in the manner of a fevered bank robber with a pistol to the cashier's temple. One such crisis arose when my cousin Emmett got married. I was fourteen at the time, and Mum and Dad decided that I should have a suit for the big occasion. The suit part I didn't mind, but when they both insisted on accompanying me to Dinkin's, a shop that actually billed itself as a 'Young Gentlemen's Outfitters', I began to worry. Then they set their hearts on a light grey number which was OK from a distance but, on closer inspection, proved to be festooned with tiny little ships. Despite the public nature of the scene, or perhaps because of it, I threw the teenage fit to end all teenage fits.

'NO!' I bellowed, like a stuck pig. 'No, no, no, no. NO.' I was quite the orator in those days.

'You can't even see the ships!' Mum argued, quite accurately, in fact – even I had to admire the delicate stitching. But they were there, no doubt about it. Nothing was more certain, as far as I was concerned, than my total humiliation at the hands of some seventeen-year-old girl singing 'Popeye the Sailor Man' at me while the bride and groom thanked the priest.

We argued back and forth for a while, drawing sniggering glances from other shoppers, until I grew frustrated and decided to go nuclear.

'OK then,' I said, folding my arms, 'I'll wear this crappy suit if you really want me to. It might look all right . . . WITH MY NEW EARRING.'

That was the end of the sailor suit. I ended up wearing this shit-brown thing with corduroy lapels, and thought I looked good enough to eat.

Such crises were few and far between, however. They may have had a serious Achilles' heel when it came to male jewellery, but Mum and Dad knew what made teenagers tick and, generally speaking, adopted a sensible policy of *laissez-faire*. As a result, I failed to find anything worth rebelling against in any serious fashion and reached my twenties with few complaints. The same could not be said for Deirdre, whose early teenage antics made me positively ashamed of myself. Next to her, I behaved like you might expect the Dalai Lama to behave when Mr and Mrs Lama paid an unexpected visit. Puked-up cider on the kitchen floor, crafty joints in her room, tiny skirts, enormous heels, make-up overdoses, reform-school boyfriends – she went through all the usual, banal seditions. But she also got herself into frequent trouble with a succession of bizarre practical jokes, several of which necessitated police action, and one that almost resulted in a fatality (long story – the key words are 'shopping trolley', 'small child', 'hill', and 'traffic'). One Christmas Eve when she was thirteen, she visited Mrs Mooney, a neighbour of ours who was pushing eighty years of age and a little woolly-headed to say the least. (My dad once found her trying to mow her lawn with a vacuum cleaner.) Deirdre knocked on her door, invited herself in for mince pies and tea, and then spent two hours convincing the poor dear that it was *New Year's* Eve. Mrs Mooney was beside herself, unable to believe that she had slept through the whole thing, even with her record.

'My daughter was supposed to come on Christmas Day!' she whimpered. 'Why didn't she wake me up?'

'It snowed on Christmas Day,' Deirdre reported. 'It was *lovely*.'

When Deirdre told me this sorry tale – through tears of laughter – I was utterly disgusted with her, and sang like a boid to Mum and Dad. Shamed to their very core, they marched Deirdre down to Mrs Mooney's to offer an apology. Which was unnecessary, as it turned out, since she had since forgotten the whole thing and was still looking forward to Christmas with her daughter.

I really don't know where this nasty streak came from, but it disappeared overnight when Deirdre was about sixteen. Since then, she'd been what you might call 'colourful', but good-natured and kind at heart. She certainly didn't deserve to be dealt a hand like this – which, if you ask me, is the surest way to get one.

I glanced at my watch and was surprised to see that it was almost nine. Motivated as much by hunger as anything else, I crept out of my room and went to test the water. Deirdre's room was just down the hall from mine, and I was halfway there before I realised that I was walking on tiptoe. Feeling faintly ridiculous, as usual, I knocked on the door, hoping a baleful sob would not be my reply.

'Yup,' she said from within.

'It's me,' I whispered.

'Well, duh.'

'Can I come in, then?'

'Have you got any vodka?'

'No.'

'Gin?'

'No.'

'Meths?'

'No.'

'Well, come in anyway.'

I opened the door, wincing at its squeaking handle, and closed it behind me as gently as possible. If you'd asked me what all the tiptoeing and whispering was about, it would have taken me a second to realise that I was trying to hide the fact that I was even talking to Deirdre without Mum there to witness it and approve – or more likely disapprove – of my technique. Deirdre was lying on her bed, doodling on a notepad, and was clearly feeling better. Very robust, our Deirdre.

'Oh, for fuck's sake,' I spluttered, noticing a Brad Pitt calendar on the wall. 'Not another one. What happened to River Phoenix?'

'Leave him alone, he's fucking gorgeous,' she said, with a small smile. 'And poor River's old news. Gotta move with the times.'

'He's a tit! Look at his shirt!'

'You're only jealous.'

'Of what?'

'Let's see. His looks, his money, his women, his career, his car, his house, his—'

'Yeah, all right, all right.'

This was familiar ground, and we were both ploughing it for

49

the sake of comfort. When she was (even) younger, Deirdre had plastered every available surface in her room with pictures of 'hunks', gleaned from lurid magazines with titles like *Wow!* and *Zip!* and *Whoosh!* Hunks of what? I used to wonder. Bread? Coal? Cheese? None of these unreal-looking figures – many of whom were clearly sporting lip-gloss – had ordinary names. There were no Seamuses or Hughies or Jimmys, only Zachs and Lucases. I ribbed her constantly about it, even after the ugly day when she found a battered *Penthouse* at the back of my wardrobe. ('What the hell were you looking for in my wardrobe?' I bellowed, mortified. 'Pornography,' she told me with a shrug.) She eventually grew out of the hunk-wallpaper phase, but still kept a special spot on the wall for calendars featuring more upmarket himbos. And I still took the piss.

'Did I tell you my Brad Pitt joke?' she asked, looking hopeful and salacious all at once.

'Is it something to do with Cockney rhyming slang?'

'Aww. Yeah.'

'Heard it.'

'Bollocks. Right then, what do you call a man with no arms and no legs adrift in the ocean?'

'Is this clean?' I asked, wagging a finger.

'Squeaky.'

'I give up.'

'Bob.'

A crap joke, undoubtedly, but we laughed ourselves sick for a full minute. As the guffaws subsided, I idly picked up a jar from Deirdre's dressing table, which was laden with all manner of creams and unguents promising 'healthy skin' and 'clear skin' and 'radiant skin'. A tiny label on the one I picked up proclaimed that the magical potion within could 'hold back the ravages of time'. I pointed out that for a teenager, this seemed a little over-cautious.

'Well, I don't want to end up wrinkly and wanked out like you,' Deirdre sniffed, charitably.

It was apparent that the ice was as broken as it was going to get. We both looked around for a second, unsure of what to say. Deirdre eventually ended the silence.

'So . . . I suppose you've got some advice. Let's hear it.'

I shook my head slowly. 'Not really,' I admitted. 'Mr Feeny doesn't sound too impressive, though.'

She bit her lip and rolled her eyes. 'He's a gobshite.'

I waited for her to elaborate. She didn't.

'Well, you must have liked him quite a bit at one stage,' I said, not intending it as a reprimand and cringing at my tone. 'Er, I . . . you know. If you . . . you know, when you . . .'

'Yeah, yeah, I get it. I suppose I did. He is a good-looking bloke. Older. Had all the chat, too. Nice car. Money. Lots of money, obviously.'

'Obviously? What does he do, then?'

'What do you mean what does he do? *Feeny's*. He's a Feeny.'

I shrugged.

'Feeny's *Motors*. Oh, for fuck's sake. Cars, Joseph, *cars*. They sell cars.'

'And, what, are they famous for it?'

'Practically, yes. Around here, anyway. They're rolling in it. Jesus Christ, you can't not have heard of the Feenys. Minted. Absolutely fucking minted.'

'Anyway. Where did you meet this high roller?'

'Chip shop.'

'Of course.'

'Rich people eat chips too, you know. He was behind me in the queue and we got talking. As you do. He was very flirty. Paid for me chips and all.'

I nodded. 'It's a beautiful story, Dee. Have you sold the movie rights?'

'Fuck off. Anyhow, we ended up going for a drink and, eh, here we are.'

'I think you're leaving a bit out.'

She looked at her nails and sighed. 'Yes. Well. As I say, he had all the chat.'

'And none of the condoms.'

Deirdre shot a filthy glare at me. 'Is this you helping?' she yelped. ''Cos if it is, it's shite.'

'Sorry, sorry. That slipped out. I suppose there's no use crying over spilt . . . spilt . . . help me out here . . . spilt . . .'

Deirdre stared at me innocently. I could tell she was enjoying my attempts at mature discourse, despite the subject matter.

'It wasn't a one-night stand, if that's what you think. I was with him for a few weeks. And, by the way, I only shagged him once. It was horrible, too.'

I blushed crimson. 'So what are you going to do?' I said, changing tack.

'What am I going to do? I'm going to get fat and have big tits and backache and nausea and then I'm going to go through the unbearable agony of childbirth. Have you got another idea?'

We looked at each other for a second and it was clear that she would consider no other option.

'No,' I said. 'That sounds like a plan.'

'It's not a plan, Joe, it's a fucking inevitability. If you really want to help, you can get that message across to your mother.'

'Hmmm. Your mother.'

'Yes. Your mother. I think she's in denial. More than usual, even. She thinks that maybe, if she can just worry and flap enough, maybe I'll get unpregnant.'

'How did you tell her? That can't have been many laughs.'

She shrugged. 'I just told her. I said I was sorry to have to tell her more bad news, but there was sod all I could do about it.'

'And what did she say?'

'Oh, you know, shame this, grave that.'

'She'll get used to the idea.'

Deirdre raised a weary eyebrow. 'She'll have to, won't she?'

I nodded grimly. Something Mum had said was bothering me.

'What do you think she meant?' I asked. 'When she said that Dad wouldn't have put up with it?'

Deirdre shrugged. 'Who knows? The woman's not rational. Feeling inadequate, are we?'

'Of course I am. That's my job.'

'Well, I wouldn't worry about it. It's my problem, not yours.'

This was no help. I could no more wash my hands of family responsibility than I could walk on water.

'So . . . what about Mr Feeny?' I said, after a pause.

'His name's Brendan.'

'Whatever. Are you going to talk to him again?'

'Certainly not. I hope he dies of bowel cancer. While staked out on an anthill. Somewhere hot.'

I gave her cheek a mock pinch. 'That's my girl,' I said, suddenly wanting to see the back of this conversation. 'Now let's go gang up on your mother.'

'OK,' said Deirdre. 'But I get to be Bad Cop.'

*　　*　　*

We did a good job of ganging up and what remained of the weekend was relatively sane. We tried our best to present a united front to Mum, smiling inanely and mouthing bland reassurances about how it would 'all work out in the end'. She actually calmed down quite a lot and seemed to appreciate the effort, even if she didn't necessarily agree with the sentiment. Shouting and door-slamming were kept to a minimum, and on the Sunday afternoon Mum even allowed herself a couple of 'Me! A granny!' comments. Deirdre and I responded to these with great screaming fits of laughter, hoping to encourage further levity. It didn't work, but at least the situation didn't deteriorate. By the time Sunday evening rolled around and I had to catch my bus, the atmosphere had settled into a state that a political correspondent might call 'tense but cordial'. Deirdre was still pregnant, Feeny was still an asshole, Mum was still in knots, and I was still powerless to help. But at least we had gotten over the initial bump. No matter what else happened, I would never again have to go through The First Conversation With Mum Since Deirdre Announced Her Pregnancy.

The bus back to Dublin on Sunday was entirely nun-free. I realised that I hadn't used Sister Frances' line about a baby being a joy, regardless of circumstances. I filed it away in a brand-new mental folder called 'Nuns – Advice From'. It sat awkwardly in my mind alongside the existing folder, 'Nuns – Running Away From'.

5

'So where were you all weekend, then?' Go-go said.

I plopped some milk into my tea and stirred grimly. 'Don't even get me started. I was at home. Don't even ... I was at home, all right?'

Go-go slurped his coffee and nodded, not in the least perturbed by my snappiness. 'Home, eh? You always come back in such good spirits. I presume there's some catastrophe afoot?'

'Lucky guess,' I said, and pulled up a chair. Go-go sat opposite me, next to our financial controller, Geraldine, who ruffled her newspaper and tried to pretend that she wasn't listening. Which she was. Always.

'What is it this time? Nothing serious, I hope?'

I glanced at Geraldine and caught her curious eye, to her embarrassment.

'I'll tell you later,' I said, gesturing slightly so that Go-go would take the hint. In fact, I badly wanted to hear his take on it. But it would have to wait. 'So, any crack with yourselves since Friday? How's Norm's nose?'

'Broken, of course. Three frigging hours we waited in casualty, you know.'

'Jesus! You didn't wait too, did you?'

'Ach, I said I'd go with him, so I stuck it out.'

I shook my head. 'He'd never do it for you, the fucker.'

Go-go shrugged. 'Let's hope we never have to find out. Anyway, I don't intend getting into fights with girls any time soon, so we may never know.'

Geraldine's ears pricked up almost visibly at this. Her eyes widened slightly and she stared so intently at her page that I feared it might burst into flames. Terrible actress, that woman. She could be found in the kitchen at work most Monday mornings, scouting for gossip from the weekend. Go-go and I often embellished our social post-mortems for her benefit, adding models and rock stars, car crashes and police raids. These details would then come back to us, hours or days later, from someone else in the office. This story, I realised, needed no gloss from us. It was shocking enough in its own right.

'He's in pain, then?'

'Seems to be, thank God. He complained enough, anyway. You know in children's comics, when someone gets hit on the nose, they go around screaming "Oh, by dose, by dose"? Well, that was Norm. A nurse came over at one stage and told him to keep it down. I mean, you know what casualty is like on a Friday night. There were people in there with bits hanging off them and things sticking out of them, and they weren't making half the racket he was.'

'He didn't seem that bothered in the pub.'

'Bravado, Joseph. Male posturing. Take it from me, he was like a banshee in the hospital.'

I laughed and made a mental note to give Norm a hard time

when I bumped into him again. 'So what did you get up to after that?'

'Not a whole lot. Saturday was a blur. Bit of shopping. Met the brother for a pint in town. Saturday night I just sat in with a video and a bottle of wine. Sheila was round.'

'Oho! Now we get to the goods. And? Progress?'

'Take a guess.'

'Oh. Well. Never mind. She's weakening, Go-go. I can feel it in my bones.'

Sheila was Go-go's ideal woman, someone he'd known in college, in Belfast. He would have hacked off his right arm for her, I knew for a cast-iron fact. We were rotten drunk on gin in his flat one night and he actually cried telling me all about her. He used the term 'love or something very like it'. Then he used the term 'an angel sent from heaven'. Then he used the term 'complete and utter ride'. Then he blubbed and fell asleep, quietly drooling on himself. I let myself out and walked home, trying to figure it out. I'd met her several times at that point, and could see the attraction. She was lovely, no doubt about it, and bright and witty and sensitive and all those other things we tick off on our little lists. But still . . . I couldn't shake the feeling that her only interest in Go-go was the periodic self-validation he provided. He had never told her how he felt, what with being a bloke and all, but she would have had to be blind and deaf not to notice. Go-go was normally calm and assured. Generally speaking, nothing fazed him. But when Sheila showed up, he seemed to suffer an immediate lobotomy. He'd drop things, mumble, giggle, scratch, fidget, snort, stare, shuffle, and generally conduct himself like a twelve-year-old schoolboy unexpectedly let loose in the *Playboy* mansion. Sheila was perfectly nice about it – she was nice, full stop – but she enjoyed every twitch and dribble, I'm sure. She was only human, after all, despite Go-go's theory about her divine origins. The worst part was that I secretly suspected her of a terrible crime, an unspeakable crime, really, something that was unforgivable in any woman, but particularly heinous in Sheila. It was my firm conviction that Sheila fancied Norm. More than once, I caught her stealing glances at him in the pub. She seemed to touch him more often than was strictly necessary, too. Most tellingly, she laughed out loud at his jokes, nearly all of which were awful, rambling yarns involving prostitutes and barmaids. I sometimes lay awake at night, wondering what might happen if they ever got together. There was no chance that Norm would turn her down, that was for sure. It just wasn't in him to say no to women. (Norm once knocked up some joke business cards at one of those shopping centre machines, advertising his services as a 'Provider of Sexual Solutions'. He even had a motto – 'If you can hold it open, I can fuck it'.) When Sheila found a new boyfriend, which she did regularly, Go-go went into a deep funk and stayed there for days. If she ever went out with Norm, God knows what might happen. Even talking about her now, Go-go had sunk a little in his seat.

'I'm going to have to tell her. I'm serious. This can't go on.'

I nodded. Geraldine seemed to stop listening so hard. She'd heard this before, as had I.

'Maybe you should,' I said. 'At least you'd know. There's nothing worse than not knowing.'

'Yes there is,' sighed Go-go, his resolve – typically – disappearing as quickly as it had arisen. 'There's knowing for sure that it's not going to happen. That's a lot worse.'

I shrugged, and we slurped our drinks, putting off the inevitable moment when we would have to take to our desks. Then Geraldine got up and folded her newspaper very deliberately.

'Better get to it,' she sighed, trying to give the impression that she was just another wage slave like ourselves. What she actually meant was, 'You pair better do some work before I have to produce a pie-chart.' Pie-charts were a Geraldine speciality. Every month or so, a copy of one would land on every employee's desk, accompanied by a stern memo from Stuart, the *capo di tutti capi*. One such memo contained the following line: 'It shouldn't take more than four minutes to perform even the most complicated toilet function.'

Quite a life I'd carved out for myself.

After I graduated in 1995, an event that post-dated my father's death by three weeks, I spent a grim summer doing nothing much, wondering what sort of future lay in store for someone with my qualifications – if a 2:2 in English and Philosophy could be so described. With some half-formed notion about creativity at the back of my mind, I wandered in the direction of advertising. I fancied myself as a copywriter, specifically, and was sure that I could shift any amount of high-fibre cereal given half a chance. Despite constant assurances that I would soon be given some real work, however, I spent my days ordering couriers, photocopying, making coffee, and stuffing envelopes, waiting patiently for the day when someone would ask my opinion about something other than their new glasses. One day, when I was simultaneously suffering from a toothache, a hangover, and the gnawing suspicion that life was passing me by, a media buyer clicked her fingers at me and called out, 'Boy! I need something faxed!' She got a big laugh. I laughed along and then wrote 'Some stuck-up cunt with different-sized eyes' (an accurate description) in the 'From' box on the cover sheet. I sent it off and walked out.

Soured on advertising, I turned, again without much thought, to its ugly sister, public relations. I couldn't quite convince myself that there were many creative elements to PR, but was at least satisfied that it was the same ballpark. Three weeks later, to my astonishment, I landed a job with Stuart. He was one of fifteen targets in my mailshot, and the only one who didn't issue a PFO by return of post. He even knew all about my hurried exit from the advertising game, because I told him the whole story at the interview. I had found myself wondering if commerce and assholes went hand in hand, and wanted to test him to the limit. He passed handsomely by laughing heartily and declaring that I had shown, and I quote, 'spunk'. Go-go had already worked there for a year and we hit it off straightaway. A new job, new people. I really thought that, for once, I'd landed on my feet instead of my arse.

Stuart Kennedy was what they call 'a self-made man'. What that made the rest of us, I'm not sure. Pre-fabbed? Assembled from a kit? Different to Stuart, anyway. He was one of those people who never seemed to conclude that something simply could not be done. When it came to work-related matters, I gave up very easily. Stuart gave up when you killed him. Of all the myriad annoying things about him, perhaps the most galling was his relative youth. He founded his company (which, after much soul-searching, he called Stuart Kennedy Public Relations) at the age of twenty-eight. Now a mere thirty-nine, he was rich, respected, and rich. Stuart had the ear of a lot of reasonably famous people: politicians, TV personalities, business people, lawyers, and any number of journalists. What he seemed to be whispering in those celebrated ears was this: 'Give me all your money.' I hesitate to use the word 'mansion', but the building he lived in was not a house as normal people understand the term. Although none of us mere employees had ever actually been there, it once featured in a weekend supplement piece entitled something like 'Rich People and the Fuck-off Houses they Live in'. In the week following that publication, seventeen of Stuart's twenty-two employees, including Go-go and me, requested a salary review. We were all refused because, and again I quote, 'Times are hard.' His car was an impressively black something or other (I'm not a big car fan) which no doubt had a jacuzzi and a squash court in it somewhere. And then there was the wife. Former model, blonde, ludicrously beautiful, perma-tanned, dressed to kill, legs up to her neck. She showed up at the office every so often and drove the male staff berserk with lust. And mirth – sadly, she had a voice like Barry White with a heavy cold. You could feel the ground vibrating when she spoke to you. Which she almost never did, except to boom, 'Do you know where Stuart is?'

My role in this mighty empire was that of account executive, a silly title for what I was rapidly coming to view as a silly job. As One-shift Brady learned in the bus station, I had a lot of trouble even describing what public relations was all about. As far as I could tell, it was all about exaggerating the good your clients had done while covering up the bad. It wasn't quite lying, I suppose, but you could certainly see it from there. Imagine you're walking along the street one day and someone rattles a can in your face and asks for a donation. Cruelty to animals, say. You fish around in your pockets and find a twenty-pence piece. You drop it in the can and go about your business. Later that day, you're driving home when, oh dear, some mutt runs out into the road straight in front of you. A squeal of brakes, white knuckles on the steering wheel – smack. You get out of the car and look around, but there's no one else there. The dead dog's wearing a collar. It's someone's pet. You could start knocking on doors and you'd probably find the owner. But you don't do that. You throw the corpse in the boot, speed off into the countryside, and dump it in a ditch. Later, in the pub, your friend asks what kind of a day you've had. 'I gave a major donation to charity,' you trumpet. 'ISPCA. I love animals, me.' Congratulations! You're in PR!

Stuart Kennedy Public Relations was housed in a reassuringly large Georgian house – actually two large Georgian houses knocked together – off Baggot Street. It had five or six major clients and maybe a dozen more for whom we did piecemeal work. Each account had an account manager for the schmoozing and major decision-making, a couple of account executives, and maybe a junior or two for the donkey work. There was quite a bit of writing involved – press releases, speeches, and whatnot – which I suppose I quite enjoyed. Unfortunately, account executives were also expected to do a lot of organising. When a client had a new product to push, for example, it was our responsibility to ensure that a) the whole world and his mother showed up for the launch and b) they all had enough vol-au-vents. Predictably enough, I was thoroughly hopeless at this. If it had been left to me, every product would have been launched in McDonald's. No fuss, no muss. No press either, of course, but that'd be a small price to pay as far as I was concerned.

I worked for three clients in all, none of which was terribly exciting. Most of my time was spent on Langley-Foster Electronics, a company which, despite all our efforts, almost no one had heard of. Langley's, as we called them, produced all sorts of gizmos (to use the technical term) that ended up inside video recorders, microwave ovens, and personal computers made by companies that people *have* heard of. In fact, the technical details of their business were an unfathomable mystery to me, but that didn't mean I couldn't function as one of their PR people – which says quite a bit about PR. In work terms, they were the most boring as well as the most important of my charges. (At least Go-go got to work on fizzy drinks and other FMCGs, which meant periodic contact with bored models dressed as oranges and bananas.) We produced a corporate newsletter for Langley's called – oh my God, the shame – 'Live Wire'. It ran to a marathon four pages and had headlines like 'HJ-147P Sets the Pace!' I've got no idea what an HJ-147P is. Some sort of gizmo, anyway. Even though this shatteringly banal publication only appeared once a month, it took a lot of putting together. There were photo shoots to set up, stories to write, facts to check, interviews to conduct. We even found space for a crossword, compiled by a Langley's employee called Brian Denieffe, who was also our all-purpose point of contact for the newsletter. Brian was like some awful parody of a boffin – brains to burn, social skills of a dunked biscuit. His crosswords were a source of frequent hilarity in the office. They had clues like '5 Across: Dielectric resonator stabilised oscillator? Not likely!'

Langley-Foster product launches were a piece of piss to organise, thankfully, since no one expected fireworks and dancing elephants from such a dull source. Generally, we just sent out information packs to the few unlucky main-stream journalists who got lumbered with such matters and found a company representative for the technical publications to talk to.

And that was about it, really, for Langley's. An occasional newsletter and the odd mailshot. This wasn't the sort of company that sponsored Grand Prix or dumped toxic waste near primary schools. They presented neither juicy opportunities nor heart-stopping crises. In fact, in the eleven months I'd been in the job, I'd come to associate the words Langley-Foster Electronics with a sort of pleasantly predictable tedium.

That was about to change.

I'd only been at my desk for about half an hour and had already had three phone calls from Go-go, who was chained to a desk on the floor above me. In the first of these, he'd wanted to know how to spell 'characterise'. In the second, he urged me to get the new Woody Allen film on video. The third call seemed to have no specific purpose, other than to waste about ninety seconds. When the phone beeped for the fourth time, I presumed it was him again, and answered with a weary sigh. I had foolishly promised to update the house style guide, and had just realised that I was way behind with it – in the sense that I hadn't even started. Nattering to Go-go all morning wasn't going to help.

'What now, for fuck's sake?'

'That's lovely talk,' said Michelle, Stuart's PA. Then, in a mock Noo Yawk accent: 'You kiss yo mudda wid dat mout?'

I winced.

'Michelle! Sorry, I thought you were Go— I thought you were Eamonn. What, eh, can I do for you?'

'For me, nothing. But you can meet Stuart in the boardroom at ten. Bring your brain. And something to write with.'

Michelle was universally adored in the office. She had the organisational abilities of a deity and knew everything about everything, work-wise. It was widely rumoured that Stuart paid her about twice what he paid account executives, but no one begrudged her. She had saved each of us at least once with reminders about this and that.

'Right. Any idea what's up?' I asked. Stuart had summoned me to the boardroom on several occasions before to have embarrassing 'chats' about my 'progress'. But we'd just had one of these meetings, not three weeks previously. I didn't think I was due another one and, as far as I could tell, hadn't made any major cock-ups. Lately.

'I think you're going to be fired,' she deadpanned. 'There was steam coming out of his ears, and he asked me to find his cattle-prod.'

I waited for her to get serious.

'I don't know, to be honest. It's something to do with Langley's, I can tell you that much. Everyone's going to be there. The four of you, I mean.'

She meant the four of us on the Langley's – ugh – team. This was all very strange. Why wasn't I hearing this from Mary, the Langley's account manager? Why was Stuart involved himself? Ordinarily, he acted as a sort of quality control officer, dipping in and out of various projects to check their progress, but never really getting his hands dirty. His real role, he often reminded us, was to get new business. This made sense. Stuart could talk anyone into anything by sheer force of personality.

I felt a vague fluttering of concern, like that feeling you get when the phone rings late at night. If Michelle didn't know what was going on, then it was something very out of the ordinary. Christ, I thought, maybe they're leaving us.

'OK, Michelle. Thanks,' I said quietly.

She said goodbye and hung up.

Ten o'clock! It was twenty-to already. Whatever it was, I wasn't going to have a lot of time to worry. I spun around in my chair to ask Barry if he knew anything about it. Barry worked on Langley's too and was more senior than me, in days served, if not in job description. Just as I caught his eye, his own phone beeped.

'Hi, Michelle,' I heard him say. Nodding then, and some hurried scribbling. Barry wrote everything down. 'What's going on?' he asked her, obviously as certain as I had been that she would know. More scribbling. He was probably writing *Michelle doesn't know*. It was a sort of mania, Barry's note-taking. 'No probs. I'll be there.'

'Boardroom, ten o'clock?' I asked when he hung up

'Yeah,' said Barry, studying his note. He had the same puzzled look that I was sporting myself.

'What's up, do you reckon?'

'Dunno,' he muttered, still staring at the notebook. '*Stuart*'s going to be there? He almost *never* goes to account meetings.'

'Maybe they've found another firm,' I suggested.

Barry shook his head slowly. 'Doubt it. They're pretty pleased with us, Mary says. Fuck knows why, but they are.'

We considered the possibilities in silence for a moment.

'*Stuart*'s going to be there?' Barry said again.

'I've hardly ever been in an account meeting with Stuart,' I said. 'Maybe twice. Three times.'

'Hmmph. Maybe it's good news.'

'Like?'

Barry shrugged. 'I dunno, maybe they're so pleased that they're giving us all a little bonus.'

We snorted at the very idea.

'There were a whole shit-load of typos in the last "Live Wire",' I said. 'Tarnsistor. Accunting. Hodilay. Maybe we're going to get a bollocking.'

'I've been here for two years,' Barry said. 'Take it from me, Stuart doesn't call the whole team into the boardroom to tell them how to use a spell-checker. Nah, it's something big. Big-ish, anyway.'

'Well, we'll soon find out,' I observed.

'That we will.'

I turned around again and tried to find a pen that worked.

Stuart Kennedy PR didn't have a board, but we still referred to the big meeting room on the ground floor as the boardroom. Somehow 'the big meeting room on the ground floor' didn't sound so professional. It was a very large space with a lush black carpet and grey walls, upon which hung various framed prints and industry award certificates. We'd won several of these over the years, for Best this and Biggest that. The fat little trophies that accompanied them lived in a display cabinet in Stuart's inner sanctum, but the rather cheap-looking certificates were on display for the masses. I'm sure this said something important about him, but I'm not sure what. The awards were dished out at an annual black-tie ceremony, usually presented by some half-assed celebrity from RTE. The occasion was known – by grown men and women – as the PR Oscars. The sheer lack of originality in that phrase made me want to shrivel up and blow away.

The boardroom was dominated by a long black table in which you could see your reflection, and a dozen of God's own chairs. We humble grunts welcomed almost any chance to swivel and bounce in them. They were deliciously springy and made a satisfying creaking sound when you shifted your weight. Sitting on one, no matter how low you were in the food chain, you couldn't help but feel like a player.

Stuart was last to enter the room, of course, accompanied by Mary Lennon, the Langley's account manager. I didn't like Mary, I must admit, even though – or perhaps because – she was chillingly good at her job. The other account managers I encountered were friendly and approachable. Mary was about as approachable as K2. She was just so . . . PR. That was rapidly becoming a Bad Thing in my book. My own enthusiasm for the job began to wane almost as soon as I started, in fact, but I told myself that I was only in it – temporarily – for the money. After all, my movie script would soon catapult me onto the world stage at which point I could drop the pretence and run a mile. *Ha ha, Jay. Yes, I did work in PR for a brief period. Terrible business. Such phoneys!* Mary, on the other hand, lived and breathed it. She never looked happier than when she was running around at an event, jabbering into a mobile phone, slapping journalists on the back, and checking the temperature of the gin and tonics. Seeing Mary in action was like watching a personal injury lawyer actually chasing an ambulance.

'Good morning,' Stuart said breezily as he took his seat at the head of the table.

We all responded in kind. He *seemed* pretty cheerful, at least. Maybe it wasn't bad news after all.

'Everyone keeping fine?'

Nods and smiles from the three grunts. I saw Barry make a note. What the hell was that? *Stuart said Good Morning?* Lisa, the other Langley's account executive, smiled a little too hard. She lived in dread of Stuart, for no obvious reason, and probably feared that this was a set-up of some kind that would culminate in her being dismissed and, possibly, tarred and feathered.

Mary sat at Stuart's right hand, with her professional face on. Hardbitten. No shit from no one. I would have bet my left leg that she had a biography of Margaret Thatcher at home.

'Well, let's get to it. This is about Langley-Foster Electronics. Anyone who hasn't realised that yet is fired.'

Chuckles all round. Lisa's face had now split into a ghastly leer.

'I met with Andrew Holland at the weekend,' Stuart went on, 'and he gave me some very important news. As you know, Langley's is run out of Phoenix, Arizona.'

This was vintage Stuart. 'Met with.' 'Out of.' If he could have clicked his fingers and been American, he would have. Andrew Holland was the chief executive of the Langley's plant in Dublin. Or rather, in Stuart-speak, he headed up the Dublin operation.

'It seems that top management in the States have had their calculators out and have decided to rationalise Langley's European activities. Now, Langley's have three European plants at Dublin, Edinburgh, and—'

'Copenhagen,' Lisa blurted, her eyes bulging.

Good God. It was like watching a SPECTRE agent trying to impress Blofeld.

'Yes, Copenhagen,' Stuart said, testily. 'And what do they do in Copenhagen, Lisa?'

Talk about digging yourself a hole. Lisa gripped her pencil like it was a life-raft and struggled to remember the most basic fact about Langley's – that they did their R & D in Denmark and their manufacturing in Ireland and Scotland.

'Emmm . . . testing?' she said after the longest five seconds in human history.

'I suppose so,' Stuart conceded. 'But try to call it Research & Development, eh? It sounds so much better, don't you think?'

Lisa swallowed hard, nodded and, to judge from her expression, silently vowed never to speak again. Stuart was back on track instantly, in any case.

'So . . . for very good operational reasons, the Copenhagen plant will survive any cutbacks. That leaves us and Edinburgh. Andrew has been told to prepare for bad news, but as things stand at the moment, absolutely no decisions have been made. I'll say that again: no decisions have been made. However. As Langley's Irish public relations representatives, we have to make immediate plans. I've already gone over some ideas with Mary, at considerable length, and I'm relying on her – and you – to see that everything goes smoothly. The first thing, though, is to prepare a holding statement, just in case, God forbid, some journalist gets a whiff and tries to make a name for himself. This holding statement, at the moment, is all that stands between us and the abyss. So you're all going to drop everything until it's done, and done properly. Everyone on the same page so far? Good.'

Barry, I noticed, was in danger of breaking his wrist, such was the fury of his note-taking. I was reeling a little, myself, and had jotted down *Dublin – fucked? – statement.*

'I have to leave for a meeting very shortly,' Stuart continued, glancing at his watch. 'Ten minutes ago, actually. So Mary will take you through the hows and whens of what needs to be done. But I want to make a couple of points before I go. First of all, let me say this. As a company, we have never – never – dealt with an issue of such sensitivity. I want you all to understand how vital it is that we keep this thing within these walls, going forward. Listen to me, now: this is very important. Langley's employ a hundred and eighty people in Dublin. Not huge numbers, but significant. Newsworthy, for sure. You're not stupid people. You can see the headlines. But if we do our jobs, there is no need for this to become a story before it has to. Which it may not, in any event. Now I know how people talk about their jobs in the pub or whatever. I do it myself. It's perfectly natural. But this is not just another gig for us. Sure as anything, you tell your best mate that you're dealing with this potential closure thing, and the next thing you know, he tells his sister and she tells her boyfriend and he tells his dentist and he tells his nephew who, what do you know, is doing work experience in the *Evening Herald*.'

He paused for emphasis, something he had down to a fine art.

'You think I'm being paranoid. But. This gets out, and I trace it back to someone in this room, I won't just fire you, I will sue you. I don't care if you haven't got two pennies to rub together, I'll sue you anyway, for the satisfaction of it. Is that clear?'

We all nodded that it was. Lisa's hands, I noticed, were almost imperceptibly trembling. Barry had even stopped taking notes. Mary was scowling and trying to catch eyes so we'd see how tough she was, too. The tit.

'The other thing I want to say is that I know that you three are not the three most experienced people in the building. Barry, you're here, what, two years?'

'Just over,' said Barry.

'Joe? Not even a year?'

'Nearly,' I said, as positively as I could. 'About eleven months.'

Stuart nodded. 'Lisa? Somewhere between the two?'

'Eighteen months, just under, Stuart,' she said, her voice wavering a little.

He pursed his lips and nodded some more.

'It's not ideal,' he said. 'But when this is over – and it might be over very soon, it might turn out to be nothing – you'll have gotten some valuable experience, take it from me. I'll be working very closely with you on this, and don't forget that you've got a great account manager, too.'

The great manager tried to look humble and came across as mildly retarded.

'But even she is new to this sort of situation. As am I, for that matter. So try not to be intimidated. It's big work, it's important work, it's brand new to all of us, but you can do it. You absolutely can.'

There was a spontaneous mumble of assent from each of us.

'I have every confidence in you, all of you. Now, are there any questions before I go?'

Again, this was Stuart to the bone. Drop a bombshell over the course of a minute, maybe two, and then fuck off, going forward.

Barry cleared his throat and sat up a little. 'When, eh, when is Andrew expecting to hear from Phoenix? I don't think you said.'

Stuart smiled. He'd omitted this obviously vital piece of information to see if anyone was awake, the bastard.

'He's been told that a decision will be made sometime before the end of November. So we're talking about weeks. Which is pathetic, really, but the big guys in the States don't really give a shit, pardon my language, but they don't. They have their eye on the bottom line and nothing else. They're money guys. This is a financial issue. Period. They own the Dublin plant like you own a tie.'

I tried hard to think of a good question but was put off by his use of the word 'period'. Why didn't he just go and live there, for God's sake? The best I could do was to worry about my own skin.

'Um, what do we do,' I asked, 'if the phone rings, like, today, this morning maybe, and it's some journalist saying he's heard something?'

Stuart shrugged. 'Well, a) that won't happen, I'm sure. Andrew only heard himself on Friday. And b), even if it did, you'd play dumb. Which I know you could manage.'

I smiled a watery smile. This was a joke, wasn't it?

Stuart smiled back. 'You don't know a thing. *Closure, Mr Journalist? Are you insane?*'

I tried to look reassured.

Stuart shook his head with conviction. 'That's not going to happen any time in the immediate future, I mean today or tomorrow. But it might happen one of these fine days, which is why Mary and I spent our Sunday working the basics out. Make no mistake, you've got to get your asses in gear, but quick. OK?'

I nodded. Suddenly, it was if a spotlight had fallen on Lisa. Barry had asked his sensible question. I'd asked my panicky question. She couldn't just sit there mute. Stuart looked around quickly to see if anyone had anything else, and when no one made a move, he started to get up. Lisa bit her lip and squinted with the mental effort. I had to feel for her. He'd actually made it to his feet before she raised her hand, like a schoolgirl, and said, 'How many people work there again?'

Stuart's shoulders slumped.

'One hundred,' he sighed, 'and eighty. I'm late. I'll see you all again soon.'

He was at the door when a better exit line occurred to him.

'By the way,' he said, turning on his heels. 'I want you all to realise that this is not bad news for us. If Edinburgh closes, all well and good. If Dublin closes, then we lose a client, sure, but in the best possible way. We get to handle a closure. We get experience. We get a big fat fee. And maybe some new clients. In the long run, we'll be better off.'

My toes clenched.

'This could be a great opportunity for us,' he smiled.

With that, he was gone.

'Fuck me,' said Go-go through a mouthful of sandwich. 'That's not what you want to hear of a Monday morning, is it?'

I shook my head and took a gulp of milk. 'It sure fucking isn't. I tell you what, though, that guy can cram a lot into a five-minute meeting. Which is more than can be said for Deputy Dawg. We were in there until fifteen minutes ago with her, and we'll be in there again all afternoon. It takes her half an hour to clear her throat.'

We munched in silence for a moment, perched on our usual stools by the coffee shop window.

'So what's the gist?' Go-go asked.

'For the moment, all we're trying to do – the four of us, mind you – is write a holding statement in case word gets out before it should. Stuart doesn't believe in the too many cooks thing, by all accounts. The basic line is that no decisions have been taken yet, but yes, it's true that the company is looking into rationalising its European operations, yada yada, no immediate threat to Irish jobs, and so on, but watch this space, sort of thing. And just in case it does close, Christ, we have to get into all sorts of hairy shite. Dealing with the Minister, media training for Andrew Holland, all that guff.'

'Jesus Christ.'

'I know. It'd turn your stomach. A hundred and eighty people out there. I don't care if the economy is picking up. They're still going to be in trouble. But that's not even the worst bit.'

Go-go raised an eyebrow.

'The worst bit,' I reported, 'is that Stuart is fucking *delighted*. You want to have seen him. He's like an expectant father. He didn't even try to hide the fact that he wants it to be Dublin. He said it was an "opportunity" for us. Never mind losing the account. And *certainly* never mind the job losses.'

'The bollocks.'

'Yeah. All morning, I was thinking about those people working away out there, oblivious. You know? Brian Denieffe, poor bloody Brian, trying to think of crossword clues for "Live Wire". No idea that we're over here, rolling up our sleeves and chewing our pencils and trying to think of a way to calm down any hack who happens to find out that there's a good chance the place is going to shut.'

Go-go exhaled dismissively.

'I don't know about this job, sometimes,' I went on. 'Even the all right bits make you feel kind of sleazy. But this sort of shit . . .'

'I know.'

'The sneaking around . . .'

'I know.'

'The . . . pretence . . .'

'Yup.'

'It's dishonest, that's what it is. It's fundamentally dishonest. At least when you see an ad, you know it's an ad. PR . . . hides.'

We looked out the window morosely at the other office workers scurrying about in the drizzle. Their jobs probably made them feel tired and fed up and insignificant and wasted. Ours did these things, and then made us feel evil, too. Well, maybe not evil . . . but it was hard to feel entirely clean, working in PR. I wondered if Barry and Lisa felt that way. Which reminded me.

'Jesus, Go-go, you should have heard the scare tactics from Stuart.'

'What scare tactics? About what?'

'About keeping it quiet. You know Stuart, he's brash and kind of forceful, but he's never nasty.'

'Exactly.'

'Well, he threatened to fire and then sue anyone who let it slip that Langley's might be closing.'

'Get fucked!'

'He did. Swear.'

'Christ! Was Lisa there?'

I couldn't help but snigger. 'She was, under the table some-where.'

Go-go sniggered along with me.

'She nearly fainted, honest to God,' I said.

'He couldn't do that though, could he?'

'Ach, I don't think so, but it just goes to show you how seriously he's taking it. He thinks we're going to get a certain reputation if we play it well. He's probably got his fingers crossed for a recession too, so we get loads more closures to handle.'

I suddenly heard myself talking.

'*Handle*. My God. We're *handling* these people's misery. I think I want to take a bath.'

We sat there for another minute or two in grim silence.

'Better go,' I said when I happened to glance at a clock over Go-go's head. 'That bitch says we can only have a half-hour for lunch.'

Go-go slid off his stool and wriggled into his trench coat. 'You still have to tell me what happened at the weekend,' he said.

'Yeah, I know. I'm trying to deal with one crisis at a time. I'll give you the potted version on the way back.'

'OK.'

I sighed deeply. 'I wish it was.'

The afternoon session with Mary was torture. For a start, we were sequestered in her horrible office, huddled together around her horrible desk with our knees touching, notepads at the ready. We had to move because Stuart was playing host to what could only be described as a murder of communications students and had commandeered the boardroom. He had groups of one kind or another in every other week, it seemed. I put it down to ego, but Michelle maintained that Stuart 'just wanted to give something back'. She said it with a straight face, too, bless her. I bumped into them when I left Mary's office to look for some statistics about the Edinburgh plant. The students all looked very bright and . . . clean. They resembled nothing so much as a group of Japanese tourists, shuffling around together as Stuart pointed to this and that. ('Hohhh!' they cried. 'Ahhh!') I caught his eye as I came around the corner and he smiled a conspiratorial smile at me.

'Making progress?'

The students turned and looked at me without expression.

'Always,' I said and only barely managed to stop myself doing the combination finger-gun and wink number. Loosening the forced grin that had gripped my visage, I suddenly felt my self-esteem fall to the centre of the Earth. What was next? High-fives?

I crept away as Stuart led them into the boardroom ('Yes, we've won several industry awards actually, Samantha') and went back to Mary's.

'Knock, knock.' She glared at me when I just walked in unannounced. I paused, trying to gauge if she was serious or not.

'Well, I knew who was in here, Mary,' I said slowly. 'I was only gone about three minutes. At most.'

'How? How did you know for sure? Have you got X-ray vision now too?' She was smiling one of those Don't-Fuck-With-Me non-smiles.

'Yeah,' I grinned. 'Nice underwear, Lisa, by the way.'

Barry and Lisa laughed way too hard at this, trying to help me out. Mary harrumphed and thrust a hand out for the file. 'Anyway. You found it, then. Eventually.'

I passed the file to her and dropped onto my chair.

Three more weeks of this shit, I thought. At the very least.

For the first couple of days, we wrote and wrote and then rewrote and rewrote in an atmosphere that I found oddly familiar, but couldn't place. It wasn't until late on Tuesday, as I chewed my biro and listened to the tick of the ugly carriage clock in Mary's office, that I put my finger on it. I was in a submarine movie. Stuck in a tin can that may or may not be about to get torpedoed. All that was missing was the sinister red light and the fearful echo of the sonar.

Stuart was around constantly, jabbering instructions on the phone, or hovering over our shoulders as we made the latest changes to the rapidly growing array of drafts, each of which had its champion among us. It was strange having him around so much. Educational, too – his attention to detail and ability to focus seemed almost supernatural. I never once saw him slouch or yawn or scratch or express even the merest hint of ennui. The man was a PR Terminator. As the drafts began to merge and a sort of super-draft took shape, it almost stopped making sense to me, I'd read it so often. But Stuart read it aloud, again and again, as though for the first time. You had to take your hat off.

On Wednesday afternoon, Andrew Holland paid a visit to inspect progress in person. Michelle, who was clued in by then, told us that she met him in reception and thought he looked 'fucked over'. He'd been on the phone to Stuart constantly all week, she said. To our utter relief, Barry, Lisa, and I were not invited to the meeting. It might have been interesting to hear what went on first-hand, but by that point, it was more important to us to get a couple of hours to ourselves. These weren't idle hours, of course – there was hardly an idle minute all week – but at least we had a break from Stuart and Mary. When Andrew left, we trooped into the boardroom to hear how it had gone. Stuart was ebullient, clapping backs and shouting for more coffee.

'Andrew's delighted,' he told us, as we took our seats. 'Well, not delighted, obviously, because he's very scared by the whole thing – but he's, what, *reassured*. He's reassured by what we've achieved in just a couple of days. His main fear, I'm sure you understand, was that the news would get out before he'd had time to scratch himself, let alone consider his tactics. He's been in touch with Phoenix every day, obviously, but they're stone-walling him completely, so his nerves have been a bit frazzled. Now at least he knows there's someone in his corner doing good work.'

Stuart paused briefly to let us all nod and smile about how great we were.

'The holding statement, thank God, is very nearly there. He made a few changes, suggested a point or two, but it's, what, about an hour's work. So unless some bastard journalist calls before the end of the day, we're safe on that score.'

Barry made a note of this fact.

'Now we can focus a bit more on to some of the other things that we've been looking at . . .'

And off he went. What we thought was going to be a ten-minute debriefing on his meeting with Andrew turned into a one-and-a-half-hour lecture on What Else Needed To Be Done. The central theme was that now we had the safety net of a good holding statement, we could get down to the real work. In other words, we could proceed as if the decision to axe Dublin had already been made. As Stuart droned on, I realised with mounting horror how much there was to do. We had to get meetings with the relevant politicians and civil servants (phrasing ourselves very carefully), organise media training for Andrew, prepare draft press releases for this and that eventuality, and generally start to think more deeply about how the story would play. This was the deep end of the PR pool, as far as I was concerned, and I didn't relish any of the tasks ahead. In fact, I was just beginning to worry in earnest when Stuart suddenly snapped his fingers and pointed in my direction.

'You're due to start work on another "Live Wire" one of these days, are you not?'

I blinked at him. 'Yeah ... one of these days. I hadn't really thought about it much, to be honest, Stuart, what with everything else.'

'Well, start thinking about it. It goes ahead, as though nothing else was going on, OK? Get yourself out there before the end of the week. Business as usual.'

Oh great, I thought. How am I supposed to wander calmly around Langley's taking my little notes and joking around with everyone, knowing what I know? I couldn't do it. The hypocrisy. The *duplicity* of it. No. No. I would have to refuse. For the sake of my self-respect.

'Sure thing, Stuart,' I said.

I believe I may even have done the old *you got it* pen point.

6

'Karate,' Norm said with his strange new voice, all honking nasal discord. 'Kung fu. Fucking ju-jitsu, I dunno. One of the martial arts, for def.'

He took a gulp of his pint and pursed his lips thoughtfully. We were in Jolly's again, to no one's surprise. When we did the pre-pint ring-around no one could think of anywhere better. Norm added that he was hoping to bump into what he was now calling his 'assailant'. He claimed to have a thought or two he wanted to express to her.

'Trained, that one. Knows the body's weak points.'

Stevie shook his head sadly. 'It's a miracle you survived, big man.'

I gave a deep sigh. 'We thought we'd lost you there for a while.'

'Fuck off. She could have fucking killed me. Sure doesn't Bruce Willis kill a guy in that movie about the guy who was a footballer and then becomes a cop or whatever he did?'

'Bruce Willis kills loads of people,' Stevie said, acting confused.

Norm wrinkled his face in disgust and winced at the resulting pain. 'By punching him in the nose is the point! He punched him in the nose and killed the bastard!'

'So what you're saying,' I asked him, looking puzzled, 'is that this girl who boxed you on the nose got it from Bruce Willis?'

He scowled at me, scarlet. 'What I'm saying, smarthole, is that a punch in the nose from a karate expert can fucking kill you, all right? I thought they were supposed to learn these techniques and then not use them.'

Stevie could withhold laughter no longer. 'Expert?' he sniggered. 'Techniques? You got slapped by a wee girl and your nose broke like a wafer. Big drinkawater.'

'Cunt.'

'It's a nice bandage, though.'

'Ah, fuck off.'

'Definitely your colour, beige.'

'Fucker.'

'And c'mere, Norm,' I said. 'Was it sore at the time? Go-go told me you seemed to be in awful pain. Roaring, you were, he told me.'

Norm sipped his pint slowly. His blackened eyes narrowed even further. His brow furrowed and darkened. Stevie and I exchanged glances. He was obviously getting properly mad, so we let our giggling tail off, and passed a silent minute or two with our drinks.

'Where is Go-go, then?' Norm said eventually, indicating that he had decided not to opt for the sullen mope.

'Guess,' I said.

'Sheila,' they said simultaneously.

'Cigars all round. Yeah, she rang him at work and said she

wanted to come around and see him. She was there at the weekend, too.'

'Something happening, do you think?' Stevie asked.

I shook my head dolefully. 'Not so far. He lives in hope.'

'I don't know what he sees in her,' Norm said. 'I mean, she's a good-looking girl and all, but Jesus, you don't devote your whole life to her.'

'Good-looking? Good-looking?' Stevie squawked.

'She's top of the range,' I said. 'You'd be all over her like a cheap suit.'

'She should be so lucky,' he honked, adding, for good measure: 'Lucky, lucky, lucky.'

The conversation drifted on through the usual topics. Kylie Minogue's hot pants, early eighties children's television, the price of CDs. Eventually, we got around to work – something I couldn't talk about, although the imminent trip to Langley's was weighing heavily on my mind. Norm, who did something to do with telecommunications – none of us really understood what – had no such restrictions. Apparently, he'd taken dog's abuse in the office about his nose. Characteristically, he lied profusely about the injury's origin. Uncharacteristically, he told Stevie and me about it.

'I said it was some big huge fucker with a Welsh accent. Must have been six-two, if he was an inch. I told one of the girls he had a weapon, too.'

'What kind of weapon?' Stevie asked.

Norm fingered his jet-black mini-quiff, a sure sign he was pleased with himself about something. 'I said it was a row in a pool hall, and he hit me with the butt of his cue.'

We tut-tutted disapprovingly.

Damien Owens

'Let me guess,' I said. 'You were dazzling this psychopathic man-mountain with your mastery of the green baize, and he couldn't stand the humiliation.'

'That too. I also said he was making off-colour remarks to some of the ladies present, and I asked him to stop.'

There was silence for maybe ten seconds. Stevie broke it, shaking his head slowly. 'I don't know where to begin with that. Do they not *know* you at work?'

Norm shrugged. 'I try to separate my professional life from my—'

'— shockingly disgusting real life?' Stevie interrupted.

'Did you call them "ladies"?' I wanted to know.

He nodded. 'I actually said "off-colour remarks" too. And when she wanted to know what they were, I acted shy and said I didn't want to repeat them.'

More stunned silence from us.

'Jackie, this was. Red hair. Cute enough. I think she likes me. She brought me back some buns after lunch on Monday.'

'What are you, a fucking elephant?' said Stevie.

'I'm a big bun fan, always have been. Good sign that she noticed though, eh?'

'It's a pity she didn't notice you're a boozy sexist cunt,' I observed.

Norm drained his pint and sighed contentedly. 'She'll find out everything there is to know about me some of these days, if she plays her cards right.' He pointed at us in turn as he rose to go to the bar. 'Pint? Pint?'

We nodded oh-go-on-then-I-suppose-so nods and settled another half-inch into our seats.

'So, any crack at the factory?' I asked Stevie, knowing full well there wouldn't be. Stevie worked as an accountant at a company

84

that made paper towels. The most exciting work-related anecdote he ever told involved the spotting in town of a fellow accountant who was supposed to be in bed with flu at the time. The drama unfolded over the course of a week, during which time we were all on tenterhooks, awaiting each development with breathless interest. (By contrast with some of his other stories, this was the OJ trial.) The climax of the tale came when the outlaw in question received a stern memo from someone called Mr Lacey. Stevie gave us the impression that this character was a sort of cross between Jeffrey Dahmer and Montgomery Burns, but we were unimpressed. You can't live in fear of someone called 'Lacey', we advised him. It's like being afraid of Mr Frilly.

'Not really. It's been a quiet week,' Stevie said.

I nodded firmly, hoping to imply that there was no need to tell a story for the sake of it. It didn't work. He gave me a lengthy update on his ongoing battle of wills with the woman in the canteen who was stingy with the soup ladle. Thankfully, he was interrupted by Norm's return from the front line.

'He never said a single word to me,' Norm said, distributing pints and settling back in. 'Not a word. Apart from "You. What?"'

We looked over to the bar where Leonard was grimly shoving a glass up against the Bacardi optic, his off-white shirt (his very off-white shirt) stuffed half in, half out of his polyester trousers. There had been speculation on the phone earlier that we might not be welcome after the weekend's fracas. Norm seemed disappointed that this was not the case.

'It's not like he wouldn't recognise me,' he went on. '*Look* at me, for fuck's sake.'

Stevie shrugged. 'He knows we've got money. Or rather, he thinks we've got money. Fuck him. Forget about it.'

I tried for a moment to work out why we should be feeling wronged here, but soon gave up.

'You were up home at the weekend, weren't you?' Stevie asked me, after another couple of pints. His family lived about ten miles from mine and he had even attended the same secondary school as me, although he was leaving just as I was starting. I met him on the dreaded bus one Sunday evening, not long after I'd moved to Dublin. Our friendship was born of a mutual loathing for public transport.

'Yup,' I said. 'Can you not see the scars?'

Their shoulders slumped slightly in anticipation of another whining monologue. Although Go-go was my primary sounding board – or punching bag, if you prefer – for all things domestic, both Norm and Stevie were fully au fait with the grisly details.

'What now?' said Norm. 'Let me guess. Your mother challenged you to an arm wrestle and you—'

'Deirdre's pregnant,' I reported.

There was a momentary lull.

'I take it back,' said Norm. 'That's a real problem. You'd think you'd have mentioned it by now.'

'Maybe I'm in denial,' I said. I wasn't sure if I was joking.

'Is she being all right about it?' said Stevie.

I nodded that she was. 'You know what she's like, Stevie. Things bounce off her.'

'They don't bounce off your mother,' he said gravely. 'Things go right through your mother.'

He'd only met the woman once. Afterwards he told me that she seemed really nice, but could probably do with a holiday. This was as good a description of her as I'd heard.

'Yes. Well. She's not overly delighted. But she'll get used to the idea.'

'She'll have to, won't she?' said Norm.

'My sentiments entirely.'

And at least one nun's, I thought.

'Who's the daddy?' Stevie asked. 'Anyone you know?'

I frowned in contempt. 'Ah, yes. The daddy. Brendan Feeny, he calls himself.'

Stevie's face lit up. 'Not one of the *Feeny* Feenys? From home? The car Feenys?'

I nodded. 'How come everyone's heard of these people except me?'

'You don't pay any attention, that's why. Jesus. She won't be stuck for cash. They're rolling in it, that crowd. The house is only a few miles from us, at home. Fucking huge. Blow-ins from Dublin.'

I hesitated for a second, debating whether I should tell them the whole story. Ah, fuck it, I thought. I'll only end up telling them later on. And besides, I kept the big secret, about Langley's.

'Thing is,' I said, 'he's denying it's his. He said she was a bike and it could be anybody's.'

I imparted this information in a casual, offhand manner. But they looked genuinely shocked by it. Mouths agape, eyebrows arched, they stared at me, waiting for me to continue. But I had nothing else to add.

Then Norm spoke up. 'I presume you went to this shithead's house and broke something painful?'

When Norm was acting hard, his Dublin accent grew heavy and stagey. I found this almost as annoying as his reaction.

'What, like his nose, maybe?'

He let that go. 'You mean you didn't?'

'Of course I didn't! Fuck's sake. This isn't the Wild West, you know. And I'm not exactly the physical persuasion type, am I?'

Norm looked at Stevie and Stevie looked at Norm.

'Well,' said Stevie, in a conciliatory tone, 'you had a word with him at least?'

'Jesus fucking Christ! I was only there for a day. You two should get together with my mother. She was oiling her shotgun for me as well. What the fuck am I supposed to do about it? If he's all that big a bollocks, she's better off without him.'

'What about honour?' said Norm, in the most grown-up tone he could muster.

Now this, I really couldn't stand for. It was like being lectured about sobriety by one of the Rolling Stones. I was getting agitated now, and couldn't keep my voice at conversational level.

'WHAT THE FUCK ARE YOU TALKING ABOUT? *Honour?* Is that . . . *What?* What the fuck is . . . ?'

'All right, all right,' he said. 'Don't start shouting at me. I'm just saying.'

'What? What are you just saying? I should find this guy and beat him up until he admits he's the father? Is that it? Am I missing something?'

Again, Stevie intervened. 'I think what he means is . . . is that you can't do nothing.'

I heard the next line in my head before he even said it.

'After all, you're the man of the house.'

I almost laughed. Almost. 'Go-go didn't give me this shit,' I said. 'He just listened and nodded and said he hoped it all worked out.'

'Go-go, no offence to him,' said Norm, 'is a big woman. You want to listen to Stevie and me.'

When push came to shove, things always broke down this way. Although the four of us were pretty tight, it was a doubles match at heart. Norm and Stevie versus Go-go and me. Sides were taken, and often.

'Well, he talks perfect sense, as far as I'm concerned,' I said to Norm.

'Perfect sense, in this case, being anything that avoids you facing up to your responsibilities.'

Suddenly, this had the potential to become a real fight.

'Listen to me,' I said slowly, through my teeth. 'I am not going to get into a stand-up row with this asshole, all right? He is not *worth* it. As far as I'm concerned, and Deirdre too, as far as we're all concerned, he doesn't exist. Get it?'

Norm sat back in his chair a little, and said nothing. Stevie sipped his pint and waited three beats for me to calm down.

'But it's not all of you, is it?' he said, in a quiet voice. 'You said your mum wanted action too.'

I shook my head in disgust. '*Action. Honour.* Listen to you. You watch too many shitty movies.'

'I just hope you don't let her down. That's all.'

That was enough for me. I got to my feet and plucked my jacket off the back of the chair.

'Ah, Jesus Christ, sit down,' said Norm. 'We're only trying to help.'

I was already moving away. 'Well, you're doing a fucking terrible job.'

They mumbled ruefully about having more pints and changing subjects. I shook my head no.

'Just keep your advice to yourselves in future,' I said, and headed for the door.

Regrettably, my big exit was marred by Leonard, for the first

time in recorded history, calling out 'Good night now, safe home.'
Bastard must have found some money or something.

I stomped home in a serious sulk, going out of my way to find
stones and cans to kick. For fuck's sake. Action. Pair of pricks.
Norm especially. Sometimes he was funny to have around, and
sometimes he was just a pain in the ring. We only knew him in the
first place because he was Stevie's cousin, someone his mum had
forced him to look up when he first moved to Dublin, years ago.
He referred to us openly as his culchie mates, and clearly thought
of us as bog-hopping yokels who wouldn't last ten minutes in the
mean city streets if he wasn't there to act as a guide. Which was,
of course, bullshit of the highest order. For one thing, calling us
his culchie mates implied that he had, secreted away somewhere,
a set of real Dublin mates. If he had, I never saw any of them. For
another thing, Norm knew Dublin like I knew Bangkok, despite
having lived there his whole life. He could get lost going into
town shopping. Worst of all was his risible pretence at nails-hard
street-wisdom. Never mind the permanent Scorsese act, he was
about as hard as my mum, as The Girl With The Ass Who Broke
His Nose had memorably demonstrated. Even his curious success
with women owed nothing to charm or grace. It was due almost
entirely to neck. I wasn't really surprised then that he was going
along with this cretinous shotgun theory. But I didn't find it as
easy to account for Stevie's attitude. He may have been a little
vacant, Stevie, but you could never accuse him of being reckless.
Why he was badgering me along with everyone else, I had no
idea. Maybe he was drunk. I knew I was.

As ever, stress and unpleasantness got me thinking about the
screenplay – my ticket out of <insert difficult situation here>.

As soon as I got back to the flatlet, I put the kettle on for coffee and fired up the Mac, which trembled and whirred for fully sixty seconds before coming alive. For reasons that weren't quite clear to me, I associated coffee with creativity. It made not the blindest bit of difference, I hardly need to report. Most of my writing sessions – especially those begun in desperation – ended with shocking profanity and a PacMan marathon. (PacMan was the only game my computer could handle. I once tried to install a real game, and the thing had a fucking fit.)

'Right,' I said to the thin air, settling in at the rickety desk. 'Let's get something done.' Within the hour, I was sullenly chasing ghosts and gobbling power pills, having added all of three lines of dialogue, two of which were 'Are you serious?' and 'Yes, I am.'

My screenplay was called *Come to Beautiful Earth*. I reckoned it was nearly two-thirds finished. The premise was that good old Earth, unbeknownst to us, is the planetary equivalent of Torremolinos, sucking in thousands of tourists from all over the galaxy. Disguised (badly) as humans, the alien holidaymakers flock to Niagara Falls, the Amazon rainforest, the pyramids, and so on, taking group photos and getting far too drunk. The central character was an alien holiday rep whose Earth name was 'Jonathon'. He gets into all sorts of wacky scrapes. Only I didn't think of them as wacky scrapes. Or zany adventures, either. I thought of them as bitingly satirical set-pieces. The Hollywood marketing machine, I told myself with a resigned shrug, would probably call them wacky scrapes. But that's the price you pay.

Jonathon's job as a tour rep is nothing but drudgery and tedium. He suffers all the usual rep torments – aliens who've lost their passports, their girlfriends, their luggage, all that. I had any number of hilarious aliens-abroad gags. My favourite sequence involved a drunken Vermalian (you know, from the planet Vermal) getting arrested for pissing acid off the Eiffel Tower and having to call Jonathon to bail him out of a Parisian jail cell. It was a lot funnier than it sounds.

Jonathon, understandably, longs for some adventure and romance, which arrives in the form of 'Karen', a being from home who has come to Earth on her honeymoon. She's just married a creepy insurance-salesman sort of alien who treats her like dirt and . . . well, you can guess the rest. I'm not saying I thought it was art. I'm saying I thought it was *saleable*. I saw Jim Carrey as Jonathon, and maybe Cameron Diaz as Karen. Julia Roberts at a push.

I'd been working on the thing for around six months. During that time, I had written enough material for maybe four full-length screenplays, but threw most of it away on the very reasonable grounds that it was complete and utter bullshit. The material that was left, though, in my humble opinion, was pretty good. Go-go, for one, had read it and declared himself impressed. Having said that, Go-go had no taste whatsoever in movies. Among his all-time favourites, he counted *Dirty Dancing* and *Police Academy*. ('The first one,' he assured me, as if that made any difference.) What's more, being Go-go, he wouldn't have had a bad word to say about my screenplay even if it had been the sort of thing that Jean-Claude Van Damme might turn down for being too crass and witless.

I wasn't even a movie buff, particularly – or a keen writer, for that matter. Like everyone else who studies English, I had tossed off a few execrable short stories in college, but had long since given up on prose. Too much like work. Then, not long enough after I started in PR, I found a second-hand book called, tantalisingly, *How to Write a Screenplay*, and thought I'd give it a shot.

What the hell made me think that a first-attempt screenplay hacked together by a nobody in Dublin would even get read, let alone made? Let alone made with Jim Carrey and Cameron Diaz. Perhaps my cockiness was due to the overwhelming conviction I shared with ninety per cent of cinema-goers that I Could Do Better Than That. Who in their right mind has sat through *Under Siege* or *Independence Day* and thought, Wow, those Hollywood screenwriters are a talented bunch? Or perhaps it was simply my childishly romantic belief that I deserved a break and this was going to be it. Whatever – *Come to Beautiful Earth* was going to be a smash-hit movie. That was a given. In some strange way, I almost relished my soul-destroying job with Stuart and my pathetic flatlet because they served as the rags in what would shortly become a rags to riches story. I spent many happy hours trying to imagine what my first Beverly Hills mansion might look like, with my first Porsche parked outside and my first starlet wife lazing by the pool in the hazy afterglow of a life-altering sexual experience.

It was a question not of if, but when.

7

Even in the best of circumstances, I never enjoyed my monthly trips to Langley-Foster Electronics. For a start, their receptionist invariably treated me like something she found stuck to her shoe. I had no idea what I was supposed to have done to offend her, but whatever it was, it worked.

'Joe,' she sighed, as I stumbled in out of the rain that horrible Friday morning. Every time she said my name, she wrinkled up her nose in thinly veiled contempt. Maybe she had a thing about PR people. Which was fair enough.

'Hi, Angela,' I chirped. 'How are things?'

'Fan-*tas*-tic. The customary ten minutes late, I see.'

I laughed a hollow little laugh. 'Yeah. Ha ha. I think I've got it now.'

To anyone else, my inability to remember exactly where the place was might have come across as mildly charming, in a Mr Magoo sort of way. But to Angela, it just seemed to underline her conviction that I was a hopeless cretin who was probably stealing their stationery when no one was looking. It was hardly my fault – Langley's was tucked away at the back of a labyrinthine industrial estate, which, I was sure, employed mirrors somehow to make it even more difficult to navigate. Without exception, all of my journeys out there ended with me wedged between the front seats mumbling faint assurances that it was around here somewhere, while the taxi driver sighed deeply and drummed impatiently on the steering wheel.

'I'll call Brian and let him know you've finally arrived,' Angela said.

I loved the 'finally'.

'Thanks,' I said and took a seat. Miserable bitch.

I sat there on a squeaky leather chair trying to act casual. They had strewn a few business and technology magazines on a glass-topped coffee table and I thumbed through one idly, not even aware of what I was looking at. Three times, I looked up and caught Angela glaring at me.

She knows, I thought, my stomach churning. Receptionists know everything. She's caught wind of it, somehow. She knows, and she knows I know.

Happily, not two minutes had passed before Brian bounded into reception, clapping his hands together and beaming broadly.

'Joseph Flood! The very man,' he gushed, greeting me, as usual, with at least twice as much respect and enthusiasm as I deserved. Brian was old enough to be my father but always acted like an impressionable youth around me, bouncing nervously from foot to foot and fiddling with his substantial salt and pepper fringe. I had a terrible suspicion that he dressed up when he knew someone from Stuart Kennedy PR was coming to see him. He struck me as the type who would be impressed by PR. In anyone else's case, I would mean that as an insult. In Brian's case, I mean it as an expression of pity. He was sporting a shiny green suit, whose hue and texture reminded me of having the flu. The nauseating effect of the suit was not alleviated by his sunny yellow shirt, black tie, and dung-coloured brogues. The shoes had clearly seen better days. The shirt, I fancied, was new. I know it sounds unlikely that this ensemble might be the result of careful planning, but I called at Langley's unexpectedly one summer's afternoon and found Brian decked out in a dizzying outfit that owed more than a little to H.P. Lovecraft. This was Brian dressed up, no question.

'Howiye, Brian,' I said, rising to shake his clammy hand.

'Never better,' he replied, going into his trademark head-bob routine. 'Busy, you know? Kept going. The only way to be, eh?'

I agreed that yes indeed, being busy was a fine and joyous thing. The best approach with Brian, I had long since decided, was to agree with everything he said. If you could articulate your continuing assent without ever resorting to actual words, then so much the better. He would simply talk to himself while you stood there nodding. If you challenged him in even the slightest way, you could forget about the next half-hour. Not in a nasty way, of course, but . . . A nervous talker, Brian, to say the least. And, hey look at this, quite possibly out of a job in a few weeks' time. As we walked to his office, I had to consciously force myself to keep my oily PR grin fastened on.

'So are you busy yourselves?' he asked as we made our way down the shiny white hallways, more hospital than factory.

'Sure when is it ever any different?' I smiled, weakly. *Smile, fuck you, smile like you've never smiled before.*

'Right enough. When is right. But sure that's the way to be, eh? Kept going.'

We kept up this harmless banter – or rather Brian did – until we reached a small meeting room on the first floor.

'Here we are,' he said, ushering me in. 'Have a seat, sit, sit. Will you have a coffee? Course you will. Milk? Sugar?'

He disappeared to get the drinks before I even said I wanted one, let alone how I wanted it. When he left me alone in that boxy little room, with its plastic pot plant, and its framed inspirational poster (a picture of a soaring eagle subtitled with the word 'Freedom!'), I felt a blanket of self-loathing settle around my shoulders. Brian loved this. It wouldn't have surprised me to hear that it was his favourite part of his job. He was out there somewhere stirring coffees and hunting for biscuits, looking forward to telling me what was newsworthy in Langley's this month. The development of some incomprehensible new gizmo maybe, or a popular promotion from the ranks. I was convinced that Brian saw his connection to 'Live Wire' as a foot into the glitzy world of the media.

After a couple of minutes, Brian returned with the coffees. Mine had unwanted sugar, but I didn't mention it. He might have killed himself.

'Now,' he said, settling in. 'Get that notebook of yours out. There's been a lot going on.'

Predictably, Brian's definition of 'a lot going on' was nothing like mine. Three women from the plant had given birth in the same week. The company bowling team had beaten hated enemies Ericsson in a tense encounter at the Stillorgan Bowl. Some big shot from Sony had written a nice letter, thanking 'the team in Dublin' for knocking out a rush job on some video gizmos. (These were the big stories, the two-hundred-and-fifty worders, by the way.) As he summarised the recent dramas, Brian slurped his coffee excitedly, and slid duff baby Polaroids and incomprehensible gizmo specs across the table at me. I jotted down names and asked silly technical questions, feeling flushed and somewhat disembodied, as if I was badly stoned, not sure if I was saying things or just thinking them. I kept wanting to clap my hand over my gob, certain I had just blurted out something like 'You're doomed! Dooooooooomed, I tell ye!'

Brian, oblivious, prattled on for a tortuous hour and a half. By the time he sucked the cap of his biro once more for luck, cast his eyes heavenward for a second, and finally said, 'I think that's everything,' my writing hand was throbbing severely and my self-esteem was wrapped around my ankles. Relieved and frankly exhausted, I gathered my notes and shook my hand back to life. Brian shunted his chair carefully back under the table and clapped his hands together once again.

'Now,' he said, grinning. 'What about a bite to eat?'

There were several good reasons for not wanting to eat lunch in Langley's. First and foremost, I already felt like Himmler visiting a synagogue. Brazenly having lunch with the staff, like any other visitor, seemed like pouring salt in the wound. Secondly, the food there was usually stodgy and taste-free. Thirdly, it would mean more conversation with Brian. He had yet to come up with a crossword for this issue, and had already given me an extensive summary of the difficulties involved. No doubt he would continue this theme over the lukewarm shepherd's pie.

But I had skipped breakfast again that day, and my stomach was shuddering noisily. Plus, and I'm embarrassed to say this, I knew that Brian really liked it when I stayed for lunch. Sad, but true. I'm sure of it.

Jesus Christ. You make these tiny little decisions all day, every day, and you don't know. You just don't know. Anyway, I said yes.

So we went for lunch.

* * *

Langley's staff canteen was, how shall I put this, a tad functional. I know staff canteens are not traditionally admired for their elegance and class, but this place really seemed to go out of its way to rob you of your appetite. White. White, white, white. White was big all over with Langley's, but you'd think they'd have made an exception where food was involved. Everything was gleaming, the walls, the floor, the tables, the crockery, the trays, the *chairs*, for God's sake. It was like eating in an operating theatre.

My meeting with Brian – such as it was – had ended at bang on one, so the place was creeping with people. As we joined the lengthy queue, I began to worry that I had made the wrong choice. I could be halfway back by now, I was thinking, munching on a chicken tikka sandwich and ignoring some taxi driver. It took nearly ten minutes to reach the serving area, which time Brian filled by telling me about the extortionate price of his daughter's school books. I didn't say a single word the whole time, so he started an argument with himself about whether or not they should be free. In no time at all, I went from ashamed and embarrassed to ashamed and thoroughly pissed off. My mood didn't improve when I saw – and smelled – the sweet and sour pork that was slapped onto my luminous white plate by a miserable-looking woman in a similarly dazzling white outfit. When I was about eight, a cat belonging to a neighbour of ours had kittens, and I watched the whole thing. Although it was impressive at the time, I forgot all about it until I saw that sweet and sour. Lunch was going to be a sandwich on the way home after all.

Once out of the queue, we spent an enjoyable five minutes rotating on the spot like robot sentries, trying to find a place to sit. Thankfully, one came free right under our noses.

'Quick!' said Brian, bounding two feet to his right. Then he stood silently wriggling like a man in urgent need of a urinal, while our predecessors stacked their plates and things on their trays.

'Bit of good luck, eh?' he said when they'd gone and we were seated. 'Sure that's all you need. Bit of good luck.'

I nodded that, controversially, I too was in favour of good luck.

My first taste of the so-called sweet and sour was also my last. All I did was dip the tines of my fork into the syrupy red goo and then lightly brush the result against my lips, but I can still taste the bastard today. Brian had opted for fish and chips. It didn't say on the menu what kind of fish we were talking about. FISH was all it said, with ominous pedantry. Something paper-thin and greasy, at any rate. Even Brian, whom I had thought immune to Langley's culinary deficiencies, seemed to have trouble with it. There was conversation, of course, inasmuch as my dining companion jabbered noisily about whatever happened into his consciousness. Personally, I was sinking lower and lower into my ugly mood, guilt and shame compounded by boredom and hunger. And frowning so heavily, right after a concerted stretch of counterfeit smiling, was starting to give me a fearsome headache.

'The thing about country music . . .' Brian said.

'Steven Spielberg . . .' Brian said.

'If the current can't flow . . .' Brian said.

'Seen from above . . .' Brian said.

'The dearest form of credit . . .' Brian said.

I tried to detach myself from the verbal assault by guessing the origin of the lumps in my lunch. When that lost its appeal – after I uncovered something that looked suspiciously like a human tooth – I began to glance around me, quite openly, out of pure boredom. Inexcusably rude, I know, but Brian was not the sort to notice, let alone care.

'The little Mexican mouse . . .' he said.

'But not quite parallel . . .' he said.

In my paranoia, it seemed that everyone in the place was laughing happily, unaware of the dangling axe. Swapping silly work stories, perhaps, that no one else would find funny. Or talking about last night's *Frasier*. Or maybe just retelling awful jokes they'd been e-mailed that morning. I surveyed the scene, imagining fine cross-hairs superimposed over my line of vision. A raspy Hollywood voice (Charles Bronson? Clint Eastwood?) whispered *Bang! You're gone* as I moved from face to unknowing face.

Big fat bald guy, looks a bit like Stevie. *Bang! You're gone*. Cute-ish blonde, horrible glasses. *Bang! You're gone*. Angry-looking manager type. *Bang! You're gone*. Girl With The Ass Who Broke Norm's Nose. *Bang! Y—*

Oh sweetfuckingjesus. It was her. Unmistakable. Not twenty feet away. Over Brian's shoulder. Just sitting there with two other girls. Ordinary girls. I think I gasped.

She was wearing a dark blue T-shirt, baggy grey trousers and a pair of complicated-looking trainers. I knew they must be cool because I thought they looked silly. Her hair was longer than it had seemed in the pub, and darker too. She had a bunch of it between her fingers and was absently stabbing herself in the mouth with it. The harsh light of Langley's canteen made shiny ghosts of everyone else, but not her. She retained some sort of indefinable poise that we had all lost in the glare. As I gazed unblinking she seemed to pop out of the background, like she was more there than those around her. It was like looking at a Magic Eye poster. Only enjoyable.

She was doing a lot of smiling and nodding as her friends nattered away, their heads almost touching sometimes, conspiratorial.

I hadn't seen her smile properly at our previous encounter, what with the fighting and so on. It was a good smile. A fucking *great* smile, actually. I felt a poor imitation of it creep over my own confused and exhausted face. And she was having a salad, I noted. Of course. Salad! Why didn't I think of that? They can't go too far wrong with salad. So she's smart, too, I thought, admiringly. I stared in wonder for maybe ninety seconds, oblivious not just to Brian, but to everything. If someone had tapped me on the shoulder and asked me where I was, I would have had to give it some thought.

Ah yes. Where I was. Langley's. She obviously worked there. *Bang! You're gone.* My stomach lurched. I was suddenly back on Earth. With Brian.

'But there's no E on the end, so that didn't fit either,' he said.

'Sorry?'

'No E on the end. So it didn't work out.'

I opened my mouth for half a second and then closed it again.

'In the crossword. Didn't fit.'

'Oh! Yeah. Didn't fit. Terrible. Terrible.'

'I'll crack it, don't you worry. Sure all you need is a bit of good luck. Isn't that right?'

I might have nodded. I don't know. I was lost again, having suddenly noticed that The Girl With The Ass Who Broke Norm's Nose might just as easily have been called The Girl With The Tits Who Broke Norm's Nose.

The big question was: could I talk to her? The smaller question was: if I did, would she thump me? Maybe she wouldn't even remember me. Norm was the one she'd seen up close. What would I say, anyway? *Hi. I don't know if you remember me. Last Friday in Jolly's? You broke my friend's nose? Yeah. Hi.*

On the other hand, I could—

'You're not even listening to me, are you, Joe?'

Brian was staring at me beadily from under his fringe. He looked deeply hurt.

'Oh, sorry, Brian,' I said, meaning it. 'I got a bit lost there.'

He gave a small miserable nod. It would have broken my heart any other day. 'I know I witter on a little bit sometimes,' he said. 'But it's only because I—'

'You don't happen to know that girl's name, by any chance?' I asked, cutting him dead. 'Behind you – DON'T TURN ROUND! – behind you, in the blue T-shirt, grey trousers.'

A twinkle appeared in Brian's eye.

'Aha!' he whispered, barely moving his lips, although the girl in question was behind him and couldn't even see his face. '*Cherchez la femme*, eh? And there's me, thinking I was boring you. Sure you're dead right. When I was your—'

I leaned forward. There was no time for this. 'Yeah, right. Got it. Now. Do you know her *name*?'

He winked at me – he actually winked – and then he went into the ludicrous looking-behind-you pantomime beloved of indiscreet people all over the world. It was a textbook performance. First, he looked into the middle distance over my shoulder. Then he issued a small cough. Next, he picked up a sachet of sugar and gave it a thorough but apparently absent-minded shake. Then he went in for the kill – an enormous stage yawn, combined with a two-armed stretch, and topped off with a leisurely head roll of owl-like dimensions. When he snapped back into a regular shape, he was nodding.

'Catherine,' he said, with some confidence. 'Catherine . . . Catherine . . .'

'Yes?'

He tapped his chin. 'Catherine something. I don't work with her, myself, but we were introduced. She hasn't been here long. Feckit, I'm hopeless with names. Catherine ... Catherine ... something. Ah, look at you! You're all smitten. So you're single then?'

'Brian, I'm so single, I'm barely here myself.'

'So, are you going to go over? Talk to her? Ask her out?'

'Certainly not,' I said, trying not to stare over his shoulder. 'Whether I know her first name or her last name or her frigging star sign, it makes no odds.'

'Why not?'

Because our last meeting ended in a punch-up, I thought, but didn't say. I gave the other reason – which was, in any case, the real reason. 'Ah. You know. I'd never have the nerve. She's in a different league.'

Brian looked intensely pleased to be having this racy conversation. 'Do they still have leagues, then? I thought they were done away with years ago.'

I combined a smile and a frown with a small snort. 'I bloody wish. No. They've still got leagues, Brian. And she's in a different one to me.'

'But sure you never know, eh? Faint heart never won fair maiden. Or lady, or whatever it is.'

'I think it's lady. And no, it didn't. On the other hand, faint heart never got a plate of Langley's sweet and sour poured over its head either.'

'She's eating salad,' Brian said, firmly. 'I saw.'

'Good point. But not good enough.'

We stared at the ruins of our lunch in silence for a moment.

Then Brian lit up. 'Maybe I could have a word with her. Find out if she's available, at least.'

I nearly choked.

'NO! Jesus, Brian. No. No. No. Please, *please* don't even think about doing that.'

Christ. What went on in his mind?

'You should at least find out if she's free. She might have a boyfriend. Or a husband, even. She could be a mother. Sure maybe you're worrying for nothing.'

I gazed at her anew, my brow corrugated. It was certainly possible. Likely, even. She had some bloke in tow in Jolly's.

'Stop helping, Brian,' I said.

But he wouldn't leave it alone. He was really enjoying himself in his new role as wise old hand with insider knowledge. Not content with the old faint-heart line, he began trotting out other well-meaning but thoroughly impractical platitudes. They were all there, all the greats – strike while the iron is hot, she can only say no, who dares wins, God loves a trier. All perfectly true. All perfectly useless, when she's sitting over there, and you're sitting over here and the space between might as well be mined. Approaching girls wasn't so hard when you stood a reasonable chance. It was different when you knew they were too good for you. When that was a brute fact – like gravity.

'It's not like you work here,' he said. 'What have you got to lose? Sure she doesn't know you from Adam.'

This was another one of those moments when I could choose between hearing the almost certainly futile advice of a near-stranger and keeping my dignity.

'Hmmm. The thing is,' I said, 'we have sort of met.'

Dignity-schmignity.

'Oh! Good! Sure that's a start, is it not? Where did you meet her?'

'A pub. It was in a pub. In Rathmines. But we didn't really meet. She, eh, she had a sort of a row with a friend of mine.'

Brian was on the edge of his shiny white chair now, eyes bulging. 'What kind of a row? Was he after her too?'

I shrugged. 'Nah. It was all about a . . . it was . . . he . . .'

Brian nodded for me to go on. I stole another peek at Catherine (what a fucking *brilliant* name for a girl). I wondered if her knuckles still hurt. If they ever did.

'I can't really remember what it was about,' I said, finally, opting to maintain at least a shred of honour. 'I was rotten drunk, to be honest.'

Brian nodded. 'But there'd be no hard feelings though, if the row was with your friend, and not you. Do you not think? Sure couldn't you go over and say hello at least. Apologise for the chap that she had the row with. Clear the air. Do you not think?'

An apology. Hmmm. Now, there was something to be said for this idea. Maybe I could get some clear blue water, in her head, between me and those other bozos. *Yes, I'm afraid they were very drunk. No excuse for that kind of thing. Admire your gusto.* Done right, it would make me look downright gentlemanly. Statesmanlike, even.

I was just talking myself into it, trying out lines in my head, when Catherine and her friends suddenly got up from their table.

'Agh! They're leaving!' I wailed.

Brian swivelled round quickly, not even trying to disguise his actions this time. They had tidied up the table in a second and were already on the move, taking their trays over to the clearing station.

'Go! Go! Go!' he hissed at me, like a sergeant pushing a reluctant paratrooper out of a perfectly good aeroplane.

I felt a huge surge of adrenalin and launched myself out my chair, only to come to an immediate halt. This is all wrong, I thought suddenly. I don't do this. Not with girls who look like that. I sit here and fret until it's too late to do anything and then I bitch about it in the pub later. That's me; I don't know who this leaping-out-of-chairs bloke is. I stood rooted to the spot for a moment, considering.

Forget about it, Joseph. Look at her, for God's sake. What the hell were you thinking about? Never in a million years. She'd probably scream if you even said hello.

I was still thinking these things when my treacherous legs started to move of their own accord, carrying me in her direction. I glanced behind me and got a vigorous thumbs-up from Brian. In the heat of the moment, I even returned the gesture – which must have looked very cool. Eat your heart out, Steve McQueen.

I held back a step until Catherine had deposited her tray, and then I pounced. Well, when I say pounced, I mean I cleared my throat noisily and then quick-stepped after her, my hand hovering over her moving right shoulder until she paused just long enough to allow me to bring it down with a force that was more slap than tap.

She did a one hundred and eighty on the spot, so quickly that the tips of my fingers stayed in place on her shoulder.

We looked at each other briefly.

'Hello, Catherine,' I quivered, withdrawing my arm.

She stared at me, puzzled. It wasn't dawning on her. 'Hello,' she said, tentatively.

I swallowed hard. 'Hello,' I said, again. (Fucking *genius*.)

'Um . . . do I know you?' she asked, giving a tiny hint of her world-class smile.

I scratched the tip of my nose, embarrassed. 'Well, thing is, ha! Eh, thing is . . .'

'OH JESUS! You're one of the wankers! From the pub!'

Everything went grey for a second. I felt my knees give a little and thought I could hear the ocean. She hadn't shouted exactly, but people heard. I could feel them staring.

'What the hell are you doing here?' she spat. 'And how did you know my name? Holy shit, are you *stalking* me or something?'

She started looking around frantically, for what I don't know. A security guard, probably.

'No, no, wait a second,' I sputtered. 'Hang on, now. Calm down. I'm here working, I had a meeting with Brian Denieffe. He told me your name. It's nothing sinister.'

Stupidly, I turned slightly and pointed back at our table. Brian waved at us enthusiastically. Then he did the thumbs-up again.

'That weirdo,' she shivered. 'He gives me the frigging creeps as well.'

There was no real answer to that, so I ignored it. Frankly, I was hoping she wouldn't ask me if I was in PR.

'Brian's all right,' I said. 'He's just a little . . . Look, never mind Brian, this is nothing to do with him. I only asked him if he knew your name because I wanted to come over and apologise about last Friday. That's all.'

She stared at me, shark-eyed.

'It was a stupid, stupid conversation. In the pub. A stupid, laddish, blokeish, childish conversation that no one else was supposed to hear. Not that that excuses it! It doesn't. I know it doesn't.'

Now that I was actually talking to her, there didn't seem to be any good way to disassociate myself from the Jolly's episode. But I could still go with the abject remorse strategy.

'I'm really, really sorry.'

More staring. A long pause.

'You were right to be upset.'

The stare wavered. Was that a flicker at the corner of her mouth?

'I would have been too, in your shoes.'

Definitely. She was trying not to laugh. I knew the signs. Women were always trying not to laugh at me. I took a breath and plunged.

'You, eh . . . you broke his nose, you know.'

Her eyes flashed from half-hooded contempt to saucer-like delight.

'No!' she cackled, clapping a hand over her mouth. She even gave me a get-outta-here shove, which I filed away. For a brief moment, she doubled over laughing, issuing great whooping guffaws. It couldn't have been less ladylike, or more sexy. I mentally pinched myself. Then I physically pinched myself. Was this actually going well?

'He deserved it,' she said, calming down and obviously remembering that I was one of them. 'Fucking prick.'

I nodded vigorously.

'He *is* a prick, a lot of the time. But I'm not.'

Oops. Too much? This was supposed to be an apology, not a chat-up. Or rather, it was supposed to sound like an apology, not a chat-up. Catherine pursed her lips and said nothing, daring me to go on, to utterly humiliate myself if I felt like it. Which, of course, I did.

'I mean, you know . . . I can be a prick too, as much as the next guy. But I'm not . . . I'm not a *habitual* prick.'

'My, my,' she said, ignoring my self-aggrandisement. 'You're not very loyal to your so-called friends, are you? I'd hate to be counting on you for support in a time of crisis. Going around telling total strangers what pricks your friends are.'

'Well. I'm a bloke. You know? That's what we're like.'

I'd learned a long time ago that women will forgive almost anything if you just own up at the outset to being a bloke. They think it's a disease. They're not far wrong, either. There was a hiatus, during which Catherine bit her lower lip in a way that made my head swim. Then, apparently working her way through the A–Z of sexy gestures, she tucked some hair behind a perfectly formed ear.

'Lookit,' I croaked. 'All I want is that if I happen to bump into you in Jolly's some night, or even out here, you won't throw anything heavy at me.'

She half closed one eye and swung her weight onto her right hip, considering. 'Well, for one thing, you won't bump into me in that pub again. Shithole that it is. The barman in there is the rudest man I ever met in my life.'

A pause for comic effect.

'*One* of the rudest men, anyway.'

I giggled nervously.

'All right,' she said. 'Apology accepted. Incident forgotten. Now, let's get on with our lives, will we?'

I nodded enthusiastically, and extended a hand. 'Very big of you. Appreciate it.'

She hesitated and shook my hand slowly and deliberately. For the few seconds of contact, I thought I might be levitating.

'Goodbye, then,' I said, giving her hand an involuntary little squeeze – at which point she snapped it back. 'You know, that barman usually isn't there on Saturday afternoons. You might try Jolly's again then. I think I will. This Saturday, I mean. Tomorrow, like. At about four.'

This was *unheard-of* boldness, from me. I felt possessed – possessed by some entity with a lot more nerve than I had.

She shook her head as she retreated. 'Blokes,' she said. 'What are you like?'

I watched her catch up with her friends, who were eyeing me with female suspicion. Then I returned to Brian, light-headed.

'Well? *Well?*' he said. 'Did you apologise?'

I nodded, still staring at the space where she had most recently been standing.

'And? What did she say?'

'She said that was fine,' I sighed.

'Good!' said Brian. 'That's the main thing, eh? Did you ask her out?'

I shrugged. 'I *think* so.'

8

I spent the rest of that Friday afternoon at work in a pleasant sort of fog, humming little tunes to myself and doodling aimlessly on the edge of my notepad. I replayed everything that had happened in the canteen over and over again, fast-forwarding through the sweet and sour, and pausing on the playful shove and handshake from Catherine. The shove, especially, was a source of delight. I mean, you more or less have to shake someone's hand when they offer it. But you choose your own shoves.

I told myself repeatedly that there was no way she was going to actually – ha! – show up in Jolly's the following day. As if. That would constitute such a violation of everything I knew about the universe that it would be more frightening than thrilling. Instead, I tried to content myself with being really chuffed that I had managed to go over there and speak to her. At all. It was a good sign, and a boost to morale. With this triumph of social daring under my belt, I could really start to shine back in my own league, back with the ordinary girls.

Yeah, forget about Jolly's, that's a non-starter. This is what I told myself every couple of minutes for the rest of the day.

*　　*　　*

At around five, just as I was beginning to clock-watch in earnest, Stuart summoned everyone to the boardroom to sum up the week's activity with regard to Langley's. It was a thoroughly pointless albeit brief meeting, since he and Mary had been in more or less continuous contact with Barry, Lisa, and me since Monday morning. There was simply nothing new to say until either a journalist got hold of the rumour, or an announcement of some kind was made. We each gave a little report on what we had done and what we planned to do in the coming week. Yet more drafting and planning for Barry and Lisa, another exciting instalment of 'Live Wire' for me. Stuart used the occasion to emphasise once again what a great opportunity this was 'for us all'. Everyone nodded and mumbled along, out of habit. Having just come back from the plant, I found the whole business more nauseating than ever. What kind of people were we, to make our livings at least partially from other people's misery? Those innocent people, carrying on, oblivious?

Poor Brian, I thought. Poor Catherine.

Go-go and I left the building together, and went for a quick pint around the corner ('Just the one, mind,' said Go-go. 'Absolutely,' I agreed. 'One. At most.') He had been in meetings of his own for large parts of the day, so we hadn't had a chance to catch up. We sat in a snug at the very back of the pub and ordered drinks from a lounge girl, who looked about fourteen years of age.

'Are we getting older,' Go-go asked, 'or are they getting younger?'

'The first one,' I replied, removing a filthy ashtray from our table. Hate that.

We sat in silence then, until the pints arrived. Lubrication, don't you know.

'Right,' I said, when our whistles were wetted. 'Get this. I'm in the pub the other night with Stevie and Norm – oh! I forgot. How did it go at yours with Sheila?'

He waved me away, while he slurped his pint. 'Tell you in a minute. What pub?'

'Jolly's, where do you think?'

'I thought we were never going to drink there again.'

We both smiled and rolled our eyes, letting it go.

'Anyway. So we're sitting there, chatting away . . .'

'Did he say anything?'

'Who?'

'Leonard. About the . . . incident.'

'Oh. No. Norm seemed very disappointed. I think he'd like to get a reputation in Jolly's.'

'He has got a reputation in Jolly's. As a drunken arsehole.'

'No doubt. Anyway. I was telling them about developments at home last weekend.'

'Right. Were you talking to them since? At home?'

'No. Well, yeah. For a few minutes, on Tuesday or Wednesday, I think. My mum. She seemed all right. Bit tense, you know.'

'Naturally.'

'Naturally. So, right, I told them all about it, just the same way I told you. That Deirdre was pregnant, so on, that my mum was being . . . my mum about it, that the father was this Feeny character.'

Go-go nodded along. 'Does Stevie know him, then? Feeny?'

'Yeah,' I said. 'He does. He said pretty much what Deirdre said, that he was one of "the car Feenys", loaded, rolling in it.'

'Right.'

115

'Right. But then I told them that he was being a real prick about it, denying it was his, calling her a slut . . .'

Go-go slapped the table with an open palm. 'Whoa! Hang on. You never told me that.'

I blinked a few times in silence. 'Yes I did.'

'No. You didn't. You told me all the rest. And you said the guy sounded like a real asshole. You never told me he called your sister a *slut*.'

I paused, unsure of myself. 'It was bike, actually. He called her a bike.'

Go-go shrugged. 'Bike, slut. You didn't tell me any of that.'

'Go-go, I fucking *did*. On the way back to the office, Monday lunchtime.'

He shook his head firmly. 'No. Uh-uh. Jesus Christ, I'd have remembered. You didn't tell me. Honestly. You didn't. You said the guy sounded like a real prick and he was denying it was his. That's all.'

I could feel my face reddening.

'Well, what fucking difference does it make? He's a bollocks. We already know that.'

'Yeah, but. There's being a bollocks and then there's being a real bollocks. He called her a slut?'

'Bike! It was bike!'

'Whatever. Jesus. That's pretty serious.'

I ground my teeth, not wanting to raise my voice. 'Lookit. How is knocking somebody up and then denying it acceptable behaviour, but calling them a bike is a fucking war crime?'

Go-go gave another little shrug. 'Dunno. I'm not saying he sounded all right until you mentioned the slutty bike bit . . .'

'Bike!' I snapped. 'Not slutty bike!'

'*Bike*, then. But, you know. That's a shocker, so it is. What are you going to do about it?'

I slumped into my chair, thoroughly miserable, too annoyed to even form an answer.

A few seconds passed. Go-go glanced around him nervously. 'Joe? What the fuck's . . . ? Did I say something wrong?'

I shook my head, trying not to be angry at him.

'This is the whole point of this frigging story,' I said, finally, as calmly as I could. 'About the other night in Jolly's. Norm and Stevie kept wanting to know what I was going to do about it, about Feeny. I thought they were out of their fucking minds. I even told them that I told you the whole story and you never mentioned any of this "what are you going to do about it" shite. And now *this*.'

Go-go stared at his knees. 'Well. Sorry. But you can't let him get away with that.'

I fixed him with a frosty stare. 'If you tell me I am the man of the house, after all, then you're getting this fucking pint over your head.'

He said nothing. We sat in miserable silence for a couple of minutes. I broke the deadlock, as ever, with poor-quality humour.

'Well. We'd better make plans then. Where I am going to get a gun? You know anyone? Something hefty. We don't want him just wounded. Or maybe a knife? What do you think? Go-go? Knife? Open him up? Or, how about, slit his throat?'

He shook his head, and smiled. 'Right. Fine. Let's change the subject. This is getting us nowhere. You want to hear about Sheila or not?'

I sat upright again, and beckoned the juvenile lounge girl. So much for one pint.

'What?' I said, trying to shake off my anger. Neither of us wanted an argument. 'Is there something to hear?'

'Nope. Not a thing. But I'm going to tell you anyway.'

It was an unwritten rule, really, that Go-go got to drone on about Sheila and I got to drone on about home, and neither of us was allowed to complain. It kept us both sane. Well, relatively sane.

She had called round to his on Wednesday, as billed. His flat-mate, Simon, an utterly humourless solicitor was out (soliciting?) and, for the thousandth time, Go-go thought that this could be the night. It wasn't.

'We got on really well, so we did,' Go-go said.

He began nearly every report concerning Sheila in this way. As if getting on really well with girls made the blindest bit of difference.

'There was wine, and I made dinner, and we just sat about talking and laughing for hours.'

I could picture this very easily. Go-go and Sheila sitting around in his (quite plush) flat, eating and drinking and laughing. They *did* get on really well. But he seemed to think that was enough, bless him.

'Jesus Christ. You'd want to have seen her.' He shook his head sadly at the thought of it.

'Oh yeah?' I said. 'Looking well these days?'

'*Jesus.*'

'Yeah?'

'I mean, *fuck me.*'

'Yeah?'

'How does she stay that colour, do you think?'

I shrugged. 'Dunno, Go-go. It's a good colour.'

'She's fudge-coloured, all frigging year. Fudge. I dunno. How does she do it? She never goes away. She's too smart for sunbeds. How does she do it? Fudge. I'm telling you.'

'I know. I have met the girl, you know.'

'Wee skirt thing. Cardigan. T-shirt. Never gave it a moment's thought, probably.'

'Yeah. But the effect . . .'

'The *effect* . . . I could hardly look at her. I'm talking about physical pain. You know what I'm on about? Painful, almost.'

'I know.'

'Do they know? Do you think? They must know. What they're doing? The effect?'

I shook my head. 'Who knows?'

All this women talk made me desperate to tell the Catherine story. But I had to let Go-go say his piece first. Fair's fair.

'What have we got?' he said, getting worked up now, that second-pint feeling. 'Men? To embellish ourselves with? Nothing. They've got jewellery, make-up, perfume, they can do weird shit with their hair, they can sit just so, they can do that laugh, you know, the *laugh*, they can . . . you know . . .'

'Yeah.'

'You know?'

'Yeah. I know.'

He paused, shaking his head slowly. 'And what are we? We're jeans and a jumper. Scratching ourselves and farting.'

We mulled this over in silence for a moment.

'So . . . did you . . . you know . . . say anything?' I asked him.

He shook his head glumly. 'Ha. Of course not. But I was going to.'

'You were going to.'

'Yeah. I was going to. Two or three times.'

'But?'

He shot me a look. 'What do you mean, *but?* You know as well as I do.'

I nodded. 'It isn't easy.'

'No. It isn't. Not when you really care what the answer is.'

The pub was starting to fill up with the post-work crowd. A couple peeked into our snug, which could have seated them easily. We gave them such a burning glare that they turned and perched themselves on high stools at the bar.

'She's single these day, too. Loving it, she says.'

Sometimes Go-go seemed to really enjoy talking about Sheila, the way everyone enjoys talking about the people they fancy. But sometimes it looked like a lot of work for him. Sheila was the only subject that could bring him down. It was starting to do so now.

'This can't go on for ever, Go-go,' I said.

He exhaled slowly and said nothing.

'You'll have to say something. Sooner or later. It's not good for you.'

He raised an accusing eyebrow at me. 'Hang on. This is the pot calling the kettle backward. Since when were you so bold? You spend your whole life fancying and not saying.'

I could hold back no longer. Besides, it would get Go-go's mind off Sheila. That's what I told myself, anyway.

'Well,' I said, moving to the edge of my seat. 'Thing is. You're going to love this. Wait'll you hear. Guess who I met today? In Langley's. In the canteen.'

He thought for a second, lips pursed. 'Dunno . . . no, wait . . . Caroline thing?! From Kirwin's?'

Caroline Hogan was a photographer's assistant from a firm we used all the time. I'd met her twice, during my first couple of weeks at work, and still talked about her nearly every day.

'Nope,' I said. 'Guess again. More recent.'

He chewed a lip, mental gears turning. 'Oh! Your woman. The newsagent.'

This was a new assistant in my corner shop. I'd been in there every evening since she started, buying bars of chocolate I didn't want.

'No, for God's sake, *wrong*. What the hell would she be doing in Langley's canteen?'

He pulled a face. 'How the fuck do I know?'

'Look. I'll give you a hint. Ready? "Owww, by dose, by do—"'

'NO WAY! The girl?! With the punch?!'

I sat back, contented. 'The very one. Sitting there in Langley's canteen. Two tables away.'

'Shit! So she's maybe going to lose her job?'

My smile disappeared almost audibly. 'That's not the point. Point is, I was *talking* to her.'

What does it say about us that the idea of actually literally talking to a girl who looked like that was so shocking? But it was. Go-go's eyes bulged from their sockets. His mouth hung open. He was gurgling a wee bit, too.

'You talked to her,' he said when his senses returned.

'Yes,' I said, cocky.

'You went over and you talked to her,' he said.

'Yes.'

'You did.'

'Yes.'

He looked at me like I had just revealed that I could fly, only I didn't do it often. 'I don't know what to say.'

'Ask me what her name is.'

'What's her name?'

'Catherine,' I intoned, respectfully.

Go-go nodded appreciatively. 'Very nice. Kate. Katie.'

'*Catherine*,' I told him.

'Well, how the hell did this happen? Were you drunk?'

'It was Brian's idea, really,' I said.

'It was Brian's idea,' Go-go said, back in astonishment mode. 'That you talk to the girl from the pub. Brian. Crossword Brian. Odd-socks Brian.'

I nodded once again.

'I'm going to need another drink for this,' said Go-go.

Another couple of pints rolled by with the story, and earnest discussion of its ramifications.

'Brian,' Go-go said, about two dozen times. He phrased it as a question, a statement, and a profound expression of wonder.

'I know,' I said. 'I'm telling you. If he hadn't been there, egging me on, I would never have gone over. Not in a million. I could have killed him at the time, mind you, going on about faint hearts and whatnot.'

'But he's *mad*.'

I played with the end of my tie, embarrassed for Brian, and guilty about my own patronising opinion of him. 'Well. Even so. He was right, in this case. Granted, he's not right that often, but when he is right, hoo. He's right big style.'

Go-go could only nod. 'And so, what, it's all set? Tomorrow in Jolly's?'

I shifted my weight in my seat. 'Well. You know. She didn't really say she'd be there.'

'She didn't say no. So you're one up on your normal performance already.'

'Very droll.'

'Saturday afternoon's a good idea.'

'Isn't it?'

'No chance Norm or Stevie will be there.'

'Precisely.'

'They never go in the afternoon.'

'I'm not as stupid as I look.'

'And it won't be all that dark yet. She won't feel threatened.'

'Very important.'

'I dunno about Jolly's though.'

This was a good point. By any standards, it was a dump, albeit *our* dump. Plus, it held unpleasant memories for Catherine. I assumed. Maybe it was the best night out she'd had in ages.

'I was on autopilot, Go-go. It just slipped out. I was so dumbstruck I'm lucky I didn't ask her to go cockfighting or something.'

'No, no, don't get me wrong, you did well, wee man. A tour de force.'

We clinked glasses.

'She'll never show up, of course,' I mumbled.

'Ah, now. She might.'

'Nah.'

'You never know.'

'I think that'd be pushing it a bit. Me asking her out and her showing up. I'm happy enough with the first bit. S'progress. If I can get the gumption to approach someone like that, then the sort of slappers we normally bump into should be a piece of piss.'

I really thought I believed that.

'Did she ask what you were doing out there?'

123

'No. Well, not really. She did mention stalking. I told her I was out seeing Brian, and she left it at that.'

'So . . . you didn't let anything slip?'

'No bloody way. Stuart would have me hung, drawn, and quartered. And then hung again.'

'You want to be careful tomorrow, though. Jesus. In a pub? Drink flowin'. Chit-chat, chit-chat, next thing you're getting on her good side with a quiet word in her ear.'

'No way. I'm a professional, Go.'

This broke us both up for nearly a minute.

'All codding aside, watch what you say. You're bound to get talking about work. That's what people talk about.'

'That's a whole other problem on its own. I think she's smart, you know, clued in. She's not going to be impressed by fucking PR, is she? I fucking hope not, anyway. Imagine the girl who'd be impressed by PR.'

He made no reply, and we settled into a comfortable, slightly tipsy silence. After a minute or two, it was clear that we had finished with Catherine. Mentally, we both turned over egg-timers. It was his turn again.

'See. Now. The thing about Sheila . . .' he began.

I caught the lounge girl's eye and held up two fingers.

We eventually lurched our way out of the pub four hours later, when they started sweeping around our feet. Eschewing Go-go's slobbered offer of a shared taxi, I meandered home on foot, making plans. Clothes were probably a big thing with Catherine, I figured. Both times I'd seen the girl, her stupefying physical appearance had been amplified by simple, elegant duds. (I was ignoring the trainers in this assessment. I didn't understand trainers.) So far, she'd seen me twice in the same shitty not quite blue, not quite grey, shiny, crumpled, too short in the legs, too long in the arms, comes-with-a-free-tie suit. To my lasting shame, I had another like it, only worse. In the wrong light, that one was mauve. Even in the right light, it was just this side of purple. It made me look, and feel, like someone playing a Sarf Landan pimp in a poorly lit episode of *The Bill*. My awful work clothes were a serious bone of contention with Stuart. He brought it up at my six-month assessment, arguing – correctly, I admit – that I was supposed to be in the image business. His protests fell on deaf ears, however. In my mind, even then, when I was still relatively keen on the job, spending perfectly good drinking money on fancy suits would constitute an unpardonable concession to PR.

This was different, however. I resolved to make a serious effort for the afternoon encounter with Catherine. It would mean, regrettably, a morning trip into town shopping. It would also mean developing some sense of style in the next twelve hours. But I was determined. If anything was going to fuck this up for me, it would be my personality or my looks, not something as trivial as a poorly chosen shirt.

Then there was patter to consider. Norm's shattered snout would provide boundless hilarity, no doubt. On the other hand, I didn't want her to associate sweet, sensitive me with that raving lout. I would have to exercise caution. Work, we'd established, was very definitely out as a topic of conversation. She was bound to ask what I did, but I could gloss over the details. Maybe if I just said it was something media-related, she'd move on, and I could tell her about *Come to Beautiful Earth*. (In reality, of course, I worked in the media in the same sense that a prostitute works in the leisure industry.)

As I swayed and bobbed along the street, dodging the pools of

Friday-night sick, another thought occurred to me. I would have to be very careful about my alcohol intake. The temptation with tricky girl situations was always to drink, drink, drink until you forgot your nerves and revealed the real you: a drunk. Since she already had me pegged as an associate of pissed-up losers – if not actually a pissed-up loser myself – I would have to take it easy. One or two, to ease the tension maybe.

On the other hand, ha ha, she wasn't even going to show up, so what was I worrying about?

It took me nearly an hour to make it back to Grosvenor Gardens, probably because I couldn't walk in a straight line. By the time I put my key in the filthy front door (first time, confounding the stereotype), I was solemnly knackered and, worryingly, already feeling the beginnings of the next day's hangover. Then, as the door shut behind me and I kicked my way through the pizza delivery and window-cleaning flyers that permanently littered the hall, I was suddenly lost in a paralysing déjà vu. There was a yellow Post-it note – if not two – stuck to the phone.

JOE: RING HOME FOR AN IMPORTANT MESSAGE, it said.

I must have looked very silly, standing there, leaning too far forward, and then too far back, my face twisted in puzzlement, trying to figure it out. Had I gone back in time? Was it last Friday again already?

I looked at my watch. Quarter to one. I looked at the note. IMPORTANT MESSAGE. Fuck. Fuck, fuck, fuck. Well, if I wake them up, I wake them up, I thought. They should have thought of that when they said it was important.

Not bothering to raid my change jar, I fumbled for some pound coins in my pocket and stumbled phone-ward. Only when my mother picked up on the very first ring — beating her previous record — did it suddenly occur to me to wonder what this was all about.

'Mum?' I said, idiotically slapping my forehead, as if that would sober me up.

She answered with a sob, and then a moan. Just as I drew breath to ask what the hell was wrong now, she added a wail.

'What?' I urged. 'What is it?'

A big wet sniff from the other end. 'It's Deirdre,' she said. My stomach jumped into my chest.

'What about her?'

'She's in an awful state. If you saw the state of her, Joseph.'

'Why? What happened?'

'She was out, tonight, in some pub. Hanratty's, I think she said.'

I shovelled more coins in, almost unconsciously.

'And she ran into him again,' Mum said.

'Who? Feeny?'

'Well, who do you think? Yes. Feeny.'

My skin crawled all over. 'And?' I said.

'Well. There was a row, anyway. In public. In a pub, oh my God, the thought of it.'

'What kind of a row?'

'Oh, I don't know the ins and outs of the whole thing, I couldn't get any sense out of her. All I know is there was a row and there was shouting and name-calling and everybody heard and I suppose the whole town knows now and she's in her room in bits. I had to give her a brandy to try to get her to sleep, hysterical she was, and me here on my own, as usual, and—'

'All right, all right,' I interrupted. 'Well. Should I have a word with her or what?'

'She's asleep, I think. Holy God, I hope so, anyway. You can talk to her when you get here.'

My breathing stopped.

'Whoaaaa, wait. Hang on. When I get there?'

My stupor was vanishing, quick.

'Well, Holy God, Joseph, you'll have to come home. There's no two ways about it. I'm on my own here. You didn't see her. She was like a madwoman, tearing around the house, kicking things, screaming her head off. I had to restrain her, Joseph, I had to sit on her, practically.'

I could not believe that this was happening.

'But . . . what good will it do, me coming home? She'll have calmed down in the morning . . .'

I felt bad about Deirdre, I really did, but – Catherine. Mum allowed a two-second pause, to indicate the full extent of her disgust with me.

'Well, now. That's a very helpful attitude to take. We can always rely on you in a crisis, can't we?'

'But she'll . . .'

'No, no. You're absolutely right.'

'It's just . . .'

'No, stay where you are. That's fine.'

'I . . .'

'No problem. So long as we know where we stand.'

She brought out her big gun now – the open-ended guilty silence. There was no point in trying to explain about Catherine. She had decided that I should be at home, and that was that. I could have had neurosurgery scheduled for the next day and it wouldn't have mattered. There was no point in pressing the issue on the basis of a may-or-may-not-be date with a virtually unknown girl, whose second name, for God's sake, was still a mystery. I gave in, almost immediately.

'Fine,' I spat. 'Fine. Fucking *fine*. I'll see you tomorrow.'

I hung up before she could complain about the swearing.

Upstairs, I went through a raucous pantomime, a parody of angry self-pity that would have embarrassed even the least asked-to-be-born teenager. First, I slammed – threw, really – the door of the flatlet behind me, causing the Mac to bounce alarmingly on its little table. Door firmly shut, more shut than it had ever been in its life, I paused inside, baring my teeth and snarling. When that stance grew boring, I tore my tie off and wildly cast my eyes around for something that would survive an enthusiastic kicking. Nothing looked sturdy enough so I settled for stamping both feet on the ground while clenching my fists and hyperventilating. More swearing, then a sixty-second machine-gun blast of scalding bile in which I actually shocked myself with the variety and scope of my profanity ('Cunting bastard fucknuggets!' I hollered. 'Bastard hooring shitflaps!') This career-best performance was rounded off with another frenzy of pointless forehead-slapping and, oddly, a strange sort of spastic chicken dance, all poking neck and flapping arms. It was the sort of thing that is normally accompanied by a David Attenborough commentary.

It took me a quarter of an hour to calm down to a more benign level of fury, in which I no longer posed an immediate physical threat to myself or the flatlet's delicate furniture. Exhausted, livid, sweating, drunk, depressed, and bruised, I collapsed onto my bed, head in hands. So this, I thought, is how it's going to be. For ever. Dropping everything to attend a domestic disaster every couple of weeks from now until I die in this fucking flatlet, alone and poor, aged forty-something. There was no point in hoping that things would soon improve at home. Evidently, things were never going to improve at home. And I would always be on call because I was the only man in the family, and that was all they wanted – they just wanted someone male to be there when the fan got hit with shit. For what, I didn't know, because I never made any difference. Symmetry, maybe. Yes. That was it. When everything went pear-shaped, they wanted a man around because, otherwise, the picture looked wrong.

By the time I got home, I knew for a fact, everything would be fine. Or as close to fine as it got in our house. Deirdre would be giggling at me, taking the piss, asking why I came home at all, sure didn't I know how Mum overreacted. Mum would be glaring at me incessantly, saying almost nothing, but letting me know that there was no point in coming home in future if I had to be dragged kicking and screaming. I would mope around for the duration of my stay, drinking several dozen cups of tea, staring at the fire, switching the TV on and then immediately off, sighing gravely and imagining that, had I stayed in Dublin, I would now be giggling and wriggling under crisp white sheets with Catherine . . . what's-her-name. Catherine, whom I couldn't even call to say I wasn't going to show up. Not that she was going to show up, I brooded, my features constricted into a whorl of misery. Fat fucking chance. I sat there for nearly an hour, in a pose not unlike Rodin's *Thinker*, only much more pissed off. I was trying to think of someone I could blame for the whole shit-storm. For my absurd family life, my loathsome job, my pit of a flatlet, my never-to-be-finished screenplay, my never-to-be-dated date, my untied shoelace, my running nose, my rapidly worsening headache, and my sudden overpowering, crippling hunger.

130

After I had exhausted the possibilities – including, at one stage, pinning the whole thing on Norm – I rose and shook myself like a wet dog. There was no point in prolonged mopery. I knew that the world wouldn't change if I frowned hard enough. I knew because I had tried that, and it didn't work.

So, rubbing my face and exhaling briskly, I turned my thoughts to food. There was a pizza in the freezer, I was sure. That is, there was a pizza in the letterbox-sized part of the fridge that was palpably cold. (I used to wonder if certain areas of my fridge figured in bacteria holiday programmes – *Come to the second shelf of Joe's fridge! Balmy conditions, all the bacon you can eat!*) My consistent failure to defrost the fridge, whatever that is, meant that the space available for actually freezing food – cooling it, really – was even smaller than the manufacturers intended. That's how I knew there was a pizza there. I distinctly remembered hammering it into the slot with a frying pan.

When the pizza was installed in the oven, I swallowed a couple of painkillers and a few pints of tap water, shivering at its quality. Slightly refreshed, if a little nauseated, I tried to think more positively. There was nothing I could do, for the moment, about home or work or the flatlet or Catherine. But I could do something about the screenplay. It hadn't grown in any significant way for nearly a month. Three or four times a week, I read through large parts of it, nipping and tucking, but not really accomplishing anything. That had to change. It wasn't going to write itself, and if I didn't want to spend the rest of my days winking at Stuart, I would have to get serious. Emboldened, I gave the pizza a quick check – the cheese hadn't even begun to melt – and sat down at the Mac.

Absolutely no PacMan, I told myself, aloud.

9

Next morning I barely made it onto the eleven thirty boneshaker home. I was still sound asleep an hour before it was due to leave, having been up until well after four in the morning, banging the keyboard with evangelical fervour. Suddenly, amazingly, *Come to Beautiful Earth* was going somewhere. Jonathon and Karen had snuck away from her crass fiancé, whose name was Ian. They were on the run, cracking wise while they took in the real sights of Earth, off the beaten track, away from the alien tourist hordes. Cue lots of uplifting shots of humanity in its natural habitat, as well as at least one good excuse to get Cameron Diaz, I mean Karen, into a bathing suit. I underlined Ian's bad-guy status by having him reveal the real face under his human mask. Imagining millions of the studio's dollars going on fancy CGI, I described his head as a cross between a hallowe'en pumpkin and a jellyfish. With fangs. And a forked tongue. Just to drive the point home, I made him devour a puppy. We never get to see Jonathon and Karen without their masks, but there are lots of close calls – like the way you never see the neighbour's face in *Home Improvement*. Exactly like it, in fact. Plagiarism, I think they call it. Before I knew I was even making progress, I had the happy couple giving it toes around Manhattan, with Ian in murderous pursuit. I still didn't know exactly how the thing was going to end, but I was out of the rut and feeling confident.

I was so engrossed in the rapidly expanding screenplay, in fact, that I worked out a lot of my anger about everything else. By the time I crept into bed, yawning and brushing pizza crumbs off myself, my status had been upgraded from certifiable to merely hugely annoyed. My final thoughts as I descended – collapsed – into sleep were not of my unwanted family responsibilities, nor even of the howling Catherine fiasco, but of the certainty that I would spend my next birthday in Hollywood. Indeed, I was out of bed and moving in the morning before I even remembered why I was going home.

Regrettably, my relative contentment quickly wore off as the bus stole away from Dublin. Last person aboard, I took the only available seat, next to a cadaverous youth with a razor-sharp Adam's apple that shuttled up and down every time he cleared his throat. Which he did every ten seconds or so, grimacing and emitting a whiny *hurrrrururrr*.

Progress was slow. The bus was like something you'd see in a Delhi traffic jam, and it was pouring rain – which started the second I left the flatlet (like in a cartoon). To compound the misery the radio was blaring out some heartfelt blather about the phenomenon of the New Lad which, to my mind, is a fancy term for what we used to call 'a prick'. Before long, I had sunk into my seat and was picking over the Catherine wound. Suppose she did show up. Suppose she had nothing better to do at four o'clock on a Saturday – who does? Suppose she actually *showed up*. Oh, fuck me.

I felt sick, all over again. How would I explain my absence? *Oh, yeah, sorry about that, I had to go home. My sister got into an argument.* These thoughts immediately, and somewhat predictably, gave way to a spasm of rage about home. As a rule, I always tried to steer clear of thinking thoughts like 'This isn't fair', because I knew that way madness lay. Nothing was fair or unfair. That was how the universe worked, Stephen Hawking said so. But still. I squirmed in my sticky seat on that poxy bus that miserable morning, as the ectomorph next door gently hawked for the four-thousandth time, and I thought, truly and honestly, without any self-pity whatsoever, just as a bald statement of fact: This isn't fair.

My mother elected to nod at me, rather than say hello, when I arrived home. She was coming down the hall when I turned my key in the door. She just gave me a little nod and retreated into the kitchen. I followed her in silence, afraid to say anything in case I didn't get a reply. At least The Dog was in there. I started towards him, but with typical contrariness, he blanked me and legged it out the open back door. I closed it behind him, relieved that I had at least thought of an opener.

'Bit chilly to have the door open, is it not?'

She shrugged. 'I was going to leave a bin-bag out. I thought I heard someone rattling round the front door.'

'That was me.'

Nothing. Not even a nod. She looked wrecked, I thought. Really shattered.

'Here, gimme,' I said, grabbing the sack, 'I'll leave that out.'

She probably interpreted that as me thinking I was a big help, when really I thought the exact opposite. By the time I came back in, she'd moved into the living room, taking up

The Pose. By the fire, with head in hands. On autopilot, I went back to put the kettle on, then took the chair on the other side of the fire. As ever, my own complaints suddenly seemed shameful.

'Is she all right today, then?' I said.

It took her a second or two to reply.

'Not really, Joseph. But sure what do you care?'

She said this with real weariness, in sorrow, rather than in anger. Ordinarily when she used this line, the tone was bitter and accusatory. It never failed to get to me, and I tended to scream my response. Not this time. She sounded so beaten and exhausted. I was suddenly struck with the notion that maybe that this was what she actually thought about me.

'Of course I care,' I said, meekly. 'Why is she so upset?'

Mum flicked at a piece of carpet fluff with her foot. She seemed disembodied. 'Well, how would you feel? Someone calling you a tart and a slut at the top of his voice in a pub with the whole town listening?'

I felt as if someone had been spotting me a large weight, and they'd just let go.

'He didn't say that again? Did he call her that again?'

She gave me the mother of all dirty looks. If you'll pardon the pun.

'Yes, Joseph, he did. But sure Holy God, you didn't give a damn when you heard that last weekend, or last night, so you needn't bother yourself pretending to care now.'

Five . . . four . . . three . . . two . . . one . . . zero.

'Lookit, Mum,' I said, as calmly as I could. 'I'm getting very, very tired of this "you don't care" line. It's insulting, and I'm . . . just . . . sick of it. Look at me, I'm here, for God's sake, two weekends in a frigging row.'

That came out wrong. I admit it. She gave a brief mock laugh and shook her head in contempt.

'Oh yes, you were full of concern on the phone last night. It was all I could do to stop you getting a taxi down from Dublin on the spot. And two weekends in a row. Oh, I know how lucky we are, Joseph. To think that you might take time out of your busy schedule for us, well . . . we're very grateful.'

Sometimes I think my mother invented sarcasm. It was my turn to come over quietly disappointed.

'OK. All right. You know what I'm saying and still you want to twist it. OK. That's fine. If that's what you really want to think, then there's no point in me even talking to you, is there? I mean, why would you want to talk to someone as selfish as me? A hard-hearted bastard like me?'

I got up slowly, expecting her to intervene. 'Where are you going?' 'Of course I know you care.' 'I didn't mean it.' 'I'm a foolish old woman.' Something along those lines. Nothing. Not a word.

Once out of my chair, I walked slowly to the door, still awaiting her response. She made none. I hadn't even considered where I was going. Sighing for all I was worth, I turned the door handle, very deliberately, like someone learning to use a prosthetic hand. Silence from the fireside. The door creaked open and I shuffled forward a couple of feet into the hall. Here, I even allowed myself a little pause – a very obvious little pause – to no end. Was she really going to say nothing? I couldn't believe it. This was what she really thought of me?

Leaving the door open in case she wanted to say something, I went down the hall at a snail's pace. I got quite a way before she spoke. Relieved and smiling to myself, I trotted back, just as she reached the living-room door.

'What was that, Mum?' I asked.

'I said close the bloody door, it's freezing,' she said. Then she closed the bloody door.

Frankly, I was in minor shock about the way this visit home was panning out. Even by our standards, it was turning into something to remember. I sat in my room for a few minutes, chewing my lip and pondering the mess. Stupidly, I began to make comparisons. Go-go tried not to enthuse too wildly about his trips up north but, when questioned, he did let the occasional detail slip. His family sounded, to me anyway, like the Waltons on E. 'What did you get up to at home, Go?' I would innocently ask, half hoping they'd been at each other's throats. Go-go, always sensitive about my own domestic purgatory, would paint the picture in the broadest possible strokes. But I got the message. Fishing with Dad, golf with Mum, movies and pubs with younger siblings. The only concession to misery he made was having dead grandparents. But even this simple tragedy was fodder for family togetherness. They always visited the graves as a unit, he said, laying flowers, placing comforting hands on trembling shoulders. Huh.

I realised I was teetering on the edge of fatal thoughts about 'fairness' again, so I physically shook myself and went down the hall to Deirdre's to see how she was.

She answered my second knock.

'What?'

I coughed slightly. 'It's me.'

Pause.

'Is it.'

'Yes,' I said, 'it is. Can I come in or what?'

I heard her sighing through the door.

'If you must.'

Frosty the snow-woman. This wasn't good. She couldn't be angry at me too, surely?

'I'm very fucking angry at you,' she said, before I even closed the door.

She was sitting cross-legged on her bed, wearing a ratty old cardigan and a pair of old tracksuit bottoms. Depressed clothes, for sure. She looked as rough as my mum. Worse.

'I would just fucking love to know,' I said, my patience instantly torn despite the shock of her appearance, 'what I'm supposed to have done to everyone.'

She shook her head slowly, sadly, a move she had stolen wholesale from her mother.

'It's always "supposed to have done" with you, isn't it? I mean, are you actually asking me? Are you really, sincerely, standing there and asking what it is that you did?'

I considered for a second.

'Yes,' I said. 'I am. I really, honestly don't know. I do my fucking best, you know, and I come home and all I get is abuse. Ha, I don't even get abuse any more, I get fucking ignored. Will someone please tell me what the fuck I did that is so awful?'

Not the most sensitive tone, I know. But by now I was back, mentally, where I had been the previous night in the flatlet. For all I knew, Catherine was sitting in Jolly's at that very moment, looking at her watch and starting to wonder.

'Mum told me all about your enthusiasm for coming home,' Deirdre said. 'I'm very touched.'

I blinked at her.

'And *that's* what I'm supposed to have done? That's my crime? I dared to suggest that maybe I didn't need to come running home every single time there's a minor crisis and this is what I get? *This* shit? I can't fu— It's . . .'

I moved my lips soundlessly for a second.

'I don't know even what to say, this is so ridiculous.'

'Yes,' she said, 'you're very often stuck for a response these days, aren't you?'

She gave me one of those puckered scathing looks that only women can do.

'And what the hell does *that* mean?' I yelled, flapping my arms. 'Jesus! I can't fucking believe this. I mean! What the fuck does that *mean*?'

'You know fine well what it means.'

'I bloody don't! What response? What's ... is ... Has everyone around here gone stark fucking mad?'

'Don't shout at me, Joseph.'

'Jesus Christ! You're turning into your mother! Right before my eyes!'

'I am not.'

'You fucking are!'

'I fucking amn't.'

'Yes you fucking are.'

We stared at each other in silence for a moment, unsure of where this was going.

'What do you mean about a response?' I said, in a calmer voice. 'What response? To what?'

She looked at me like she had never encountered anyone so dim in her whole life.

'A response, shit-for-brains, to *him*.'

Him, then. The shotgun theory again.

'Feeny, you're talking about?' I said. 'And what? You'd like me to kill him for you, is that it?'

It came out more venomous than I intended and her eyes dampened immediately. Oh great, I thought. Here we go. That sounds harsh, I know it does. It isn't meant to. But there's only so much blubbing a person can see before it begins to lose its impact.

'Ah lookit, Dee, I'm sorry. I don't mean to get so rattled. Your mother has me driven insane. Tell me about the row.'

'I don't want you to kill anyone, you stupid fucker. And it wasn't even a row,' she said in a fragile voice. 'A row is two people having a disagreement. This was one person shouting at me in fucking Hanratty's in fucking front of fucking everyone.'

I sat on the edge of the bed, still nodding uselessly. 'What did he say?'

'*Shout*,' she insisted.

'What did he shout, then?'

'He shouted that the baby wasn't his and I was a liar and a slut.'

More nodding from me, helpful as ever.

'In fact,' she sniffed, teetering on the edge of real tears now, 'he roared out that I was a *money-grabbing* slut.'

'What?'

'That's what he said. A money-grabbing slut. In front of everyone.'

I stared at my toes, which were tapping involuntarily. 'Money-grabbing' was particularly harsh.

'Well, it's no wonder you're annoyed,' I said. 'That's a fucking terrible thing to say. Did you say anything back?'

She shrugged. 'Ah, you know. I called him every filthy name I could think of. I must have looked like a real harpy. Probably just underlined everything he thinks of me already.'

I shook my head and tapped her clumsily on the ankle.

'You were damn right,' I said. 'You can't let him get away with the likes of that.'

She sniffed another little sniff.

'Things are bad enough,' she said. 'I didn't want to get pregnant, you know. I never asked for it. But I'm going to make the best of it. But I don't need this sort of shite on top of everything else.'

'You'll make a good mother, Deirdre,' I told her.

This was true. I always thought she'd make a very good mother. But, when I thought it to myself, I added 'eventually'.

'Thanks,' she said, and a brief smile flickered.

Ah, the thaw, I said to myself. Spring has come at last. Deirdre easily matched her mother in her ability to get angry, but she lacked the old girl's stamina.

'So, how did it end? In the pub?'

'Well, I just walked away from him. I was so mad, I was afraid of what I might do. Everything was spinning, I was that annoyed. Jesus Christ. And it started out nice and friendly. I mean – considering the last time we met. He was all chat and said he was sorry we fell out.'

I snorted. 'Fell out? This was when he called you a bike? Funny kind of falling out.'

'Yeah. Well. He didn't apologise for *himself* exactly, but he said he "regretted" the way that particular conversation went. As if we were both at fault.'

'Very gracious.'

'That's him. Anyway, we chatted away, and I don't know, stupid me, I sort of presumed he was accepting his responsibilities in some way. I thought he was admitting it was his and we were going to make plans of some kind.'

'But . . . ?'

'But I was sadly fucking mistaken, Joseph. We were having one of those conversations you see in bad sitcoms, where people

142

are talking about different things and each of them thinks they're talking about the same thing and then it dawns on them both and there's this awful moment when they realise.'

'So what did he think you were talking about?'

'Well. He thought he had made it perfectly clear that he wasn't the father of this baby and he wasn't going to have anything to do with it. He only came over to me in Hanratty's, by all accounts, to say he *regretted* that it had turned nasty when he was *explaining*, that's what he said, "explaining" this to me last week.'

I shook my head in silent bewilderment. This guy was taking the piss.

'Go on,' I urged.

'So . . . he was . . . wishing me luck, basically. Whereas, I, dim-bulb, thought he was . . . you know . . . owning up.'

'You must have been gutted,' I said.

'I was stunned. I couldn't believe it. I called him a coward and a bastard and a spineless rich-kid, and *that* was a stupid choice of words, because then he launched into this crap about me being after his money.'

I whistled, shaking my head. 'I can't get over his nerve. What a *cunt*. I still can't picture him, you know.'

'You'd know him if you saw him. Big tall bastard, long-ish blond hair, always got a tan, always just back from somewhere hot. Wears combats and big fuck-off trainers all the time, it's like a disease with him. He must have thirty pairs of each.'

'I still can't see him. They live out near Stevie, don't they?'

'Yup. You'd know the house, too, if you saw it. Huge big thing.'

'Nope. Can't picture that either.'

She rolled her eyes in exasperation. 'Jesus. Do you ever pay any attention, ever, to anything that happens around here?'

I shot her a glance. She continued briskly. 'You'd know it if you saw it. Here – will we go out and have a look? She's not using the car.'

I was startled.

'What for?'

'Just to see it.'

'But why?'

'Just.'

'But I don't want to see it . . .'

'Why not?'

'Well, why should I?'

She shrugged. 'It might all come flooding back to you. Maybe he'd be there himself, strolling about the well-manicured lawns.'

She said this with a smile, trying to lighten the tone. But I smelled a rodent.

'Oh,' I said, folding my arms, 'Oh, I get it. You want me to just happen to bump into this cretin and maybe, oh I don't know, give him a little slap? Fuck me. That's it, isn't it? It's fisticuffs you're after?'

'Of course not!' Deirdre said (too eagerly, I thought). 'Don't be so dramatic. All I'm saying is it annoys me that you don't even know who I'm talking about and you don't seem to have any interest in finding out. *That's* the response I want from you, not a fucking fight. I want you to get the full picture.'

I mulled this over.

'What full picture? What do I gain by driving past the house?'

She slumped back onto her pillows.

'Right. Fine. Don't, then.'

There was a tiny pause, during which she fiddled with the zip of her cardigan and sank even further into the bed. It had been a good five minutes since I'd felt this guilty. I almost missed it.

'OK,' I said, slapping my thighs. 'Come on then. If you really want me to see it.'

'Nah,' she said, and squirmed slightly. 'You don't want to.'

I grabbed her hand and pulled her upright. 'You can stop the act, Dee. I've already said yes.'

She slipped off the bed, smiling slightly, and I gave her a disdainful look.

'Do you write down your mother's moves, or just remember them?' I asked.

'I videotape the really good ones,' she said.

The first row was over who should go get the car keys. I pointed out, quite accurately, that her mother wasn't even really talking to me, so the job should be Deirdre's.

'Uh-uh,' she told me in the doorway of her room, where the problem first occurred to us. 'She'll ask too many questions. You're a better liar than I am.'

This wasn't a dig, from her. This was flattery. And patently untrue.

'Oh stoppit,' I said. 'You could lie for Ireland. Remember when you told Dad you were failing biology because you were embarrassed to learn about reproduction?'

She smiled at the memory.

'Yeah, that was a little bit of lying history. If I say so myself.'

'Exactly. It's a gift. You shouldn't waste it. Now go tell your mother we're doing something . . . plausible.'

Still smiling, she crept down the hall and disappeared into the kitchen. She was out again within a minute.

'Come on,' she hissed up at me, jangling the keys.

I went down the hall like a burglar. Deirdre shushed me when a floorboard creaked. She put an index finger to her lips and shushed. This was how we spent our time at home. Creeping around. Shushing each other. We should have acted normal from the day he died.

The second row was about who would drive. We had this one on the front doorstep.

'I never get to drive anywhere!' I complained. 'It's not fair!'

A logical argument, and a mature one.

'*I'll* do the driving, *you* do the looking,' Deirdre said.

She took off in the direction of the car and I trotted after her.

'Not fair!' I spat, again.

'Shut up and get in.'

'Bitch.'

'Arsehole.'

We got in. In fairness to us, we made it out onto the main road before the third argument.

'Turn that shite off!' Deirdre moaned, when I settled on a radio station.

'Leave it alone!' I yelped. 'Just keep your eyes on the road.'

'Fucking Morrissey? Are you taking the piss?'

'Don't touch it! Just drive. And it's The Smiths.'

'It's fucking Morrissey!'

'Morrissey was in the fucking Smiths!'

She paused. 'Was he?'

'Of course he fucking was!'

'I thought that guy was called Simon something?'

I glared at her, trying to gauge if she was joking. I glared so long that the song ended before I could think of something to say.

'Anyway,' I said, changing tack, 'what did you tell your mother? Tractor ahead.'

'I *see* it, I see it. I did you a big favour, sunshine, not that you deserve it.'

'Favour?'

'Yup. I told her you had come over all big-brotherly and wanted to go somewhere quiet for a chat.'

'Did you?!'

'Yes.'

I was oddly touched. And embarrassed. Fact was, I didn't exactly volunteer for the road trip, let alone any big-brotherliness. She shouldn't have had to lie.

'And she bought it?'

'Seemed to, yeah. She had that face on, the pleasantly-surprised-but-looking-for-the-catch face. You know the one.'

Deirdre turned to me and adopted a puzzled and highly suspicious look.

'Watch the frigging road!' I splurted, laughing at the accuracy of the impression. This was exactly the look my mother would have sported if she had ever won the Lotto. *What do you mean, millionaire? What's behind all this?* She had all but forgotten how to greet good news. She couldn't remember what you do.

'So, what, I'm golden boy now?'

'Ha! Certainly not. But your stock has definitely risen. She was giving out shite about you this morning. She had me really annoyed.'

'I noticed.'

'Yes. Well. She said that you said that I'd be fine in the morning and there was no need for you to bother.'

'Look,' I said, 'I think what Feeny said to you was despicable, and you were quite right to be upset. But you're hardly suicidal about it, now are you?'

She said nothing for a second.

'I always bounce back,' she said, finally.

We drove along in silence for a while. I debated telling her about Catherine, in my defence, but decided not to. There was nothing she could do about it. Why make her feel guilty? It wasn't her fault. It wasn't even her mother's fault. It was, as bloody usual, fucking nobody's fault.

'I still don't know what you think is going to happen when I see this house,' I said after a mile or two. 'I mean . . . is there any chance that this guy is going to be around?'

'He's probably in the pub, the bastard.'

'No, not now, I mean around, as a . . . father.'

I thought she was mulling this over, but it turned out she was trying to decide how loud to shout. In the end, she decided on Very Loud Indeed.

'Weren't you even listening?' she bellowed. 'Didn't I just tell you he more or less told me to fuck off? Isn't that why I'm so annoyed to begin with? What's the matter with you?'

'I know all that,' I bristled, hoping we weren't about to start arguing again. 'But I mean . . . is that his last word?'

She almost choked.

'What do you think? He's bargaining? I say father and he says nothing and we settle in the middle on uncle?'

'I only—'

'HE CALLED ME A MONEY-GRABBING SLUT!'

'All right, all right, keep your knickers on.'

As soon as I said it, I could feel the follow-up forming in my throat.

'Which, by the way, you should have done in the first place.'

Deirdre screamed, and for a moment I thought I'd made a huge mistake. Then she punched me as hard as she could in the bicep, laughing.

'You cheeky fucker,' she said. 'I've a good mind to tell Mum that you said that. And that you had to be coerced into doing me this one kindness.'

I acted contrite and terrified, and we cracked up. This was how we got our giggles. Me laughing at her unplanned pregnancy, and her laughing at my complete inability to be of any help.

It took around fifteen minutes to reach Feeny-land. The last part of the journey involved a detour down a tiny side road. At least that explained why I hadn't seen the place before. It was the sort of road you need a good excuse to go down. When we were still about a mile away, Deirdre began to froth.

'Wait'll you see it,' she said, practically bouncing in her seat. 'You go on about your boss's house, but I bet this beats it. I mean, *massive*. It's—'

'I get it, I get it,' I said. I was beginning to find her enthusiasm for Casa Feeny a little disturbing. 'I'm sure I'll be very impressed.'

'You will,' she said. 'Ugly as sin, of course, but you gotta be impressed by the size of the thing.'

'You're talking about his house, correct?'

'HAHAHAHAHAHAHA,' she howled, face like stone. 'Take the piss, then.'

'Thanks. I will.'

A minute or so later she began to slow down. Noticeably.

'Um. Why are we going so slowly?' I said.

'It's coming up,' Deirdre said. She was slightly out of breath.

I couldn't think of anything to say. It was too weird. We trundled along at about twenty miles an hour. Then we went around a long, gentle bend and there it was, on our left. Even when I saw it, it didn't ring any bells. If I'd seen it before, I would have remembered. It was the most offensive private dwelling I ever saw, before or since. 'Huge,' she said. Yeah. It was. It was huge in the same way that the Grand Canyon is a huge crack in the ground.

'Fuck me,' I whistled.

'I told you,' Deirdre said, slowing down even more. 'Didn't I tell you?'

I turned to look at her. She was beaming.

'It's absolutely disgusting,' I said, with real sincerity.

She nodded. 'Isn't it, though?'

I gazed at the house, stupefied, as it slid past us. Even if it had been of average size, it would have been deeply unpleasant. For one thing, it was pink. Honestly. It was pink. Pink. It was a pink house. And it had stained-glass windows. Dozens of them. From our moving vantage point, it was difficult to see what they depicted, but I was fairly sure I spotted a golfer. There may have been a lion, too. The structure was perfectly symmetrical, two sprawling wings jutting out of a fat torso. There were three garages. The garage doors were a slightly different shade of pink from the rest of the house. Nice touch, that.

'Look at the frigging garden!' I said.

'I told you,' Deirdre said, again.

It made our own enormous lawn look like a window box. It was measured in acres. Lots of them. I was still marvelling at it when Deirdre stopped the car entirely.

'What are you doing?!' I hissed. 'What are we stopping for?'

'Just getting a better look,' she shrugged, yanking the hand-brake.

I immediately began to cast nervous glances around, like a soldier caught behind enemy lines.

'What the hell's *wrong* with you?' I said. 'Move! Move! Someone will see us! Move!'

'Oh, take a pill,' she said, not even looking at me. She was looking at the house. 'We're not breaking any laws.'

My mind whirled.

'Deirdre,' I said, as calmly as I could. 'What's going on here?'

'What do you mean?' She was still looking past me to the house.

'You know full bloody well what I mean. This is getting fucking creepy. I don't know what you're trying to achieve. Do you want someone to come out, is that it? Jesus. You do want a fight. That's it, isn't it?'

Finally, she looked at me.

'For fuck's sake, Joseph,' she sighed. 'You couldn't beat me up. You were talking about "fisticuffs", for Christ's sake.'

'Well, exactly,' I said, not even a little bit hurt. 'So . . . what is it then?'

I said that, and then suddenly I knew. It was kind of obvious, really.

'Oh,' I said. 'Oh. Oh. I just got it. You want me to approve.'

She didn't speak, but looked at her knees.

'You want me to approve of the guy that got you pregnant. Despite everything. He may be a real asshole but at least he's rich.'

She began to speak, then stopped herself, and I concluded that I was right. It was sad. Disappointing. Didn't she know that I would support her no matter who the father was? It didn't matter how much money he had, or how little, or whether he lived in a cardboard box or a monstrous pink mansion. What mattered was his ability to be a good father, a role that should begin with acknowledgement of paternity. Something he had singularly failed to achieve. In fact, he had not only failed to admit he was the father, he'd called my sister a slut. No. I didn't like the sound of Brendan Feeny one little bit. The fact that he was clearly rolling in it didn't make him any more appealing.

Looking back, I suppose I should have said all these things out loud, instead of just thinking them and letting Deirdre drive us home in morbid silence.

10

By the time we arrived back at the house, Mum seemed to have cheered up considerably. There was little doubting the reason. I was, she obviously thought, at long last starting to play my part.

'So,' she said to me in the kitchen, 'did you have a chat, then?'

Deirdre vanished into her room as soon as we got home. Mum hadn't seen her miserable, confused face.

'Uh, yeah, we did,' I said, affecting a smile.

She nodded, smiling back. Evidently, she had done one of her patented emotional backflips.

'Well, good. I'm glad. She looks up to you, Joseph. She needs your support.'

'Right,' I said, thinking of the silence we had just endured in the car. I could have said *something*, for God's sake. But, as usual, I was too scared of making things worse. So, I said nothing. And made things worse. Hmmm. There was a pattern emerging here.

'Did she not come back in with you?' Mum asked.

'Oh, she did, yeah. She's in her room. Tired, I think. It's tiring for her, all this, I'm sure.'

Mum nodded in sad agreement.

'So. Where did you go?' she asked, filling the kettle. Clearly, I was back in the neutral, if not the good books. I grabbed a couple of mugs and started poking around for biscuits. For a moment, I considered telling her the grim truth. We hadn't gone for a cosy sibling chat. We had gone on a quite frankly disturbing road trip to Feeny's ghastly lair, the point of which, by all accounts, was to demonstrate that Deirdre may have gotten accidentally knocked up, but hey! at least she got knocked up by someone with money. No taste, maybe, but lots and lots of moolah.

'We just drove around,' I said. 'You know. Chatting.'

Mum nodded again, looking increasingly pleased.

'And is she in any better form? You know I was very worried about her last night.'

Again, it was perfectly obvious that I should tell the truth here. Comfortable half-truths and their big brother, outright lies, were a large part of the problem in my house. But I chickened out. Again.

'She seems a bit better now, yeah. Eh, calmer. You know.'

'Good. I get so upset, Joseph, when I see her in a state. Especially with her father gone.'

My turn to nod. 'He, uh, he doesn't sound too hot. Feeny, I mean.'

Mum's lips tightened and she shook her head. 'I don't like to think about him, Joseph.'

She poured the tea. Her hand was trembling ever so slightly.

'No. Me either,' I said.

'What did she say about him? Did she say anything?'

I exhaled forcefully and hopped from foot to foot. 'Ah, you know. Nothing pleasant.'

Mum sipped her tea and waited for me to go on. I didn't.

'We might as well sit down,' she said. 'It's free.'

I smiled briefly, and we took seats at the kitchen table.

'So . . . did she say something unpleasant about him?' Mum asked, not letting it go.

Feeling distinctly uncomfortable, I scratched the tip of my nose and instantly regretted it. I might as well have held up a sign saying I AM NOW LYING OR AT BEST BEING ECONOMICAL WITH THE TRUTH.

'She's a bit . . . confused. That is . . . I mean . . . she says she hates his guts, which is understandable, after the way he's treated her . . .'

Mum gave me a very serious look. 'But?'

What the hell, I figured. I could give her the gist without telling her about the bizarre staking out the house episode.

'Well . . .' I began, and faltered immediately. 'It's just that . . . well . . . she seems to be more impressed by the guy's bank balance than is strictly healthy.'

Mum looked at me, apparently nonplussed.

'That's only my opinion,' I concluded. 'I mean – I could be wrong.'

'What are you basing this on?'

I shifted from butt-cheek to butt-cheek, exactly as I shifted from foot to foot when I was talking to her standing up.

'Not much, really. She mentioned how rich they are quite a bit, I thought. If she told me about their enormous frigging house once, she told me a dozen times.'

I was hoping Mum would tell me I was talking rubbish.

Ordinarily, she needed precious little excuse. Instead, she nodded soberly.

'I thought I was imagining that,' she said, staring morosely into her tea. 'I hoped I was imagining it, I should say. Even last night, in the throes of it, in hysterics she was, she kept repeating, over and over, about their house and this car business of theirs. I didn't know what to say. She was just panicking, I thought, you know – rambling. But when I thought back, she's said that sort of thing again and again. "They're loaded, Mum." "He's not short of cash, Mum."'

The Dog began to scratch at the back door. We ignored him.

'I didn't know what to say to her,' she continued. 'Mother of God, Joseph, who cares how much money he's got? I don't care if he's Bob Gates. He's not much of a man, judging by the way he treats women. And that's all that counts.'

Bob Gates. For God's sake. I had to pinch my thigh and bite my tongue simultaneously to stop myself correcting her. I managed, but only just. Quite a triumph, though, for me.

'It's strange,' I said, choosing my words carefully. 'The feeling I got was that she was trying to . . . impress me. And you too, by all accounts. You know? Make us think it was all OK. Not so bad, really, 'cos the family's rich.'

I gave a rueful little grin. 'She doesn't think too much of us, eh? If she thinks we're that shallow.'

Mum didn't miss a beat. 'She doesn't think too much of me, you mean. She thinks the world of you.'

I swallowed hard and felt my eyes widen involuntarily.

'That's not true, Mum,' I spluttered. It wasn't. She waved me away, as she took a long sip of tea.

'I'm not stupid, Joseph. She thinks I've lost it, since Gerry. So do you.'

My mouth went dry and my palms went wet.

'No,' I said.

I tried to think of an addendum.

'No,' I said again.

She actually smiled at me, then. She did the morphing thing, and smiled at me, like she used to.

'Well, I suppose I have lost it,' she said, her voice heavy. 'But I'll get it back. Some of these days.'

Suddenly, I felt tears growing fat in their ducts. This was a good example of a phenomenon I have noticed again and again. You can be hard as nails, I can anyway, when everyone and everything is going wrong. But as soon as someone shows you a kindness, or hints at an end to the misery – you crack wide open.

'Things haven't been too great for any of us lately,' I said in a small croak.

It was something to say, something obvious, neutral. There was a real danger that I would start blubbing. I didn't want to. Maybe I should have.

'We'll get there in the end,' Mum said, curiously calm.

I wasn't even sure what we were talking about any more. Were we talking about Deirdre and her baby? Or were we talking about ... everything?

The Dog scratched at the back door again. I grabbed the chance to leap from my chair, take a good deep breath, and get my act together. When I opened the door, he waddled in and, making soft snuffling sounds, dropped his head on Mum's lap where it was gently patted.

'What'll we do, then?' I said. 'About Deirdre. We'll have to find some way of letting her know that we don't care about Feeny, without, you know, without sounding like we think she's gone nuts.'

Mum pushed The Dog's head away and he went to his favourite corner to lick himself to sleep.

'Well,' she said, pursing her lips, 'we could always try telling her.'

I nodded vigorously. A second chance. I'd get it right this time.

It was, perhaps, the first family meal I had looked forward to for two years. Usually when we sat down together, the atmosphere was utterly funereal. Thick, gooey silence punctuated by knife and fork noises, small coughs, and deep, deep sighs. But this wasn't just a meal. In the nicest possible way, it was an ambush. We were going to set things straight with Deirdre, once and for all. Let her know that we were one hundred per cent on her side, that we weren't interested in Feeny, didn't care what he thought or said, let alone what he owned or spent.

Mum knocked up a carbonara and toyed with the lighting while I nipped out for a bottle of wine. When I returned, the kitchen was filled with homely smells and some tinkly piano music was wafting from the battered stereo. It looked more like a seduction than an ambush.

'Jesus Christ, Mater,' I said. 'We don't want to kill her with shock.'

'Don't take the Lord's name in vain, Joseph,' she said, distributing cutlery. 'And what's wrong with making an effort once in a while? Especially when there's good reason.'

I couldn't help but smile. This was good. This was a chastisement from the old days, when things were normal. Don't take the Lord's name in vain, Joseph. It used to set my teeth on edge, but now it was music to my ears. So much better than her more recent criticisms of me – why don't you fix my life for me? How come you haven't brought your father back from the dead yet?

When everything was ready, I went to call Deirdre. She eventually answered my third knock on her bedroom door.

'What? For fuck's sake. What is it?'

'Come on down, Dee. We're having a bite.'

'I'm not hungry.'

'You must be.'

'Well, I'm not. Fuck off.'

Evidently she had spent the last hour constructing a time machine in her bedroom and had travelled back to her mid-teens.

'Don't be like that,' I said. 'There's wine.'

This made her pause for a second.

'Not hungry,' she said again.

I made a fist and only just stopped myself hammering the door and screaming. But that would get me nowhere, and fast.

'Ah, come on,' I said, trying a different tack. 'Your mother's made an effort. There's bread *and* butter.'

I was sure I heard an involuntary giggle.

'Come on. We'll gang up on her and try and make her swear.'

The irony of this ploy was not lost on me. I was trying to get Deirdre to show up for the ambush we had set up for her by promising her that we would ambush Mum. It suddenly occurred to me that I might be in the middle of some elaborate plan of theirs to ambush me. You had to have your wits about you in our house.

'Right, right,' she said, her voice getting closer to the door. 'Anything for a quiet life.'

I took a step back and the door swung open. When I saw the fresh tear-tracks on her face, I was more determined than ever that this would go well.

'It's non-alcoholic wine, though,' I said, looking sorry.

She opened her mouth to yell at me but caught herself in time.

'You wouldn't even know where they *keep* the non-alcoholic wine,' she said, giving me yet another punch.

It went well at first. Deirdre's legendary bouncing-back abilities were in evidence again, and the mood was infectious. Mum was as calm as I'd seen her in months, almost disturbingly so, making small jokes and tackling her glass of wine with relative gusto. She usually drank wine in tiny sips. That evening she drank in medium-sized sips. Things were going so well, in fact, that I decided to tell them about Langley's. It was exactly the sort of personal conundrum that I usually avoided sharing with them – Mum especially. Why add to the general air of misery, I used to think, by admitting that I have problems of my own outside this house?

I wasn't worried that I might incur Stuart's wrath. There was no danger of them letting the story slip to anyone. They were more likely to yawn and immediately forget that I'd even mentioned it. But to my genuine surprise, they actually seemed interested. Neither of them had heard of Langley-Foster Electronics, of course, even in its capacity as one of my clients. But they recognised my dilemma and showed real concern.

'That's shocking, Joseph,' Mum said, when I'd given them the headlines. 'What does your boss think?'

'Well, he says he doesn't care either way,' I told her, enjoying her shocked look. 'But I think it's actually worse than that. I think he's hoping it will shut. He wants to handle a closure. Good experience, he says.'

Deirdre pretended to shiver.

'Creep,' she said.

I shrugged. 'Ah, he's not that bad. It's not his fault, really. It's the nature of the business. I think maybe it's the nature of business, full stop. He's just . . . good at it.'

Mum speared a piece of pasta with her fork, and said, out of the blue, 'So why don't you quit?'

I was so stunned I suspended my own fork halfway between plate and gob.

'Sorry?' I whimpered.

She swallowed and dabbed the corner of her mouth with a napkin. For effect, I'm sure. 'If it's all that bad, then why don't you quit?'

This was amazing, coming from my mother. She had barely even registered my profound unhappiness in the advertising agency. I walked out of that hellhole on a Friday afternoon and caught a bus home almost straightaway, hoping against hope that I would find solace and, yes, sympathy at home. When I told her that night, still shaking with rage, she shook her head and thanked me for adding to her pile of woes.

'I'm sure it'll all work out,' I mumbled, suddenly embarrassed to be bothering them with my silly problems.

'Besides,' Deirdre said, 'you'll be soon be a big-shot Hollywood scriptwriter and you can forget all about PR.'

I checked her for traces of scorn, but there were none. Evidently, she was just being nice. Now I really was ashamed of myself. These people had real problems to grapple with. I had a minor crisis of conscience. Or what suddenly felt like one, at any rate.

'Don't hold your breath,' I said, although, really, I had never been more pleased with *Come to Beautiful Earth*.

'You've got to have confidence, Joseph,' Mum said, stopping me dead in my tracks again. This was the first time she had even admitted that she knew I was writing a script. I had told her about two dozen times, of course, but the most elaborate response she had previously made was a brief nod.

'I'll try,' I said, unable to come up with anything more sensible. I wasn't used to having normal conversations at home. It was confusing.

'How far are you along now?' Deirdre asked.

'Um. It's nearly finished,' I said. 'I did a huge chunk last night. As much as I've done in the last month, all at once.'

Oops. Mentioning the previous night could have proved fatal. But the conversation moved on. We talked about nothing in particular, Deirdre and I offering periodic compliments on the carbonara, which Mum dismissed as both unnecessary and undeserved. I can't say it was a laugh riot, but it was pleasantly humdrum. The sort of mindless dinner-table chatter that normal families have. I hadn't realised how much I missed it. It was so soothing, to be honest, that I began to think that missing out on the potential date with Catherine might even have been worth it. I really felt like something had changed. Mum wasn't exactly telling jokes and doing magic tricks, and Deirdre still looked troubled and exhausted, but, my God, we all seemed to be on the same side. And that was virtually unheard of lately.

We were at the coffee and tummy-patting stage when Mum decided to go for it.

'Deirdre,' she said, meaningfully, letting the word hang there. No one spoke for a few seconds.

'We want to talk to you,' Mum continued.

'Oh yeah?'

'Yeah,' I said, trying to contribute. I suppose I could have done better than 'Yeah'.

'What about?'

'About your baby,' Mum said.

Deirdre raised her eyebrows, already uncomfortable.

'We haven't talked about much else around here lately,' she said. 'What else is there to say?'

Mum looked at me. Then Deirdre looked at me. I looked at my coffee.

'Joseph and I were talking –'

'Were you indeed?'

'Yeah,' I said, again. Stick to what you know.

'– and we've both noticed something. Something we're a little worried about.'

Deirdre folded her arms and leaned back in her chair, daring us to go on.

Mum said, 'We've noticed that you seem to have a peculiar attitude to . . . the father.'

'Peculiar?' Deirdre said, almost inaudibly. 'Peculiar how? Am I not being kind enough about him, is that it? Do you think I'm being too harsh on the poor lamb?'

'No,' I said, without looking at her. 'Just the opposite.'

I could feel her glaring at me.

'I'm being too kind?' she fumed, temper rising. 'Jesus Christ! Do you want me to go over it all again, everything that prick said to me? In public?'

'You see?' Mum said. 'You see? You call him . . . that name. You're clearly very angry at him.'

'And you should be!' I ventured, looking to Mum for support.

'Yes,' she said. 'You should be. That's not a real man. Treating you like this. It's beneath contempt. It's despicable. He deserves . . . he . . .'

She trailed off, suddenly thin-lipped and white with anger.

I stole a glance at Deirdre. She looked so confused. 'You're losing me,' she said, shaking her head sadly.

'What we mean,' I said, catching my breath, 'is that you seem to loathe him as much as you should, as much as is absolutely, you know, understandable and normal and predictable, but you also, at the same time, you seem to, uh, have a . . . you seem . . .'

Mum grew tired of my fumbling and butted in.

'You go on and on about how much money he has,' she said, firmly. 'It doesn't seem . . . healthy.'

'Of course, worrying about money is perfectly healthy!' I chirped, looking at Mum, rather then Deirdre.

'Oh, yes! We're not saying that! You should be worried about money. I mean, not that you should be worried about it, everything will work out, but it's . . . a normal reaction. To your situation.'

It was so good to hear Mum being supportive, for once not recasting her daughter's problems as her own. But Deirdre looked more bewildered than ever. I made another attempt to clarify things.

'All we're saying, Dee, is that we're behind you completely. In everything. You can hate Feeny as much as you want. Or don't. Whatever. You don't have to try to make him sound better for our benefit. We don't care if he's got money or not. We don't like him.'

Deirdre twirled her coffee cup about on its saucer, apparently lost in thought.

'So you told her where we went, after all,' she said to me,

casting an accusing look in my direction. She could probably tell from the idiotic face I pulled that I had not.

'Went?' Mum said. 'Went when?'

There was no point in any further deception, now that Mum and I were on the same page. Besides, it didn't seem that important any more. A little white lie.

'This afternoon,' I told her. 'We went out to Feeny's house.'

'You didn't mention that,' she said, frostily. 'What did you do that for?'

'Well. Deirdre wanted to,' I said. Jesus. Wasn't this what we were talking about? Deirdre's attitude to Feeny?

'And you felt you had to lie to me about it,' Mum said, using one of her disappointed tones.

I could hear her mood slipping. I could *feel* it. Her old paranoia, back again, like putting on an old coat.

'It was hardly a lie,' I said. 'And aren't we getting off the point?'

'The point being my obvious insanity,' said Deirdre, deadpan. Christ, I thought. One thing at a time, *please*.

'No one's calling anyone insane,' I said, spreading my hands, trying to look calm.

'No, we're just deceiving each other,' Mum muttered, in exactly the same tone Deirdre had used. It was slipping away from me already. I could feel bad temper crawling up my throat.

'The *point*,' I howled, before immediately softening my voice, 'the point is that we all want the same thing, which is for Deirdre to be happy, and never mind Brendan Feeny.'

Mum pushed herself back from the table slightly and clasped her hands together.

'Yes. Yes. You're very keen on forgetting all about Mr Feeny, aren't you, Joseph? He can't be forgotten about quickly enough for you. Isn't that right?'

'Told you,' said Deirdre, before I could even draw breath. '*She* wants you to go for him, not me.'

'Well, if you're going to be paying social visits to him . . .' Mum said.

I put my thumb and index finger to the bridge of my nose, trying to keep it together.

'One fucking thing at a time!' I snapped.

'Don't swear at me, Joseph,' Mum said.

'I'm not!'

'Yes you are.'

'I'm not!'

'You are.'

'I'm fucking not!'

She raised her palms, case closed, your honour. I drew an enormous deep breath.

'Right. OK. Right. Right. Lookit. One, no one's calling anyone insane. We just wondered, Deirdre, that's all, just *wondered* if it's entirely healthy for you to be so interested in how much money the Feenys have, right? That's all. We were *worried*. We thought you were trying to talk the guy up for our benefit so your situation wouldn't look as bad, even though he's obviously a total asshole, right? Two, now, two, no one's been telling lies. Fact is, Mum, you weren't even frigging *talking* to me when I got in this afternoon, so I wasn't going to come bounding in telling you we were off to Feeny's. Right? And three . . . three . . .'

I rolled my tongue around, trying to find a way to put it.

'Three . . . I'm not beating anybody up. You'd better get used to that.'

Neither of them would catch my eye.

'Are we all clear?' I said, still hoping we could all come out of this in formation.

The silence went on for several seconds, and I began to hope that some sort of sanity had prevailed.

Then Mum said, her voice catching, 'You know, it's at times like this that I really miss your father.' I could certainly go along with that. We locked gazes. This could be the moment when everything gelled.

'He would have sorted this out a long time ago,' she said.

To my great satisfaction, I didn't even speak, let alone shout. I pushed my chair back, nodded at Deirdre, who was wide-eyed, and walked out quietly. My weekend bag still lay in the hall where I had dropped it a few hours before. My jacket was hanging up behind the front door. I grabbed both and slipped silently away.

11

'Am I talking to myself here?' Stuart said, and everyone sat up a little straighter in their chairs. Everyone except Mary. She was already sitting bolt upright, looking at us like we'd all just simultaneously lit farts. It was Monday morning, and none of us, least of all me, had any enthusiasm for this shit. Stuart looked from face to apathetic face.

'Haven't you had enough coffee? Jesus. Inject some, if you have to, but waken up for Christ's sake. It's a brand-new week, people. We've got work to do.'

Barry and Lisa mumbled assent. I bit down on an enormous sigh, and tried to affect the coiled spring look that Stuart was after. That is, I picked up my pen and clicked it on, feeling more limp thread than coiled spring. I couldn't remember ever having felt as low, not even in the immediate aftermath of my father's death, when I seemed to be living underwater. I actually felt better then, because I knew, at some level, that it was normal to feel that way. But now . . . surely it was supposed to be getting better by now? Instead, it was getting worse. Not for me personally, not in the grief sense, but in the rapidly growing feeling that everything at home was fucked for ever, which meant that everything, everywhere was fucked for ever. Nothing I said or did made any difference. I might as well give up, and leave them to it. At least I'd be able to keep dates.

'As you know,' Stuart was saying, 'the weekend papers had nada, zilch, so that's something.'

In fact, I knew nothing of the kind. I hadn't even thought of checking. Saturday had been . . . Saturday, and I spent Sunday in an all-day red wine fog, periodically kicking things over and then wearily uprighting them again. The Mac even got a slap. Langley's hadn't crossed my mind once since the dinner table, other than as a backdrop for Catherine-related musings, including at least one filthy daydream. But now, as Stuart wittered on in his pathetic mock-American ('sports fans', I dimly heard him call us), I bore down on the work issue with new intensity. How could I be doing this? How could I be sitting here with these people, in this awful bloody suit, planning how best to cover up . . . what? A crime. That's what. We were covering up a moral crime. Never mind business. Never mind profit and loss. There were people out there whose lives were about to be ruined, as likely as not. I felt a stab of concern for Catherine, whom I had laid eyes on twice. I'm ashamed to recall that Brian Denieffe never entered my head. And, of course, wailing about the evils of business was hypocritical of me, to say the least. I sucked on capitalism's perky tit as noisily as the next man, when it suited me (a mansion in Hollywood, anyone?). But I wasn't being logical that Monday morning. I wasn't listening either, and don't know if I heard Stuart say my name the second time or the forty-second time. It wasn't the first, though, that was fairly clear.

'Helloooooo? Helloooooo? Anyone home?'

I looked at him like I'd never seen him before. I was afraid to speak, in case I started saying what I was thinking about Langley's. I might have mentioned Catherine, and my mum too, if he'd got me going. Instead, I sat even more upright and nodded firmly. Then I nodded again, to indicate that I was nodding deliberately, and not nodding off. Stuart stared at me stony-faced, and I think I heard Lisa whimper.

'Is there something more important you should be doing?' he asked me in a prissy schoolteacher voice.

'No, Stuart,' I said and gagged at the beaten tone I managed to strike.

He clicked his tongue and went back to talking a good game, keeping half an eye on me. I tried to listen. There was nothing new in what he had to say. But he said it anyway, issuing the same instructions, spouting the same fortune-cookie go-get-'ems. It was a summary of Friday's summary meeting; appointments to keep, phone calls to make, letters to write. Every word made me sink a little lower. I gave up on trying to look coiled and quietly bit my tongue, scribbling hopeless notes like *nb include history of other thing* and *rem find name of guy who did dept thing (June)*. I had these same instructions, in an intelligible form, from Friday's meeting, but I was trying to look as if I might at least be alive and sentient. Stuart didn't seem too impressed. He glanced at me continually and flat-out stared twice. But he never said anything. I think he understood that this wasn't a hangover. Well, that it wasn't *just* a hangover. I wasn't looking too stable, I knew, with saddlebag eyes and unhappy hair. My mouth had settled into the sort of super-frown that made Judge Dredd look like one of those Day-Glo people you see in cereal commercials. I could feel it making me old before my time, before the end of this meeting probably, but it didn't seem to be under my conscious control. He could read people like a tabloid headline, Stuart, and he knew a person on their second-to-last straw when he saw one. God only knows what he imagined the problem might be. A minor bereavement maybe, or a relationship break-up. He had the good sense not to press me on it.

After fifteen minutes, he gave us further assurances that we were doing 'damned good work' but warned us to keep up the pace because this was 'the major leagues'. By now, I had succumbed to a feeling of mild panic and really thought I couldn't feel any worse about my job. But then, just as I was climbing out of the pit I had worn in the chair, Stuart clapped his hands, coach-like, and said, 'Keep it up! This is what PR is all about!'

Go-go was on the phone when I got to his desk, having trudged up the stairs, not really sure of where I was going or what I was going to say or do when I got there. All I knew was I had to talk to someone sympathetic, and fast. He was doing his professional voice, twirling the phone cable around his fingers. Deep and calm, with just a hint of luvvie.

'That's absolutely right, Margaret,' he crooned. 'Yes . . . yes . . . Well, that's what I told him, he – yes . . . yes . . . Well, exactly. I'm glad you agree. That's what we'll do.'

He looked up at me and I gestured *hurry up*. He started trying to wind the conversation down, but it took a while. I guessed that 'Margaret' was Margaret Doyle, a graphic designer we often used. Margaret worked from home and seized gratefully on any contact with human beings. Getting rid of her could take some time. Glancing over my shoulder from Go-go's corner of the room I saw Eoghan, one of his two office-mates. The other, a sweet girl called – Jesus Christ – *Mildred*, had broken her leg playing tennis and was off for weeks. Eoghan smiled and nodded at me, and I mouthed a silent hello, hoping to avoid an actual conversation, with real words and the exchange of ideas and so on. Not that there was anything wrong with Eoghan, per se. He was perfectly pleasant, very friendly and what have you. But, my God, he was keen on his job. Imagine a scale of PR enthusiasm with me at the very bottom, Go-go, Lisa, Barry, and almost everyone else somewhere in the middle. Eoghan was right up there at the very top, right under Stuart. In fact, if you think of us all as climbing a ladder to success, you can imagine Eoghan's head bobbing just below Stuart's arse, which is as good an image of him as you need.

Eoghan was nominally an account executive like the rest of us, but Stuart clearly viewed him as an adopted son and heir. Indeed, Barry and I had quietly wondered if Stuart would try to involve him in the Langley's affair. Stuart didn't co-opt him, I suppose, to avoid ruining our morale. Ha. If only he knew that my morale, at least, was not only down the toilet, but halfway across the Irish Sea.

Go-go was still trying to wriggle backwards out of the phone call with Margaret. 'Yes . . . yes . . . Leave it with me. No . . . no . . . not at all . . . Exactly. It's settled.' My not speaking to Eoghan was starting to look rude. Reluctantly, I took half a step towards his desk, which was a paragon of order, compared to mine and Go-go's. Especially Go-go's. My desk looked like the desk of a busy man. Go-go's looked like the desk of a homeless man. Eoghan's was not only neat and well organised, he even had a plant, a small spidery thing with a pink flower. Now that I think about it, there might have been some flora growing quietly on a discarded sandwich crust somewhere in Go-go's corner. But Eoghan's had been grown deliberately.

'All go, I suppose,' Eoghan said, smiling at me.

I rolled my eyes, trying to look world-weary but, you know, competent. 'Don't get me started.'

173

'Any change since last week?'

'No, thank Christ,' I said. 'There won't be a decision for a while yet, and nobody's got wind of it so far. Fingers crossed.'

'Good experience for you, though,' he said. 'At least you're not stuck doing press releases about proudly sponsoring a fecking children's fun run.'

To be fair, that didn't sound like any more fun than Langley's. Less obviously evil, though.

'*Pleased to be a part of,*' I sneered, spotting a chance to get off the Langley's topic.

Eoghan smiled and knocked the ball back.

'*Children are our best natural resource,*' he said.

I hawked up my most contemptuous tone. '*Proud of our links with the community.*'

'Yeah,' said Eoghan, slowly.

'*Part of our ongoing commitment to people,*' I chirped and immediately saw that the joke was over. Eoghan's smile had slid off his face. Workplace banter was one thing. But you couldn't slag off the biz. He stared at his plant for a moment, so I did too. I was exhausted, the previous night having been almost entirely uninterrupted by sleep. I didn't have the mental energy for trying to work out what to say to Mr PR Junior. Go-go put the phone down then and spun around.

'What can I do for you?' he said. I shuffled back into his corner.

'I want to talk to you,' I replied out of the corner of my mouth. 'Let's go outside.'

He raised a quizzical eyebrow but followed me without comment. Eoghan saw us out with a microsecond smile. Downstairs we both nodded politely at our fierce receptionist, Bernie, whose ability to hang onto her job was a source of some debate in the office. Receptionists, by definition, have to be people people. Bernie seemed to hate every living thing equally. Even Angela, Langley's front desker, was nice to some visitors. (I just didn't happen to be one of them.)

Outside the front door, we loitered on the footpath, shivering slightly.

'What's wrong?' Go-go asked.

'Everything,' I said, meaning it.

He didn't miss a beat. 'I presume it didn't go too well with yer woman then.'

'Yeah. Well. That's not the only thing that was fucked up this weekend.'

He waited for me to go on, well used to Monday-morning moaning sessions. I took a breath and plunged.

'I don't know where to start. Well, for one thing, I didn't even get to show up in Jolly's.'

This drew a startled look from Go-go.

'I was at fucking home, of course.'

'Ah. Of course.'

I raced through the latest episode, breathing only when strictly necessary, and ending with '. . . then Mum went postal and more or less formally accused me of being negligent in not having taken the opportunity, while I was out there, to beat the bastard, you know . . . up.'

Go-go whistled, impressed. It was much beefier than my usual post-home monologues.

'She says my father would have taken care of it ages ago.'

Incredulous head-shaking from Go-go.

'Now I know you're not a million miles from that position yourself,' I told him, 'but it's getting a bit much for me, to be honest, all this.'

'Well,' he said, 'I was going to apologise about that. That conversation we had in the pub on Friday. I didn't mean to sound like I thought you should, you know, do anything to him. I was just shocked by what he said to your sister.'

I nodded firmly at this, pleased to hear some sense for a change. 'Right. It's insane. And it's fucking laughable, to be quite honest, to bring my father into it. For God's sake. He was like a fucking mouse. You know? In a good way, I mean. Gentle, like. He would have ignored this prick, like I'm doing.'

'I'm sure you're right,' Go-go said. 'Your mum's just panicking a wee bit. It'll blow over.'

We stepped aside then to let a courier through. When the door swung open, we saw Bernie glare at him and spit a thin hello.

'So what else is up?' Go-go asked.

I did my pitiful shrug routine, all rolling shoulders and curling top lip. 'I don't know if I can do this job much longer. It's just . . . getting to me.'

'What is it, Langley's?'

'No. Well . . . yeah. Maybe. Fuck it, I don't know. It's . . . ah . . . bollocks. I . . . everything seems all knotted together all of a sudden. Home being the way it is, and the way that gets its frigging tentacles into everything else like the non-date that, Jesus, who am I kidding, probably wasn't even a date in the first place, and her working in Langley's and walking around in my head as this perfect example of the very people whose imminent demise I'm trying to explain away. Or, ideally, hide entirely.'

Go-go scratched his ear and exhaled, looking up the street to the corner.

'I'm probably talking shite,' I offered.

More looking away and exhaling from Go-go.

'Things haven't been easy at home, they've been fucking hard, in fact, for so long now that I don't think it's ever going to change. Which means nothing will ever change. This pregnancy is making it worse, but it was fucked to begin with.'

I paused for a moment, giving him a chance to say something. He didn't take it.

'And that girl Catherine is, like, some ludicrous parody of my ideal woman, looks-wise, at least. You saw her. I mean . . . it's not my imagination, is it?'

Go-go shook his head sharply. 'She's an attractive girl, Joe. Maybe a bit short, but –'

'It's *ludicrous*. It's *absurd*. It's a joke, that's what it is, someone's having a laugh, putting that girl in the same hemisphere as me. It's an experiment, it must be. See how much suffering a person can stand when they see their ideal pop into frigging reality right there in front of them. Someone's watching this upstairs, I'm telling you, and they're laughing.'

I pouted and slumped, slightly exhausted by all this complaining. We stepped out of the way again for the emerging courier, who was mumbling darkly about something, Bernie no doubt.

Go-go waited to make sure I was finished and then delivered his verdict.

'I think you probably are talking shite,' he observed. 'I can see you're annoyed. I'm not denying that, all I'm saying is . . .'

He showed me the palms of his hands and dropped them again.

'All I'm saying is, you might be blowing things up in your mind a wee bit and imagining that it's all a rich tapestry and you can maybe think of one good plan and work the whole thing out . . . I don't think it's like that. I know you're stressed about the way things have been at home and the way your mum is, and now this whole be-the-man-of-the-house-and-kill-the-father number . . .'

He bit his lip.

'Well, actually, that is a bit hard to take. But anyway. Home will come round all right. How long has it been now, since he died, like?'

'Two years. And a bit.'

'Well, I'm no expert, granted, but maybe that's not enough time to get over losing someone you were with day in, day out, for twenty-five years. Maybe it takes three years. Or four. Who knows? But it won't take for ever. All you can do is sit it out. And the baby might even be a blessing in disguise. New beginning, and all that sort of stuff. You never know.'

I frowned, thinking of my 'Nuns – Advice From' folder. This was the same theory. I wasn't convinced. After everything that had happened, it sounded too simple.

'I dunno,' I moped. 'What about work?'

'Well, that's easy, isn't it? You either like doing your job or you don't. If you do, you just do it, if you don't, you quit and get another one.'

I considered this. Another childishly simple answer.

'You complain about this job as much as I do,' I said, in a vaguely puzzled tone.

'Yeah, I do, but that's only me *talking*. If I really couldn't stand it, I'd walk. I mean, it's just a job, Joe. Sooner or later, everyone has to get one. Right, OK, it is kind of cheesy sometimes, but fuck it, we don't make biological weapons for use on orphanages.'

I tutted loudly, shaking my head. 'But we might write a press release for the people who do, explaining how they were only forging new links with the community.'

Go-go shrugged, and looked over my shoulder, saying nothing. He was doing his best, and probably wanted to punch me.

'And Catherine?' I said, with some hope in my voice.

'Hmmm. This is the girl you've spoken to once.'

'Yes,' I snapped.

'Well, this is clearly based on nothing, if you don't mind me saying. Other than her looks, which I can appreciate. Fancying her is fine, I did too, so did Norm, so did Stevie, so does Brian Denieffe and everybody else out there, probably . . . But. But don't go convincing yourself that you've met the one for you because of your shitty job and fucked it up because of your shitty home life, just so you can link it all up and do some extra worrying. She could be a total bitch. She took no time in breaking Norm's nose, for a start.'

'OK,' I said, grimacing at him. 'One, it was only a matter of time before Norm got his nose broken by some girl or some girl's boyfriend in Jolly's. At this rate, he's going to be killed in a duel, and I've got no sympathy for him. Two, she isn't a total bitch. I can tell, because . . . Well, I can just tell. Three . . . three, have you got any actual fucking advice on what to do, or are you just going to tell me to forget about her, which I won't, in any case?'

Anyone else would probably have told me to go learn some manners and ask nicely next time.

'It's simple,' he said slowly. 'Answers usually are. Ring her. You know. With a tel-e-phone. Brian will get you her number. Tell her what happened. Ask her out again. And this time, make sure it's obvious that you're asking her out, for fuck's sake. No woolliness. Use the words, "I am now asking you out, Catherine," if you have to.'

'But—'

'But, oh *no*, Go-go, what would she say, she already thinks I'm a dick, she probably didn't even show up, blah, blah, blah.'

So his patience was finite, after all. This was abuse, by his standards. Accurate, though. That was pretty much what I was about to say. There was awkward silence – is there any other

179

kind? – for a moment. I held out against the urge to ask him why he didn't fess up to Sheila if it was so bloody easy.

'I suppose I could try it,' I said.

'Yeah. You should.'

Then, signalling that he'd given up trying to help, Go-go broke into his Yoda.

'Do or do not,' he croaked. 'There is no try.'

I broke into a minor smile, despite myself.

'Teach you, I will,' he said, trying to pull a Yoda face, which is impossible.

'All right, I get it,' I said. 'We better go back in.'

Go-go looked at his watch.

'Sacked, we will be,' he said in his own voice.

At the top of the first flight of stairs, where we parted, I made a total arse of trying to thank him for making an effort to help.

'Don't mention it,' he said, when I had bumbled through a tortuous sentence involving twenty-five *You knows* and half a dozen *Cheers, likes*.

I was suddenly excruciatingly aware that I hadn't even asked him how his weekend went.

'Oh shit,' I said, embarrassed. 'Anything happen with Sheila at the weekend?'

He brushed me away. 'We should do some work. You especially.'

I felt like a black hole of selfishness.

'Yeah,' I said. 'OK. See ya later on. Lunchtime.'

'Can't. I'm meeting the brother.'

'Whenever, then.'

I turned to open the office door when Go-go snapped his

fingers. 'Oh yeah. I meant to say, when you were in the meeting I left a wee pressie in there for you.'

'A pressie?' I said.

'Well, a joke pressie.'

'Really? Well, thanks. I think.'

That was what Go-go was like. He gave people presents. He turned to go up the stairs and I went inside, curious. Barry was on the phone, giving somebody a hard time about something that hadn't arrived from somewhere. Marian, our other office-mate, was typing furiously in her dark little corner, the worst spot in the whole building. She was probably doing her CV. She was always doing her CV, that one, when she wasn't taking sickies.

To my horror, there were two Post-it notes from Mary stuck to my monitor. *I need the draft letter re wage rates now* the first one said. The second one, below it, in a different ink and obviously from later on said *NOW*. It was underlined twice. Thankfully, I had the information to hand, so there was no problem. But I still objected to the tone.

There was no evidence of a joke pressie on my desk, or under it, so I turned to my tiny drawer unit. My top drawer was very tight, and I had to pull hard twice to get it to open a couple of inches. As soon as it did so, I shoved it shut again. I blinked twice at the wall in disbelief, and if I'd had a bottle of rum handy I'd have stared accusingly at it, like a toothless bum in a bad movie.

There was something in there that looked very like a gun. A revolver. I looked quickly over my shoulder at Barry and Marian. Still talking and typing, respectively. I swallowed hard and tightened my grip on the drawer handle. This couldn't be. He couldn't be serious. I tried to ease the drawer open slowly, but it wouldn't budge. I tugged harder. Nothing. I felt sweat break out on my upper lip and tried again, with proper force. The drawer shot open six inches and ground to a halt, stuck again.

'Oh thank fuck,' I said aloud. Neither of them noticed.

My fucking heart, I whispered to myself.

It was a toy. A cap gun, stuck to a cardboard backing with a picture of a cops and robbers scenario on it. The phone went then, making me jump an inch off my seat.

'Did you get it?' Go-go said.

'You *fucker*,' I hissed, 'I thought the fucking thing was real.'

He hooted at me, seriously pleased with himself. 'Yeah, what with all the arms dealers I know and all.'

'I nearly shit,' I told him, giggling now too.

'Well, so long as you're not offended or anything. I'm not taking the piss, it's just something I thought of in the pub on Friday night. I knew you were annoyed at everyone, and I thought I'd, you know, lighten the tone.'

'Thanks,' I said. 'I'll treasure it always.'

'Right. Let me know when you've made the big call. I want to see if any of my wonderful advice works out.'

'Yeah. We'll see. Listen, I have to get this letter to Mary, she's going to kill me.'

'See ya, then.'

'Right.'

We hung up, and I thought how lucky I was to have such a friend. His simplistic answers didn't really appeal to me, but at least he tried. Maybe I was exaggerating how bad things were. And maybe it was silly to let everything become linked in some hellish knot in my mind.

The least I could do was ring Catherine.

12

I spent the rest of the morning in Mary's office being told off. Most of the telling off was about the draft letter. I do believe she changed every word of it except 'Dear'.

'I thought it was fairly clear what we were trying to say here,' she said, repeatedly. I said very little, reluctant to defend my part in this shabby affair. Mary also found time to wonder if I thought it appropriate to disappear without trace for 'half the morning' while all this was going on. I had no sooner formed a mumbled semi-apology than she informed me that, by the way, my performance in the recap meeting that morning had not gone unnoticed by Stuart. She said he told her to make sure I knew that he had his eye on me. I stared at her quizzically when she said this, half tempted to tell her that I knew she was trying it on. Stuart was not the sort of man to pass on criticism through half-assed intermediaries. This was Mary acting big. I let it go, though, not wanting to add to my stress level.

By the time she let me go – lunchtime – I had decided that Go-go was right about one thing. It was time I stopped whining – or rather, scaled down my whining – and took positive action.

When I got back to my desk, I eschewed Barry and Marian's offer of soup and a sandwich in the pub. They left me alone and I picked up the phone.

'Hi, Angela,' I sputtered nervously when she answered with a surprisingly breathy *Langley-Foster Electronics, how may I direct your call?* 'It's Joe Flood, from Stuart Kennedy Public Relations.'

Angela's breathiness turned instantly to the cold scorn she seemed to reserve for me alone.

'Joseph,' she said, in the tone people use when describing bad weather. 'I presume you're looking for Brian?'

'You presume right,' I said. 'I just—'

The phone clicked, beeped and beeped again, then Brian answered.

'Joseph Flood! The very man!' he bellowed. 'How's the form?'

'I'm fine, Brian,' I assured him. 'And yourself?'

'Oh, never better,' he said. 'Is there some problem with the newsletter?'

I swallowed hard.

'No, that's all fine. I think. It's something else.'

He waited for me to continue.

'Well,' I began, 'do you remember the girl in the canteen, on Friday?'

Brian honked with delight. 'Of course I do! That's the first thing I thought of when I heard you were on the phone! I didn't want to mention it myself. So how did it go?'

Oh God, he was so enthusiastic. It was highly embarrassing.

'Thing is, it didn't go,' I told him, gravely. 'I didn't show up. I mean, I couldn't show up, I had to go home for something.'

'I see,' Brian said, already deeply involved in the problem. 'Was she disappointed?'

I laughed aloud.

'I doubt it,' I said. 'But, the bitch of it all is, I don't know. I never told her I wasn't going to show up. I couldn't – I don't know her number. I don't even know her last name.'

'And you want me to get it for you!' Brian said, so pleased with himself and his role in this exciting affair that it made me unaccountably sad.

'Exactly. If you can find out her last name for me, I'll give her a call, and try to explain. Assuming, that is, she showed up herself.'

'Ah, don't talk like that,' Brian said. 'Sure why wouldn't she show up? You're too pessimistic. Bit of confidence, sure isn't that all you need?'

I couldn't think of a reply, so I let this hang in the air.

'Give me five minutes,' Brian said then, coming over all businesslike. 'I'll call you back.'

'Thanks, Brian. I really appreciate it.'

'Grand.'

'See ya.'

I felt my heart pick up speed as I put the phone down. Fuck me, suppose he just walked up to her and asked her personally? She already knew that Brian and I were associates of some kind. She'd freak completely if he came stumbling up to her demanding to know her second name for his 'friend'. I could be sunk for ever. I had no sooner worried this new worry than the phone rang.

'Brian Denieffe on four,' Bernie said, perfectly echoing Angela's leaden delivery. What was it with these people? I stabbed the blinking light with my finger and warbled, 'Yes, Brian.'

'Done deal,' he said. 'Dillon. It's Catherine Dillon.'

185

I nodded in silence, forgetting I was on the phone and he couldn't see me. I was thinking about the word Dillon, wondering how I felt about it. It seemed OK.

'Joe?' Brian said. 'Are you there?'

'Sorry, Brian,' I said, snapping out of it. 'That's great, thanks a million.'

'No problem. Sure that's what I'm here for.'

'Yes. Well. How did you find out, by the way?'

I clenched all over, sure he was going to say he just asked her.

'I looked in the company directory,' he said simply. 'She's the only Catherine in that section. Easy peasy, nice and . . . easy.'

'Right, right. Well, thanks again, Brian. I owe you one.'

'So long as you let me know what happens,' he said.

I assured him I'd keep him abreast of developments and hung up.

Now. The tricky part. The first thing that occurred to me was to wonder what Angela would say. She might even ask why I wanted to talk to Catherine. Or she might simply guess why I wanted to talk to her and laugh out loud. And then hang up. Even assuming that she just put me through, what could I say? Where would I even begin? *I don't know if you showed up on Saturday, but I didn't?* I tried to think of something to say that would paint me more like Cary Grant and less like Barry Grant. There didn't seem to be anything. As in many moments of stress, I lapsed into physical parody and started scratching my head for ideas. This positive action business was beginning to feel like a lot of trouble.

I scratched and thought and fussed for ten minutes until, more or less unconsciously, I picked up the phone and hit the Langley's speed-dial. It was as if some tiny sensible corner of my brain got fed up with all the hand-wringing and acted alone, like my legs had in Langley's canteen.

'Langley-Foster Electronics, how may I direct your call?'

'Hi, Angela, it's Joe Flood again, I—'

Sigh. Click. Beep. Then a familiar voice.

'Joseph?'

'Brian? Oh, fu—'

'What's wrong?'

'For Christ's sake. Angela didn't even ask me who I wanted to talk to, she just put me through to you. She didn't even say hello! What the hell's the matter with her?'

'Dunno,' Brian said. 'She's very nice to me. She's nice to everybody.'

'Well, she's frigging horrible to me!' I almost yelled. The tension was getting to me. 'Anyway,' I said, trying to sound normal, 'can you put me through to Catherine from there?'

There was an ominous pause.

'I'm nearly sure I can,' Brian said.

'Well, please try,' I said.

'Right you are.'

'Thanks.'

'Good luck, now.'

'Thanks.'

'You'll let me know—'

'Yes, yes.'

'Right. Good luck.'

The phone went dead. Not being transferred dead, but dead dead. I gave it a second to make sure, and then quietly stood up and wafted my arms about, inhaling deeply.

Stay calm, Joe, I told myself, strolling about. Positive thoughts. Taking action. The answers are usually simple.

187

I floated around like an idiot spouting this gibberish for a minute or so and then returned to my seat, where I snapped a harmless pencil, purely for the satisfaction of it. Then I picked up the phone again.

'Langley-Foster Electronics, how may I direct your call?'

'Catherine Dillon, please.'

The direct approach. Well, reasonably direct — I'm embarrassed to report that I affected a slight English accent to disguise myself. I'm even more embarrassed to report that it didn't work.

'Is that Joe Flood again?' Angela spat.

I almost hung up, like a teenage prank caller caught ordering a ton of manure for a teacher's address.

'It is indeed, Angela,' I croaked. Then I coughed a couple of times, hoping to give the impression that I had some sort of windpipe ailment, which might explain my sudden adoption of an English accent.

'Catherine Dillon, you said?'

'Please.'

Great choice of response. Catherine Dillon? Oh, yes *please*. Tool.

There was a click. Then a single beep.

'Yello?' Catherine said.

'Catherine!' I shouted, overcompensating for my nerves. 'Hello. Hiya. How are ye?'

'Fine, thanks,' she said, in such a friendly tone that I half thought she knew who it was, and approved. Then I realised that if she did know who it was, she probably wouldn't have sounded so friendly.

'Right, good. Eh. It's Joe, by the way.'

There was an awful silence which I again misread, assuming

it was filled with loathing. Then I remembered – duh – that she didn't know my name either.

'From the canteen!' I blurted.

On Friday, I'd been Joe, the sexist goon from the pub. Now I was Joe, weirdo Brian's friend from Langley's canteen. I wondered if I would ever be Joe from somewhere pleasant.

'Oh. Rrrright. Hello.'

She sounded confused and puzzled. That wasn't good.

'Hi,' I said, again. I was sure I could hear my heart beating. I was sure *she* could hear my heart beating.

'What can I do for you?' Catherine said, pleasant but neutral.

'Well . . . I'm not sure how to put this. I had a bit of a crisis at the weekend, and I had to go home.'

I thought she might interject at this point, but she didn't. A more perceptive person than myself might have taken this as a hint.

'So, I didn't, you know, I wasn't able to, eh, show up. On Saturday.'

A pause of about a year or so ensued.

'Saturday?' she said. My spine buckled. I coughed. I wriggled. I broke sweat.

'I was afraid of this,' I said, faux casual. 'You didn't show up.'

She thought for a second, or seemed to. 'Joe, is it?'

'Yes.'

'Joe, I don't even know what you're talking about. Show up where? When?'

This time I felt my entire stomach expand then rapidly contract, then try to escape through my nose.

'Right,' I said, glumly. 'I was afraid of this too.'

I heard her chuckle slightly under her breath. She clearly

thought – knew, rather – that she was dealing with a total moron.

'Well, I obviously did it with such skill and subtlety that you didn't even notice, but the fact is, I did, in my own little way, ask you out on Friday. In your canteen.'

'Did you?' she squealed, apparently genuinely surprised. 'I must have nodded off during that bit.'

'Thanks very much.'

'Sorry, I didn't mean it that way. But I didn't notice. What did you say, exactly?'

I shuddered, wondering if she knew full well what I had said and was just prolonging my agony.

'You were saying something about Jolly's, and what a dump it is, and I said I'd be going back there, despite everything, on Saturday. At four o'clock, I said.'

'Yeah, I do remember that, actually.'

'Yes. Well.'

'Yes, well, what? Was that it? That was you asking me out?'

I could see her point. 'I suppose it was.'

This time she laughed out loud.

'I was *trying* to be oblique,' I said, a little peeved, and hopelessly turned on by her easy chatter.

'There's oblique,' Catherine said, 'and there's completely incomprehensible. I think you drifted over the line.'

'Anyway. I didn't show up.'

'Charming. First, you ask me out in code, and then you don't show up. I'm offended.'

Wait a minute. This was banter. This was good. I pressed on. 'That's what I get for trying to be subtle. I should have hired a skywriter.'

'Or you could have tried the English language. It's very useful, you know.'

'Too much room for misinterpretation, I'm learning.'

'You think so?'

'Yep.'

This was the moment to come right out with it, and ask again. But before I could say anything, she asked, 'So, how are your friends? Still full of charming romantic tales?'

I felt my face glow.

'We've been over this, Catherine,' I said, enjoying saying her name. 'That conversation in the pub was a one-off. Ordinarily, it's strictly politics and sport with us.'

'That's not what you said on Friday. You said they were a bunch of cretins, but you were all right yourself.'

Ouch. I did say that.

'The truth is somewhere between the two,' I lied, unconvincingly.

'Hmmm. I hope you had a good reason for standing me up. That's not very nice. What if I'd been able to read minds and knew you were asking me out and actually showed up? Where would I be then?'

'You'd be in Jolly's,' I said, 'having a not very good time.'

'Exactly. And quite frankly, even if I'd known you were asking, I wouldn't set foot in that place again if you paid me.'

'I'd have paid you, if that's what it took,' I said, trying to flirt. Mistake.

'So now I'm some kind of prostitute. Thanks. You're not very good at this, are you?'

I sighed like a mopy teenager, causing her to chuckle again.

'I suppose not,' I mumbled. It was now or never. 'So. Catherine. I'm asking you again, officially, as plainly as I can. Would you like to go out for a drink?'

191

'No thanks,' she said.

Here's a tip. When you ask someone out and they say no, never, ever, ask them why.

'Why?' I said, my eyes rolling in different directions. I had imagined the conversation was going well, despite everything. I had been growing confident, or as confident as I got about these things.

'Oh. You know.'

'Is it because of the doctor thing in the pub?' I said, pathetically.

'No. Of course not. Anyway, I may have overreacted to that.'

My brain clouded over. 'What, then? Is it because I work in PR?'

'Do you?'

Shit. She didn't even know that, of course.

'Yeah, I do,' I said in a small voice. 'We do Langley's PR. That's how I know Brian, that's why I was out there in the first place.'

'I see. Well, I don't know anything about PR. And I certainly wouldn't refuse to go out with someone because of their job. Unless they were, you know, a terrorist or something.'

I could feel the tendrils of my separate problems start to entwine themselves around each other again. Positive action, my hole.

'Terrorist,' I repeated, dumbly. Then: 'You just don't fancy me. OK. I get it.'

She lost her temper slightly at that point.

'Fucking *blokes*. Look, for God's sake, I can barely remember what you look like. I couldn't pick you out of a line-up, if you want to know the truth. I don't fancy you, and I don't not fancy you – I don't bloody know you. And I'm not going to get to know you, because I'm not looking for anybody, all right? I'm single and that's how I like it. That's all there is to it.'

This had the ring of a last word on the subject. I couldn't think of anything constructive to say, so the conversation was over.

'Look, I'd better go,' she said. 'I'm sorry. Maybe I'll bump into you in Langley's some day and we'll have a cup of tea or something.'

I snickered bitterly and spoke before I knew I had even formed a thought.

'Huh. Assuming Langley's survives,' I said.

As soon as I said it, the air seemed to solidify. I stared at my wall in bug-eyed disbelief.

'What was that?' Catherine said.

I swallowed the bowling ball in my throat. 'Nothing. Never mind.'

'What did you mean by that? *Survives?* What the hell does that mean?'

I felt weak, and pressed a palm to my forehead.

'Ohhh fuck,' I said quietly. 'Oh fuck me. Look. Lookit. Forget I – ohhh, shit.'

'Do you know something I should know?' she said, her voice rising and cracking.

'I'm sorry. I'm really sorry. I shouldn't have said anything. It slipped out.'

'*What?* What is it?'

'Ohhh shit. I can't have this conversation on the phone.'

'Well, you're going to.'

'No,' I said. 'No. I'll meet you, if you like, but no, I can't say anything on the phone.'

She laughed bitterly. 'Oh, I see. You'll meet me, if *I* like. You ask me out, I say no, you start dropping bombs and *consenting* to meet me if *I* like. I'm not a fucking fool.'

'No! That's not it! Honestly. Fine, you don't want to go out with me, fine, that's OK. But if you want to talk about this, you'll have to meet me, 'cos I'm not saying another frigging word on the phone.'

Her breathing had become ragged. I could hear her gulping down air as she thought it over.

'Right. Fine. Tonight. Eight o'clock in Finlay's, in town.'

'Eight o'clock,' I repeated. 'Catherine. Promise me you won't say anything to anyone there before I talk to you.'

She hung up.

13

Finlay's was one of those trendy Dublin pubs that appeared overnight in the mid-nineties. When I say 'trendy', obviously I mean overpriced and underlit. It was all exposed brick, car-sized sofas, and low, dark tables. The staff were all physically perfect, dressed entirely in black (of course) and sporting either serious sweater meat or rippling pecs, as was appropriate to their sex. Most of these places were loathsome posing pits where wannabe models and never-were musos leaned on bars and kept their shades on at eleven o'clock at night. Finlay's wasn't too bad, though. Despite the Gap-ad staff and too-cool-to-live decor, it wasn't completely soulless. And most of the clientele looked like normal people who didn't mind if they were caught smiling in public. There were some shocking poseurs, snarling and preening, but they looked as foolish in Finlay's as they did on the street. My favourite thing about it, though, was the fact that they played proper music, not free-form jazz wank like so many of their competitors. When I arrived, a few minutes early, Nina Simone was segueing into Marvin Gaye. Not entirely my cup of latte, but at least they were real tunes, with proper notes and everything.

There were lots of seats to choose from, it being a Monday night. After some deliberation, I made my way to a table with three impressively deep armchairs. I purposely avoided the cosy sofas. I was in enough trouble with Catherine. The last thing I wanted was for her to think that I hadn't taken the hint. (Hint? Who am I kidding? She just stopped short of putting an ad in the paper.) I sat in the chair facing the door. I couldn't tell if she was serious about not being able to pick me out of a line-up, but there was no sense in taking chances. This way I could see her coming and might be spared the indignity of her walking straight past me. Only one table near mine was occupied. Three blokes, a bit older than me, quaffing Miller out of bottles. I saw one of them shaking his head in sympathy when he caught me looking at my watch, all knots and nerves.

I sat there for several minutes before it occurred to me to get a drink. Then it took three attempts ('Excuse me? Hello? Can—? Hello?') to get one of the floor staff to notice me. The girl who stopped was blonde, Scandinavian of some kind. She was quite plain, by Finlay's standards, in that she was merely startlingly pretty. Wherever she was from, she could have made the national smiling team.

'What can I getchoo?' she beamed at me. There was a hint of LA mixed in with the Abba.

'Pint of Guinness, please,' I said.

'Sure.' She disappeared to the bar, presumably still smiling.

While she was gone, I kept my eyes trained on the front door, which was quite a distance away. It opened twice. The first entrant was a tiny man with a slicked-back ponytail (I mean, really). The second was a girl of about Catherine's age and about Catherine's height. My skin contracted all over and I made a tiny noise. But it wasn't her. My skin relaxed again.

'Hereyego,' the smiling blonde said, when she returned with my pint.

'Right, thanks,' I said, going for my wallet.

She kept her smile pointed straight at me as I fished about.

'It might never happen,' she said.

'Excuse me?'

'Whatever it is det you're worrying about.'

'Oh. Do I look worried?'

She shrugged. 'It is none of my business. Sorry.'

I shook my head. 'I should smile more, eh?' I said.

'Exactly!' she said, turning her own grin up a couple of notches.

I tried to smile back, but it died halfway up my face. When she saw me freeze, the blonde leaned a bit closer, rolling her tray over onto one hip. Maybe she was afraid she'd broken me.

'Are you OK?' she said.

I certainly wasn't. I couldn't even blink, let alone speak. My brain had just accepted what my fingers had been telling it since she arrived. The simple fact was this: I was not in the same place as my wallet. I did everything in a daze that day, including getting changed after work. I remember looking at my wardrobe with disdain and then reluctantly opting for a pair of black chinos I'd owned for five years and a dark blue shirt with a small hole in the left armpit. I remember taking my wallet from the other trousers and putting it on top of the Mac. I remember telling myself not to forget it and shuddering when I briefly imagined how awful that would be.

I opened my mouth but nothing came out so I closed it again.

'Are you feelink ill?' she said.

'No,' I croaked. 'I don't seem to have . . .'

I didn't finish my sentence because that was when Catherine popped up. It was probably just as well, actually. I might have been kicked out.

'Hello,' she said, doing the hair behind the ear thing. The blonde took a last concerned look at me, then turned and hit her with the smile.

'What can I getchoo?' she asked.

'Gin,' Catherine said, flopping into an armchair. Then as an afterthought, 'And tonic.'

The girl disappeared and we were alone. Time was against me. There was nothing for it.

'You know, you're going to laugh,' I said, attempting another grin, using the blonde as a role model.

Catherine looked at me with suspicion. 'I doubt it.'

I pulled a face.

'Maybe not, actually. Thing is . . . thing is, I've left my wallet at home. I've got, lemme see . . . one pound twenty-eight in change, but that's it. I can't even pay for my drink, let alone yours.'

I thought it best to be specific. She looked at me with an expression I couldn't read.

'Do you think you're being cute?' she said, leaning in. 'You've read this in a spotty lad's magazine, haven't you? *If it's going nowhere with a bird, pretend to be completely useless and she'll come over all maternal.* It's deliberate, isn't it?'

I was shocked. I was hoping more for cold, silent contempt.

'I'm sorry,' I said. 'It was a simple mistake. I'm not *trying* to be pathetic. Jesus.'

She dropped her head and sat back. 'No, look, *I'm* sorry. I'm a little bit on edge, you know. Forget about it. I've got money. We're not going to be here all night anyway.'

'Thanks,' I said. 'I'm so embarrassed.'

'Forget about it.'

Her drink arrived then.

'I'll pay for both,' Catherine said, handing over a note.

The blonde glanced at me, with a smile so ordinary, it was practically a frown, by her standards. She had probably guessed what was going on. I must have looked pretty damn smooth. As soon as she was gone, Catherine got right down to it.

'So. Langley-Foster Electronics might not survive?' she said, looking me right in the eye.

I took an enormous gulp of my pint.

'I can only tell you this,' I said shakily, 'if you promise me you won't tell another living soul. If you can't promise me that, I can't tell you.'

She sighed. 'Look. Drop the Deep Throat stuff. I'm not an idiot. It's fucking obvious the place is going out of business. What else could you have meant? I know that's what the thing is. All I'm asking you for is the details. When and why.'

My intestines did the twist. I wished I'd put more effort into rehearsing this. But I'd been in too much of a fog all day. Also, the Deep Throat reference threw me. It took me a moment to realise she was talking about the Watergate informant, and not the porn movie.

'Right,' I said. 'OK. Well, it's like this. You're not entirely correct there. There's a good chance you won't be closing at all. It's you or Edinburgh. Fifty-fifty, we're told. Actually, they make it sound like there's so little between them, they're going to end up tossing a coin.'

Her eyes widened very slightly when I dangled this potential reprieve. 'Edinburgh?'

'Maybe, yes. I honestly don't know. Andrew Holland and his

people don't even know. They're making the decision in Phoenix, in the next few weeks.'

She looked over my head, considering this. 'But get to the why part. I don't understand. What's the problem? I thought we were doing well.'

I shrugged. This was exactly what we'd spent the past week doing. Trying to find a nice way to explain it all away.

'There are lots of reasons, apparently. Competition, mainly. New players. Everyone's getting squeezed. And it's bloody expensive to manufacture electronics in western Europe. All you greedy graduates, doing fairly simple jobs.'

She gave me a withering look. I shrank back.

'Not you personally! I mean . . . you know what I mean. There are people in Langley's with master's degrees in God knows what sticking little plastic yokes together for thirty grand a year.'

She nodded sadly that this was so.

'You might find Langley's popping up in some sweaty little country where they pay small boys five beans a week to do the same thing.'

She looked shocked now. For herself or the bean boys, I couldn't tell.

'I'm exaggerating,' I said, regretting my callous tone. 'But you get the idea.'

'Yeah. I do. So when would we close? If it was us?'

Another shrug from me, and another major gulp of booze.

'Dunno that either. Very quickly, that's for sure. Once they make the announcement, they'll pack up and fuck off as fast as they can. No point in hanging around being unpopular. We're already in touch with the relevant civil servants, and the Minister. Warning them, like, giving them the excuses – the reasons, I mean – so they don't look unprepared.'

Catherine swigged her gin, and then gripped the glass with both hands, shaking her head as she looked at the floor. With her gaze averted, I allowed myself to take her in properly, and immediately felt a little drunk. How to describe her? What about this – she made me wish I could take decent photographs.

'So what's your role in all this?' she said, looking up quickly and catching me staring at, of all things, her wrists (delicate, but not bony). This was the question I feared most. Well, no – the question I feared most was *How much will you pay me to keep this a secret?* This was second, though.

'Relatively minor,' I said, blushing. 'Langley's just happens to be one of our clients. Mind you, up until now, it's been deadly boring. Newsletters, silly little press releases, that sort of thing.'

Her eyes lit up. 'Jesus! Are you responsible for "Live Wire" then?'

My toes curled. 'To my lasting shame.'

She shook her head sadly. 'It's the silliest thing on Earth.'

I wasn't about to argue. 'Look who you're telling. I hate my job, Catherine. I really do. I hated it when it was all about crosswords and gizmos. I hate it a lot more now it's all about human misery.'

She raised a perfect eyebrow at me. 'Come on now. I think you're going a bit overboard there.'

This surprised me. 'How so?'

'Well . . . *human misery* is a bit much. It's just business.'

I didn't know what to say for a second.

'Hang on. You could lose your job here because of some fucking *spreadsheet*. You're supposed to, you know . . . *object* to that.'

'Oh, I object plenty to the idea of losing my job, thank you very much. But there's no point in getting all morally outraged about it. It's business. That's how it works. Profit maximisation, you know?'

I blinked. 'You seem very calm about all this, if you don't mind me saying so.'

She drained her gin.

'To be honest, you've just given me good news. Relatively speaking, I mean. Objectively, it's shit news. But since lunchtime, I presumed it was all over bar the shouting. I only came here to find out when we were closing, and why. Now you're telling me we might not close at all. I feel a bit better. Want another drink?'

'Yes please,' I said, in monotone. Catherine raised a finger, immediately attracting one of the male floor staff. He stared at her chest without blinking as she ordered. Bastard. That was my job.

'And, what, now you want to swear me to secrecy?' she said when he was gone.

For once, I tried to think my response through before it came tumbling out.

'Look, I told you I hate my job. It's making me feel ill, in fact. But I can't afford to lose it either. Not just yet. And I certainly can't afford to get sued, which my boss threatened to do, if we told anyone. This can't get out, Catherine.'

'Sued?'

'That's what he said.'

'He couldn't do that. Could he?'

'I don't think so, no. But I'm not sure.'

Worryingly for my Guinness, the drinks arrived almost immediately. The guy winked at Catherine when he handed over her change. I was pleased to see her recoil.

'Lemme ask you something,' she said as he slunk away.

'Suppose I had a) realised that you were asking me out and b) said yes. Suppose we'd gone to that shitty pub on Saturday. Were you planning on telling me about all this?'

Again, I gave myself time to think. I decided, since she already thought I was a fool, to tell the truth.

'Well. To be honest . . . I was going to play it by ear. If we'd been getting along well, and it looked like something was happening, you know . . . between us . . . I thought I'd probably have to tell you. Otherwise . . . no.'

She sipped her drink, nodding. 'So. Let's see if I've got this right. If you were getting somewhere with me, you were going to tip me off. "Probably." If not, you were going to let me rot. Correct?'

I could only nod back at her.

'I see.'

In the silence that followed, I wondered if honesty really was the best policy. Just then, it seemed about third best, behind dishonesty and saying nothing.

'It's shady behaviour, I know.'

'It's not so bad. You'd be in trouble if it had been the other way round.'

'Eh?'

'Well. If you'd said you were going to say something only if it was going *badly* with me, that'd be unforgivable. To use it as a tactic, I mean.'

I nodded for all I was worth, pleased to have apparently said the right thing for once. 'Right. And, just to reiterate, I didn't mean to let it slip on the phone today. Genuinely. It wasn't a ploy to get you to go out with me.'

'OK, OK, I believe you. It would have been a pretty stupid ploy. And, by the way, I am not "out" with you.'

'No. Of course not.'

'We're just having a quiet drink and discussing the situation.'

'Got it.'

'And that's all.'

'Right. So. I have to know. Are you going to tell anyone at work?'

She pursed her lips and did the hair thing again. 'Does Brian what's-his-name know?'

'No.'

'I thought you two were pals.'

'Not really.'

She could see how uncomfortable I was. 'But you feel guilty about not telling him?'

'Yes. Yes, I do.'

She waved me away. 'I wouldn't be. You're just doing your job. Part of your job is keeping quiet about the whole thing.'

'Christ. I wish I had your attitude to my job. I feel sick with shame.'

'That's twice.'

'Sorry?'

'That's twice you've said your job makes you feel sick. Why are you still doing it?'

Good God. Another one.

'You should meet my friend Go-go. You two'd get along like a house on fire.'

'Oh yeah? Mature, sensible bloke, is he?'

'Occasionally. He says answers are usually simple.'

'He's right. Why is he called Go-go?'

The unfortunate incident flashed before my eyes. There was no need to open that particular can of worms.

'Never mind,' I said. 'Now, please. Can I have an answer? Are you going to tell anyone or not?'

She looked at me over the top of her glass. 'Nah.'

'Really?'

'Yeah, really.'

I almost didn't believe her. It seemed too good to be true. 'Are you sure? Don't get me wrong, I'm delighted, I've been going frigging nuts about this all day. But . . . you must have friends there. People you want to warn.'

She popped her shoulders up and down quickly. 'Nope. I mean . . . I do have friends there. But what would I say to them? Some guy I don't know accidentally told me that there's a fifty-fifty chance we might be closing down?'

'Why not?'

'I dunno. It sounds too ropy. What if we don't close? I'd have worried everybody sick for nothing.'

'But what if you do close? You could be warning them in advance, you know, get the old CVs out.'

A curious expression settled on her face. 'Listen, I'm getting *my* CV out. In fact, I've already jazzed it up, this afternoon. I don't see why I should deliberately flood the market with dozens of engineering CVs exactly bloody like it. I want to beat the rush.'

She shrank back when she said this, hand over mouth, obviously embarrassed to sound so mercenary.

I tried to make her feel better. 'Makes sense,' I said, even though I was a bit taken aback.

She shook her head. 'No. It's a scummy way to think.'

Personally, I was getting used to feeling scummy. It looked brand new to Catherine.

'So we're both scum,' I smiled. 'Low-down, sneaky, self-serving scum. All we care about is our own hides.'

I felt a little erotic rush as she cracked a smile of her own, raised her glass and clinked mine.

'To our own hides,' she said.

'To our own hides.'

We smiled guiltily and made decent eye contact for the first time that evening. Despite everything, I allowed myself to entertain the thought that she didn't seem to actively dislike me. All right, so she had yet to see me in anything remotely resembling a flattering light, and OK, she'd made an unequivocal declaration that it was never going to happen between us, and fair enough, I was the one who just told her that she could well be out of a job within a few weeks, but *still*. Surely, I thought to myself, if she really couldn't stand me, she wouldn't be sitting here having a drink now that our official business is over. If she really couldn't stand me, she'd be making some silly excuse and leaving.

'Right, gotta go,' Catherine said then, finishing her drink as she stood up. 'I have to pick up a snooker cue for my dad.'

14

'That's a result then,' Go-go said through a mouthful of crisps. We were having lunch in his office the following day.

'Result? A fucking result? She said she had to go and pick up a snooker cue! A snooker cue! I've heard some excuses in my time, but that takes the biscuit. She could have at least made up a decent lie. A sick granny or something.'

He shook his head disparagingly. 'I thought your main concern here was that she might tell somebody the big news. She told you she wouldn't, hence – result.'

'But—'

'But nothing. You're bloody lucky to be getting out of this so easily. You could have been in serious bother. Fired, sued, killed, God knows what. Your problem – one of your many problems – is that you don't know when you're well off. You go around complaining about how fucked up everything is, and then when something goes right, you can't even see it.'

I thought he was being unfair, for once, and tried to communicate that with a hefty pout.

'And don't pull that face, either,' he snapped. 'Lookit. She doesn't want to go out with you. So that's that. Forget about it. Things could have been a whole lot worse.'

I knew he was right, I suppose, even though he was being uncharacteristically blunt. Finlay's had gone better than expected. Especially considering the fact that I showed up without any money. There was no real nastiness, and we both took something away from it. I got reassurance that the news would remain secret and Catherine discovered that she still had a chance of keeping her job. These were hardly major victories for either of us, but at least we left the place in better form than we arrived. Still. I couldn't help but wish that there had been just a tiny hint of unpleasantness. It might have made it easier, somehow. I was uncomfortable with the notion that we seemed to get along reasonably well, but still she felt obliged to make up crap about snooker cues before scarpering.

'You know what you should do?' Go-go continued, taking a small slurp of milk. 'You should worry and moan about it all day every day for the next couple of weeks. That approach usually works for you.'

I was temporarily stuck for words.

'Well, I like to stick to what I know,' I said after an uncertain pause. 'Catherine said something else that surprised me, though. She said she was worried about flooding the market with loads of CVs just like her own.'

'And?'

'Well. Isn't that a bit . . . callous?'

'Oh dear. Is she not as perfect as you thought she was?'

'It's not that, it's . . . Well. That's the sort of manoeuvre I associate with *PR*, for God's sake. Cynical, like.'

He sighed deeply, evidently bored or annoyed or both. 'It's

not the worst thing I ever heard. She's only looking after her interests. I would, in her shoes. So would you.'

'I certainly would not.'

'No? You wouldn't sneak a CV out? Course you would.'

I frowned my hardest. 'Only if I'd let my friends at work know too. She isn't doing that.'

'It's just business. I see no problem.'

'My God. This is spooky. She said something about "just business" too.'

'Business isn't a swear word, you know, Joe. People are allowed to look out for themselves. So are companies, for that matter.'

The penny finally dropped that he was having a proper go at me.

'I know all that,' I huffed.

'No, you don't. You think, somehow, that wanting to make a profit or wanting to have a career is morally wrong. Face facts. You're a fucking hippie. Without the charm.'

He wasn't joking. He meant it as a real insult. I took it as such and, as is my way, got up to leave.

'Now you're going to storm off in a mood because someone pointed out something about you that you didn't want to hear.'

I stood there glaring at him, unsure of what to say next. It wasn't like Go-go to be so . . . unhelpful.

'I'm not storming anywhere,' I said, levelly. 'I'm going to do some work.'

He sniggered, with some venom. 'Right. Because you care so much about your job.'

I was tempted to ask what the hell was wrong with him, but didn't. I didn't ask because I didn't want to know.

I've got enough problems of my own, I thought. And none of them is getting any better.

*   *   *

A pattern was quickly established for the rest of that working week. I spent the days alternately being bored to within an inch of my life by 'Live Wire' and then panicking wildly every time the phone rang, certain that it was news from Phoenix. Or worse, some journalist asking me if the name Catherine Dillon meant anything to me. Thankfully, neither of those calls ever came.

My nights were spent working like never before on *Come to Beautiful Earth*. It was my sole refuge. At the lowest points of the working day, when I felt sick with guilt about my job, sick with worry about home, and sick with, well, plain old lust for Catherine, my mind wandered in the direction of the script and the opportunity it represented – a chance to leave it all behind. To my surprise and delight, I made swift progress. Perhaps it was the desperation I was feeling, but suddenly, just like that, scriptwriting was easy. I was not only speeding up, I thought, I was getting better. The jokes were funnier and the characters were sharper. It was as if the full story was revealed to me all at once, and all I had to do was type it in. I even trawled back over what I had already done and saw a dozen ways to tighten it up. The whole thing seemed to be coming into some kind of focus. There was precious little pointless staring at the screen and only the occasional game of PacMan.

By the end of the week, in fact, I was so pleased with myself and the script that I even began to cheer up a bit at work. None of my problems had gone away, but they were diminished, lessened somehow. Twice that week I entertained childishly literal dreams of success in Hollywood. Both involved me marching into Stuart's office and telling him, with good grace and minimal gloating, that I had been offered millions for the script. One of them also featured Catherine getting wind of my good fortune and basically throwing herself at me.

'Is it my imagination,' Go-go said on Friday morning, 'or are you in reasonably good humour for a change?'

'I suppose so,' I shrugged, ignoring the slight. 'Reasonably.'

'How come? Did something happen at home?'

'Naw. I haven't even called, and they haven't called me.'

'What then? Have you been in touch with Catherine again?'

'Nope.'

He frowned at me, puzzled. 'Langley's blown over?'

I leaned across the kitchen table, and pretended to glance around for spies. 'If you must know,' I said, 'I'm on my way to Hollywood.'

Go-go nodded. 'Ah. The famous script.'

'Yup.'

'Getting somewhere, are we?'

'Yeah. I think so. I've been tearing through it, every night this week. It's just flowing out of me.'

He sniffed the air. 'There's something flowing around here, that's for sure.'

'What? You don't believe me?'

He shook his head and toyed with his coffee mug. 'It's not that. But you've had little flutters of confidence about this before, haven't you? Hollywood this, millionaire that. Ten minutes later, you're giving out about how shit it is and how you'll never get anywhere.'

'Yeah. Well. That was before. It's different now, the whole thing. It's had a major overhaul. It's actually looking pretty good these days, even if I do say so myself.'

'Am I going to get to see this new improved masterwork?'

I shook my head as I swallowed lukewarm tea. 'When it's done.'

'How come? You showed bits of it to me before.'

'I want you to get the full effect. All at once.'

'My. We are cocky this morning.'

'It's not cockiness, Go-go, it's burgeoning confidence. And I'll thank you to be a bit more encouraging. This is the only thing that's keeping me sane.'

He raised his mug in salute. 'Don't worry. I'll be the first to congratulate you if it all works out. I just hope this isn't a dead cat bounce.'

I didn't like his negative tone.

'And what the hell is that?' I sniffed.

'You know. An upward blip on an ultimately downward trend.'

I gave him a second to smile or otherwise indicate that he was joking. He didn't.

'I've got a lot of work to do,' I said, draining my cup.

'You sure have,' Go-go said.

I froze, halfway to standing, and looked him in the eye. 'Have I done something to annoy you?' I said.

He smirked and shook his head. 'Of course not. What a silly idea.'

'You're acting weird.'

'Me? No.'

'If there was some problem, though, you'd tell me?'

'Sure.'

I chose to believe him.

On Friday afternoon, I made a decision. I would Go Home, voluntarily, for an unprecedented third week in a row. In retrospect, I can't really say why. When they weren't ignoring me, they were insulting me. Relations had never been at such a low ebb, and I felt sure that none of it was my fault. On the other hand, when did not being responsible mean not feeling guilty? It would have to be sorted out sooner rather than later. And besides, I saw my recent success with *Come to Beautiful Earth* as a good omen. Maybe I was on the beginning of a roll, I thought. Maybe I could go home, get Mum and Deirdre back on-side, and then, with that triumph under my belt, turn my attention to the other biggies – work and Catherine. Yeah. Maybe things could turn around after all.

So keen was I to start putting my world to rights that I decided to get the Friday-night bus, instead of the customary Saturday lunchtime number. I even dared to leave work early, which was easy, since Stuart and Mary were both out at Langley's talking turkey with Andrew Holland. I planned to march back to the flatlet, stuff some clothes in a bag, and race into town for the six thirty 'service'. But just as I was closing the door, the cheesewire strap of my weekend bag already slicing deep into my shoulder, the phone rang. I heard Julie answer it as I fiddled with keys and swore under my breath, already sure it would be for me, some dingbat holding me up.

'Jophus!' she hollered. I couldn't tell if she was making a little joke, or was too whacked to speak properly.

'Yeah, coming, coming,' I said, bounding down the stairs. She had disappeared by the time I got there, leaving her usual herbal aroma hanging in the air behind her like the tiny clouds of dust that Roadrunner speeds away from.

'Yup,' I sighed into the receiver, not bothering to disguise my impatience.

'Joe? Hiya. It's Norm.'

This was a turn-up. I hadn't spoken to Norm, or Stevie for that matter, since the ugly incident in Jolly's when they threw their weight behind the Let's Kill Feeny campaign. I didn't expect to talk to either of them again until chance (or necessity, more like) threw us together in the pub again.

'Norman,' I said, in monotone. 'What's up?'

Norm wasn't actually short for Norman. It was a self-imposed nickname, chosen in honour of his hero, the fat guy from *Cheers*. Norm's real name was Glen. And he hated when Norm was lengthened to Norman. Which was why I did it. I was still mad at him.

'Listen, I know we had a bit of a falling out last time . . .'

'Huh.'

'Yeah. I know.'

'Are you calling to apologise then?'

He paused. 'No, actually. I'm calling because there's something I want to talk to you about.'

Bastard. Norm just didn't do apologies.

'What? Have you thought of some way for me to torture Feeny before I kill him?'

'Oh, for Christ's sake. Look, it's—'

'Listen, Norman, all joking aside, I really haven't got time for this, I've got a bus to catch.'

'If—'

'See ya next week.'

I hung up. What did he expect? I was trying to start a roll here.

15

We sat unsmiling, for the ten-millionth time, at the kitchen table. Deirdre was out. As was par for the course, we skipped opening pleasantries and got straight down to the unpleasantries.

'I have come here,' I told her, 'to try to put things right between us.' It wasn't a bad line, but I delivered it in the manner of Don Corleone addressing the heads of the five families, and felt instantly foolish.

'That's very nice of you, Joseph,' she said, 'but I'd appreciate it, first of all, if you'd explain your version of what's been going on. Because I'm lost.'

How typical was that? She could always steal the momentum, that woman. You had to hand it to her. She didn't even look surprised when I came through the door. She just said a quiet hello and backtracked into the kitchen, where I followed her still clutching bag and jacket.

'What do you mean?' I said.

'What do you mean, what do I mean? I mean, what happened last weekend? You got up and ran off. One minute, we were having a chat, and the next –' She waved a hand in the air. 'Gone.'

I choked slightly and gave serious consideration to the notion that she might be joking.

'Who are you,' I said when I recovered the power of speech, 'and what have you done with my mother?'

'I don't get that one, Joseph,' she said. 'You're talking in riddles.'

She probably practises this, I recall thinking. She probably sits in front of a mirror and practises getting the better of me. Still – I tried not to shout, determined to make progress.

'OK. Lookit. Let me recap. Last Saturday night, you and I had a conversation with Deirdre about her attitude to Feeny.'

Pause for effect.

'You do recall that, don't you? Even vaguely? Rings a tiny bell?'

'There's no need for sarcasm,' said the most sarcastic woman in Ireland.

'Right. So we're on the same track. And do you remember how that conversation, which started out so well, suddenly went all wrong?'

She cocked her head to one side. 'I remember you storming off, if that's what you mean.'

'Now we're getting somewhere,' I said, pushing her button again for the hell of it. 'Think hard, now. Just before that . . .'

I rubbed my temples and half shut my eyes.

'Wait! I'm getting something! Yes . . . yessss . . . it's coming back to me! It's a bit hazy, but . . . yes . . . yes . . . you told me I was utterly useless compared to my dad, who would have sorted all this out long ago.'

We looked at each other, hard. Then she seemed to wilt.

'I didn't say that.'

'Yeah, you did.'

She looked flustered. 'Well, I didn't mean it that way.'

'Oh? How did you mean it then?'

'I meant . . . I meant . . .'

I nodded for her to go on, to explain this to me once and for all.

'Look,' she said. 'When I said a minute ago that I was lost and didn't know what was going on . . . that's not strictly true. I think I know what's going on, and it's something you and I have to talk about. Sooner rather than later.'

Hang on. Surely I was the one doing the sorting out?

'Oh? Go on then.'

'Your father,' she said, whispered almost. 'I miss him. At times like these. I feel lost and I don't know who to turn to.'

Her eyes closed and the little anger I had left evaporated.

'We all miss him,' I managed to say. 'I certainly do.'

'I know, Joseph.'

'But I don't go around accusing you of being a poor substitute.'

She clasped her hands together, and shook her head slowly. 'That's not what I meant,' she said. 'Honest to God it's not.'

I shrugged. 'That's how it sounded. That's how it's sounded since this whole Feeny thing started. When I came home a couple of weeks ago, you said something about how Dad wouldn't have put up with it. Those were your exact words, more or less. Even Deirdre says she gets the impression you want me to kill him. Punch him out, anyway.'

Mum shook her head, her eyes closed. 'You've got it all wrong,' she said. 'I don't want that. I never said I wanted that. For the love of God. *Violence*. How could you think that?'

'Well, you've never really denied it.'

She nodded with the whole top half of her body. 'Maybe not. Maybe I . . . half wanted you to get that impression. Not consciously, but . . . oh, God. I'm so sorry. I was upset, Joseph. He's been so horrible to Deirdre.'

'No one's denying that. So. What do you want?'

'I don't know, Joseph. I want your father to be here, sorting this out.'

I flinched. 'You're doing it again!'

She stroked her forehead, apparently as confused and frustrated as I was.

'No, listen to me, now. This is what I've been thinking about all week. You'll have to stop jumping off the deep end every time I mention his name. Just because I wish he was still here, that's no reflection on you. OK? I think it's time you faced the possibility that this is your problem, as much as it is mine.'

'*What?*'

'Don't shout at me, please. Just think about it. Can't you see there's a tiny possibility that all this commotion is down to your own feelings of guilt?'

'Jesus Christ! What the hell have I got to feel guilty about?' I yelled. In fact, guilt was my constant companion. But I wasn't sure we were talking about the same sort.

She looked at me wistfully. 'See? Instant bad temper. You've got nothing to feel guilty about, but still, you're up to your neck in it.'

'Guilt?' I gasped, trying the word out.

'Guilt. You're what-do-you-call-it, you're *projecting* all this guilt onto me. You feel guilty because you're not living up to some criteria or other that you've set yourself.'

'Criteria?' I said. I'd never heard her use the word. 'I've set criteria?'

She nodded. 'Yes. I think so. I think you've convinced yourself – *you've* convinced *yourself* – that you're supposed to be the man of the house, in some way, I don't know. And then you imagine that your sister and I are holding you up to it and judging you. But we're not. When I say I wish he was here and, you know, if he was he'd sort it out and all the other . . . insensitive things I say, you have to understand that I'm not talking about you. I'm talking about him.'

I became suspicious. More so. 'How do you know what Deirdre thinks?'

'Because we spoke about this during the week, Joseph. She agrees with me. She's seen you do it herself.'

'Oh, right. You've been discussing me, have you?'

'Joseph, that's what we do in this family these days. We get together in pairs to discuss the other one. That's how it works. You and Deirdre do it to me, you and I do it to Deirdre, and Deirdre and I do it to you.'

I took a moment to drink this in. It was the most perceptive thing I'd heard her say about her family for two years. It was the first sign of proof I'd had that she was even aware that there still was a family.

'That's right,' I said softly. 'That's exactly what we do. I never really thought of it. Consciously. But that's exactly what we do.'

She swept some crumbs off the table into her cupped hand and sighed.

'Well. I never consciously thought of it either, until this week. But, like I say, I've been doing a lot of thinking. Since you left. Trying to understand why we can't all sit down together for a simple meal without everything descending into this . . . mess. Accusations and suspicion and bad feeling and temper. And there's no one to blame but me, really.'

'No,' I said, immediately. 'It's not your fault.'

She stared me out. 'Of course it is.'

I shook my head, but said nothing. We sat silently for a moment. Outside the back door, The Dog barked once and then began a steady whimper. Great sense of ambience, The Dog.

I suppose I knew straightaway that she was right – about Feeny, anyway. She never really did say that she wanted 'action'. I sort of . . . imagined it. And then I stupidly brought it up with Norm and Stevie and Go-go and let it all spiral out of control. The idea seemed absurd now. My mother, requesting a hit! Laughable.

'Tell me more about this theory of yours,' I said, levelly.

'It's the truth, isn't it, Joseph? I want to hear you admit it. You worry that you're not coming up to scratch in some way. Not filling your father's shoes, or something.'

I nodded. 'Maybe I do,' I said.

She nodded back. 'I'm only sorry I didn't see it before. I've been very selfish.'

There was a pause, during which I wondered if I was supposed to argue with her. I didn't, not because I agreed that she'd been selfish, but because I just didn't know what to say. The old familiar feeling. Out of my depth, sitting with the grown-ups, with a grown-up expression, but no fucking clue what to say. I let this feeling wash over me without guilt, trying Mum's theory on for size. So I didn't know what to say. So what? Maybe Dad wouldn't have known either.

'So where do we go from here?'

'I don't know,' she said. 'Well . . . how about this? I'll promise to choose my words more carefully when I talk about your father and what he might or might not do in any given situation, and you'll promise not to take it so personally when I slip up.'

I nodded. 'Sounds like a plan,' I heard myself say. 'And I'll go and talk to Feeny. This weekend.'

It seemed like the thing to do. She sat back, surprised. And pleased. I could tell. She may not have wanted him killed, and she may have regretted giving me that impression, but still . . . she wanted someone to have a word with him, and that someone was me. She looked so chuffed, in fact, that I had a rush of blood to the head.

'I'll go right now, in fact.'

'If you really want to,' she said, trying to suppress a smile.

'I do,' I said, even though I was already regretting my hastiness. What was I going to say to him? *Hi, Brendan, you don't know me, but you impregnated my sister and I've come here to give out shite to you.*

'I'll get the car keys for you,' Mum said.

She was grinning from ear to ear now.

16

As I drove away into the darkness, with Mum waving from the front door like a tearful dockside wife in a World War Two movie, I began to panic a little. What if this turned into a physical fight, despite my clear intention to the contrary? I'd only been in two real fights in my entire life, and was severely beaten in both of them. One of my opponents was blind in one eye, too — some childhood catastrophe with a catapult. Cathal Greeley, he was called. When we were in second year of secondary school, he blackened my left eye and loosened a tooth because I made some crude Cyclops gag. I deserved it, little prick. But it didn't bode well. Brendan Feeny, as far as I was aware, had stereoscopic vision. He might blacken both my eyes and loosen all my teeth.

My other foray into the world of pugilism came during first year in college. It was the archetypal Are-you-looking-at-my-pint? sort of affair. Some no-neck troglodyte in a Leeds United shirt took exception to my very existence and knocked me out cold, crossing the floor of a very large pub to do so. He prefaced his assault with the words, 'You think you're fucking funny, don't you?' I wish I'd said yes. But I just whimpered, 'Not really,' glancing sideways to make sure my friends were still there. They were, and helped a lot by dragging me outside by the armpits and depositing me in a taxi. Thanks.

So. If push came to shove, and shove came to punch, chances were that Feeny would come out on top, to put it mildly. I would just have to make sure it didn't come to that. I'd be reasonable, calm. Tell him I wanted to talk about this in a mature and adult fashion. There was no point in apportioning blame, it was a done deed, she was pregnant and that was that, was that. But. He had responsibilities. He couldn't just walk away. And he certainly couldn't call her a money-grabbing slut in front of the whole world. I would ask him what his plans were, what role he planned to play in his son's or daughter's life, how he would support Deirdre and, ha ha, did he have any names in mind. The more I thought about it, the angrier I became and the more I could see Mum's point. This asshole was getting away with murder. It *was* high time someone took him on. There was no disguising the fact that my father, gentle soul or not, would have done it long ago. I'd been kidding myself all along, I realised with a churn of my stomach. She'd gone about it the wrong way, but Mum was right – it was up to me. I felt my foot press harder on the accelerator.

It was raining steadily that night and the gentle swoosh of the windscreen wipers was mildly hypnotic. As the trees and hedgerows swept past, a grainy movie began to play in my head. Even though I had no violent intentions – quite the reverse – my idle fantasy was of the wise-cracking tough guy variety. Maybe the script, and movies in general, were on my mind. I was the cocky hero, natch, a bit like Bruce Willis only less irritating and sporting a full head of hair. Because I had no idea what Feeny looked like, I mentally cast Tom Cruise, whom I couldn't stand, as the villain. 'You messed with the wrong family, shit-heel,' Bruce/I sneered as he/I pummelled the hapless Cruise/Feeny, who began to cry almost immediately. 'I didn't mean no harm!' he whimpered, but there was no mercy. He fell to the floor and vainly tried to scamper away. Still the blows rained down, both relentless and unerringly accurate. As I drove along, the scene changed abruptly to a western, for some reason. Suddenly, I was more of a Clint Eastwoody sort of figure. Inexplicably, Feeny was now played by Christopher Walken. I respected Walken as an actor, but went with the image anyway. In this new scene, I found I had a six-shooter and took careful aim as I delivered the final wisecrack.

'You ain't nothing but a dirty low-down rat, mister,' I sneered. 'You're a rat and I'm the . . . sssssssssHHHHHHHHHHHHH-IIIIIIIIIIITTTTTTTTTTTTT!'

There was a man on a bicycle in the middle of the road right in front of me, not ten feet away, as I rounded a corner. Eight feet away. Six. Four. Two. Thump. I stood on the brakes, screaming briefly, and the car skidded to a halt. When it stopped, I sat there panting and staring straight ahead, but not at the cyclist. My first thought, in shock I suppose, was *Mum is going to kill me*. That car was her pride and joy. There's bound to be a dent, I remember thinking. Fucking bound to be. Slowly, I undid my seatbelt and groped for the door handle. 'Helter Skelter' was playing on the radio. The song that U2 stole from Charles Manson, Norm called it. I got out and crept around to the front. The grille and bonnet were badly dented, worse than I imagined even.

'Ah, shit,' I said – aloud, I think. 'Ah, holy fucking shit. Look at that.'

The rain felt oddly warm and the car's headlights caught it beautifully. I don't know how long I looked at the drops,

225

apparently suspended in the beams. Maybe ten seconds, maybe a few minutes. There was a pause, certainly, before I felt my legs carry me on to the crumpled figure on the ground.

'Dead,' I said, nodding to myself, when I reached him. He certainly looked dead. His bike, which lay a little further down the road, was badly twisted out of shape. It looked like a modern sculpture, one of those awful, meaningless things any child with a hammer and a bad temper could make. Its light was still working though, catching raindrops of its own. The cyclist himself was properly kitted out, I could see by the car headlights. Lycra shorts and shirt, those funny-looking shoes. No helmet though. He lay on his back, arms outstretched over his head, mouth half open. His left leg showed no sign of distress. But his right . . . His right leg was bent sideways at the knee, as though that joint was a ball and socket, capable of fancy swivelling. For a horrible moment, I thought one of his eyes was missing. But I crept closer, hands to my face, and saw that it had merely filled with dark blood. Where exactly the blood came from, I couldn't see.

I don't know how I knew it was Brendan Feeny. I suppose it was the worst thing I could conceive of, and I had come to assume that the worst thing possible was the thing that always happened.

I gazed at his broken body for a while, shivering in what suddenly felt like freezing rain, before it occurred to me to seek help. I had no phone, and there were no houses around, so I decided I'd have to stop a car. But I had no torch either, so I walked slowly to the crumpled bike, picked it up (marvelling, despite everything, at how light it was) and carried it back around the corner. I pointed it in the direction I'd come from, assuming for some reason that the next car along would come from there. I wasn't even sensible enough to rest the frame on the ground, I just stood there with it held aloft, aiming the beam into the darkness, like a sentry with a gun. Minutes passed then, I'm sure of it. It began to sink in. They're going to lock me up and throw away the key, I thought. Big brother finds out his sister is pregnant and takes off in a murderous rage. Spots the father on the road, innocently riding his bike, and wham! I'm ashamed to admit that it was this thought, of imprisonment and injustice, not the idea that I'd killed someone, that finally broke me down. From stony disbelief to foaming hysterics in a heartbeat. I bawled, taking great heaving gulps of air and rain, freezing, soaking, shaking. I couldn't keep the beam steady. It was arcing all over the place. This is what you get, I told myself, for trying to be something you're not. You're not the positive action type. You're the whinging type. If you'd just stuck to whinging, you'd be in the flatlet now, warm and dry, working on your script, edging ever closer to the good life. Instead . . . look.

Several minutes of this howling self-pity passed before I saw headlights approaching from the predicted direction. I started to scream and wave the bike frame about long before they reached me. God knows what the driver made of the scene ahead, but she slowed sensibly and made her final approach to me at a snail's pace. Deserted country road, mysterious lights – maybe she thought it was a UFO encounter. It was a white Ford Fiesta, new. I remember looking at the registration. When it stopped, I ran around to the driver's door and hammered needlessly on the window, which was already opening. The face that was revealed behind it was middle-aged, concerned, slightly fearful.

'He's dead,' I told it, in a shrill voice. 'He's dead, I fucking killed him.'

I threw up as soon as I spoke, hawking up scalding puke onto the slippery road. As I heaved and spat, bent over double, yet still holding the bike frame, the woman spoke in a voice I remember as being remarkably calm.

'Killed who?' she said. 'What happened?'

In her shoes, I might have driven off at speed. But she showed all the composure and savoir faire of an emergency services telephonist.

'Was there an accident?' she said, when I didn't answer. 'A crash?'

I straightened up and nodded so hard my teeth shook. 'He was in the middle of the road,' I blurted out, pointing. 'I wasn't speeding. I wasn't. I didn't mean it. He was in the middle of the road.'

Only then did she get out of the car. She walked slowly past me round the corner, past my car, to Feeny's body. When she saw the state of him, she shouted 'SHIT' at the top of her lungs and then looked from the body to me to the body to me.

'Have you called an ambulance?' she said, running back.

I shook my head. 'No phone,' I managed to say.

'I've got one,' the woman replied, and dived into her car.

I looked back down the road into the darkness as she made the call. I heard her ask for an ambulance and the Gardaí, and give directions. When she was finished she took a coat from the back seat of her car and hurried back over to the body. I stayed where I was, watching her cover him, but not move him. A coat's not going to help, I thought.

'There's not much we can do,' she called back to me, sounding quite shaken herself now. 'They'll be here in a few minutes, don't worry. And he's alive, he's breathing.'

I felt no relief whatsoever, curiously. But I nodded and started to cry again, certain that he would die soon anyway. Just then, a van approached from the direction we'd all been travelling in. It slowed, and then stopped entirely. When the driver saw what had happened, he pulled into the ditch as far as he could, switched on his hazard lights, and hopped out.

'Jesus Christ!' he called out in what I originally mistook for a greeting, as he trotted over to Feeny and the woman. He was a fat guy in overalls, about my age, maybe even younger. He spoke quietly with the woman, rubbing his chin and occasionally glancing down the road at me. Twice he bent over to take a closer look at Feeny, recoiling and spinning three hundred and sixty degrees, both times. Then he walked down the road to me, stopping a few feet short, as though I posed a danger to him too.

'Y'all right?' he said. 'Are you hurt?'

I shook my head, embarrassed to be crying in front of this man.

'It's maybe not as bad as it looks,' he said, and even smiled.

I shook my head again, gripping my elbows. 'Brendan Feeny,' I said quietly, apropos of nothing.

The fat man looked surprised. 'Do you know him?'

I failed to answer, but shook my head a third time.

'Well, I know him,' he went on, confused. 'To see, like. The car Feenys, down the road a bit. Five or six cars at the house, and he's always out cycling.'

His confirmation that this was Feeny barely registered with me. I took that as a given. He was suddenly illuminated by headlights then, as another car approached. It too slowed and stopped just before the corner, behind the van. The fat man walked over, hands in his overall pockets, amazingly casual, and spoke to the driver through his window. After a while, the car took off, creeping slowly past the other vehicles before speeding away. This was a family. I saw a woman in the passenger seat, two small children in the back. It was not a scene for children. The sight of them, indistinct little shapes straining to see what they'd no doubt been told to ignore, made me cry all the harder. The fat man placed a meaty hand on my shoulder.

The ambulance arrived within minutes, driving past the Fiesta and my car, past Brendan Feeny too. I stayed where I was, watching them work, three of them. Even before they had him on a stretcher, the Gardai arrived too, parking in front of the ambulance. There were two of them, a young woman I vaguely recognised from around the town and a much older man. He stayed by the victim. She approached me.

'HE WAS IN THE MIDDLE OF THE ROAD!' I shouted when she was still twenty feet away. 'I WASN'T TRYING TO HIT HIM! WHY WAS HE OUT ON A NIGHT LIKE THIS FUCKING CYCLING ON A NIGHT LIKE THIS? IT . . . HE . . .'

Everyone, the woman, the fat man, the ambulance people, the male Garda looked at me, then looked immediately back at Feeny.

'It's all right,' she said. 'It's all right, we'll take care of him now.'

I took a step back, then, thinking that looked suspicious, took two steps forward to meet her.

'My name's Joanne,' she told me.

'Joe,' I whispered.

She nodded and smiled.

'Joe what?' she said, taking out a notebook.

17

It was well after midnight when I got home. They dropped me off in a squad car, Mum's having been taken home already by a Garda.

'Try not to worry about it too much,' Joanne said, as we slowed to a halt. 'I'm sure he'll pull through. Accidents happen.'

I was almost afraid to speak, in case I started to blub again, but croaked an OK.

'Take care,' she said, as I got out.

I nodded and closed the door. I turned to face the house as they drove off and saw the front-room curtains twitch. *Don't look at the car*, I told myself walking up the drive, and then looked at the car. My stomach turned over at the sight of the damage. *A Feeny-shaped dent*, I thought. The front door opened before I reached it and my mother bounded out, as energised as I'd seen her in years. She hit me at speed, throwing her arms around me and squeezing hard.

'It could have happened to anyone, Joseph,' she said, words tripping over each other. 'It was an accident. Don't forget that. It was an accident.'

She let go to look me in the face.

'An accident,' she repeated, shaking my shoulders. 'It's more my fault than yours.'

I pursed my lips and ground my teeth. 'He's going to die,' I said.

She shook me again, but could find no definitive words of comfort. 'Maybe not,' was the best she could do.

Brendan Feeny's right leg was badly broken, as were two fingers on his right hand. That was the good news.

'The bad news, Joe,' a Garda told me in the station, 'is that he smacked his head on the road pretty badly when he landed.'

Smacked. Landed. Not the most careful choice of words.

'Did he?' I said, dumbly.

'Yes. He did. It's a bit soon to tell how he'll do. But, as of now, I'm afraid he's in a coma.'

'Coma,' I said. 'Like in a soap opera.' It seemed absurd, not something that might actually happen in real life.

They were very nice to me, the Gardai, once they'd established that I wasn't drunk. They treated me like a victim. The position of the dent in Mum's car showed that either I'd been driving in the ditch, or Feeny had been cycling in the middle of the road. In the absence of alternative testimony, they chose to believe the latter. Also, his snazzy racing bike had no back light or reflector, something I hadn't even noticed.

'I mean, what was he doing out cycling on a night like this?' someone asked me, trying to make me feel better with my own line. It didn't work.

When we were installed on the sofa at home, Mum took exactly the same tack.

'A filthy night like tonight,' she said. 'And him with no

light? Right in the middle of the road? Sure what chance did you have?'

I sipped the enormous brandy she'd produced from somewhere and said nothing.

She bit her lip. 'No helmet either, they told me. He was asking for trouble.'

'He wasn't asking to be mowed down,' I said.

'Well, no,' Mum said, patting my shoulder. 'But . . .'

There was no but. No matter how you sliced it, there was only one villain in this piece.

'She's not home yet then,' I asked, after a prolonged silence.

'No,' Mum said. 'She should be in soon.'

I looked at my knees. 'What am I going to tell her?'

'Just tell her what happened.'

'What? I finally decided to tackle Feeny and ended up killing him?'

'*Injuring* him.'

I gave her a withering look, which she didn't deserve. She looked cowed. I felt a little worse.

'She'll understand, Joseph. Everyone understands that an accident is an accident.'

'The father of her *baby*. Things are bad enough for her already. She'll never forgive me.'

'Of course she will. She's a sensible girl.'

I shook my head, then took another warming sip of brandy. It made my tongue feel thick, numb. Like the rest of me.

'I can't do anything right,' I said.

Mum got angry. 'Now, listen. I don't want to hear that kind of talk. It was an acc—'

'Oh, stop. *Stop*. I'm not just talking about this. Everything I touch turns to shit.'

233

She ignored my coarseness, for once.

'*Everything*. Work, home, friends. Women. Everything. I can't remember the last time anything went right.'

Mum sighed and gave me a smile, mock-punching me. 'That's my line. You're stealing my lines.'

'It's the truth,' I said, stroking the side of my brandy glass. 'Things are getting worse. Every day.'

I thought I'd cried as much as any grown man could in one night, but no. I felt my lip begin to quiver. My nostrils flared involuntarily and my head rolled around on its base. The tears were just beginning to tumble when I heard a key turn in the front door.

I shot up, spilling brandy on my lap. Mum stood slowly and we faced the door. After some noisy shuffling in the hall, the door swung open to reveal a slightly pissed Deirdre.

'Christ!' she yelped, taking us in. 'I thought someone left the lights on. What are you doing up, Mum? And how come *you're* home?'

I sniffed. Mum coughed.

'What?' Deirdre said, contorting her features in drunken confusion. 'What happened?'

She saw the brandy I was clutching like a life jacket.

'BRANDY! Oh shit, who's dead? The Dog! Is it The Dog?'

'No, Deirdre,' Mum said. 'C'mere, sit down.'

We all sat down, me and Mum on the sofa, Deirdre in an armchair. As she made her way to her chair, Deirdre muttered *fuckfuckfuckfuckfuck* under her breath, like a prayer.

'What?' she said when seated. 'What is it?'

'It's Brendan Feeny,' Mum said.

Deirdre was literally taken aback, flopping further into the armchair. She stayed there for a half-second.

'What about him?' she asked, sitting forward again.

Mum cleared her throat. 'He's been in an accident. A road accident. He was hit by a car.'

Deirdre nodded, as if this was confirmation of something she already knew.

'Is he . . . dead?' she said.

Mum shook her head. 'No. He's alive. But he's got head injuries. He's in a coma.'

'Jesus,' Deirdre said, solemnly. 'Jesus *Christ*.'

I held my breath.

'There's something else,' Mum said. 'The—'

'It was an accident,' I said, for the hundredth time that night. 'I didn't mean it.'

Deirdre switched her gaze from Mum to me and then back to Mum. She didn't get it.

'He was hit by our car, Deirdre. Joseph was driving it.'

Her first reaction was to jump to her feet. Then she put her hands over her face. 'Ohhh, *fuck*,' she said, sitting down again.

'I'm sorry,' I said, uselessly.

'It was an accident,' Mum said, reaching over to touch Deirdre's knee. I noticed that her tights were laddered. She probably stumbled into something on the way home.

'But . . . how? Where?' Deirdre said. 'What were you . . . ?'

I swigged hard on the remaining brandy. I was mildly buzzed myself by then.

'I came home to sort things out,' I said, hoping I wouldn't babble, but knowing that I would. 'After last week's fiasco.'

A voice in my head said, *As distinct from this week's fiasco, and the previous week's fiasco.*

'We had a chat, Mum and me, and she told me that you and her had a chat too, and we cleared the air a bit.'

I looked to Mum, who nodded her agreement with this summary.

'Mum explained that she, y'know, she never wanted me to go for Feeny in any way, that that was all in my head, which is probably true, and then I said that maybe I should go and talk to him in any case. You know. Just *talk*, ask him what he's playing at with you and the baby.'

Deirdre grew pale. 'And?' she said.

'And I was driving out there to see him, get it over with, and . . .'

She stared at me wide-eyed.

'And I came round this corner and there he was. On a bike.'

'And you hit him?'

'Yes. I hit him.'

'You were speeding?'

'No! I wasn't speeding. I wasn't. He was right in the middle of the road, Deirdre, I don't know why. And he had no back light. No helmet, either.'

'Then what?'

I closed my eyes, not wanting to see her face. 'Then I stopped a car and the driver called an ambulance and they took him away.'

I kept my eyes closed during the ensuing silence.

'He's in a *coma*?' she said.

I nodded, finally able to look at her again. 'They told me in the station.'

'The station?'

'The Garda station. They had to get a statement and . . . all that.'

Her voice dropped an octave. 'Did they breathalyse you?'

'On the road, yes.'

Tiny pause.

'And?'

Mum inhaled sharply. 'Deirdre!'

'What?!'

'What are you suggesting?'

'It's all right,' I said. 'I was stone-cold sober, Deirdre. It was an accident.'

There was nothing in my brandy glass, but I put it to my mouth anyway, breathing the vapours.

'Did they ask you where you were going?'

'Yes. I said I was going to Stevie's house. He lives out that way.'

'So, you lied in your statement?'

'I suppose so.'

'You suppose so? What if they find out how you're linked to Feeny?'

'How would they?' Mum said.

'How the hell do I know?' Deirdre snapped. 'They might though, mightn't they? I mean, it doesn't look good, does it? The whole town's seen me and him fighting like cat and dog, calling each other names. And it's no secret I'm pregnant, you know.'

I thought of One-shift Brady telling me at the bus station. The room spun.

'I don't want to think about it,' I said, quietly.

'Well, you might have to, if they come knocking.'

'STOP IT,' Mum yelled. 'Just . . . stop it. No one's getting into trouble over this. It was a simple accident, and that's the end of it.'

'Unless he dies,' Deirdre said.

I dropped my head into my hands and fought the urge to puke.

'I think you should go to bed,' Mum said, very deliberately. 'You're upset, and you're not helping Joseph.'

'Leave her be,' I moaned. 'She's got every right to be upset. Maybe I've killed her baby's father.'

I might have shed yet another tear at that point. God knows I felt like it. But Deirdre suddenly made a little choking sound. If we'd been in a play, her stage direction would have said DEIRDRE MAKES A SUSPICIOUS NOISE. Mum and I looked at her. She wriggled. She squirmed. She made the sound again.

'What?' we said together.

Deirdre patted down her skirt and rubbed her knees. Centuries passed.

'Nothing,' she said, quietly.

We all sat back then and let a grim silence settle over us. From out of nowhere, Catherine Dillon swam into my mind. All at once, I was finally able to rationalise the disproportionate attraction she held for me. It wasn't her looks, that was just the hook. It was her outsider status. She knew nothing about the appalling mess my life was in. She knew nothing about Mum and her grief-induced insanities, or about Deirdre and her entanglements. She knew I was unhappy in my job, but she probably thought it was one of those everyday things, not some half-assed existential crisis. She certainly didn't know I had put all my eggs in an unlikely basket marked HOLLYWOOD. Like the script itself, she represented a way out. It didn't make much sense, but I wanted her there more than anyone else. Norm and Stevie would laugh. Go-go seemed to be finally sick of my whinging. She was the one. Not despite the fact that she was a total stranger.

Because of it.

18

'Morning,' I slurred from the couch the next day as my mother came through the door with shopping.

'Afternoon,' she corrected, without temper. 'Did you sleep well? Did you sleep at all?'

I nodded, returning my gaze to the TV. 'Yeah. Like the dead.'

We'd all gone to bed with not much more said. I would have bet my script that I was in for a night of staring at the ceiling, stomach in knots. But I was asleep before I was fully horizontal. I shut down, actually, rather than fell asleep. Just switched off, automatically, to effect an escape.

From the kitchen: 'Not getting dressed today, then?'

I shrugged, even though I knew she couldn't see me.

'Hello? Joseph?'

'No,' I snapped. 'Yes. In a while.'

I heard the kettle filling and switched back to *Football Focus*. Ron Atkinson was saying something about somebody's balance and poise.

'I had words with Deirdre this morning,' Mum said, opening and closing cupboard doors.

I sat up a little. 'Words?'

'About the accident. About her attitude to it.'

I heard my teeth grind. 'What did you say? You weren't giving out, I hope, because—'

'No, it was all very friendly.'

She appeared in the kitchen doorway. 'I'm not stupid, Joseph, I can see how this is tough on Deirdre too, you know.'

I waited for her to say how tough it was on herself, but she said nothing, and went back inside. Cups clattered.

'She's a very confused little girl.'

Little girl?

'Yeah,' I said, unsure of where this was going. Not in the direction of maternal support, surely?

She reappeared with two cups of tea and took an armchair opposite me. 'Drink this,' she said, sliding one across the coffee table. 'You might feel better.'

'I doubt it,' I said.

She looked at me and shook her head sadly. 'Can you turn that thing off?' she asked. 'I want to talk to you.'

I sighed deeply and pressed the mute button. She ignored my childish compromise.

'Now, you're not to get all depressed about this. Joseph? Are you listening to me?'

'Seems like a perfectly normal response to me,' I said.

'I won't have it,' she said. 'There's been enough depression around here. No more.'

I adjusted my boxer shorts, suddenly aware that I might pop out of them at any moment, which wouldn't have helped.

'It's all right talking,' I said. 'You're not the murderer.'

'Who is?' she said, with piercing simplicity. There was no

answer (yet) so I watched the silent TV again. Trevor Brooking was shaking his head and laughing.

'No one's been murdered, Joseph. Even if he, God forbid . . . slipped away, you still wouldn't be a murderer. You know that. You're just feeling sorry for yourself.'

I almost choked.

'I don't fucking believe it!' I yelped. 'You're lecturing me about feeling sorry for myself! Pot? Kettle? Do these words mean anything to you?'

It was the first time that I had dared to suggest such a thing. She took a small sip of tea and replaced her cup on its saucer very carefully.

'First of all, please don't swear at me, I'm not a football hooligan. I can get the gist of your point without profanity. And secondly, I am fully aware that I have been feeling sorry for myself. It's becoming clearer to me with every passing moment. It's all I think about these days. I have neglected my family. But I had good reason, Joseph. I had good reason. I hope to good God you never find out for yourself.'

I closed my eyes, stung and ashamed.

'I'm sorry,' I whispered.

'You're sorry, I'm sorry, everyone's sorry. Let's move on. Now. About Mr Feeny. Brendan. What can you do?'

I blinked.

'What can I *do*? What do you mean? Nothing.'

'Not for him, personally, obviously. Although you might offer a prayer. Don't look at me like that. Don't underestimate the power of prayer, Joseph. I meant, in general. For you, as much as him. What can you do?'

'I don't know what you're talking about,' I said, quite honestly.

241

Another sip of tea.

'You can go and see him in the hospital. And talk to his family. They'll be there, no doubt.'

I dropped my head into my waiting hands.

'You're out of your mind,' I mumbled.

'I have never felt more sane. It would be good for you. Good for them too.'

'No.'

'It's the right thing to do.'

'No.'

'The only positive thing you *can* do.'

'No.'

'Deirdre would go with you. If you didn't feel like driving. She came shopping with me, then went off on her own, to meet that Yvonne one. But she'll be back this afternoon. You could go then.'

I ignored the part about driving, although she was dead right. I never wanted to drive again.

'What could I possibly achieve? They'd beat me to a pulp.'

'Nonsense. They'd appreciate your courage.'

'They'd appreciate the chance to fucking kill me.'

'No swearing,' Mum said, rising with her empty cup. 'Now. Let me ring the hospital, and I'll find out what visiting hours are.'

She was gone for a couple of minutes, which I spent in the foetal position, frowning my very hardest.

'Three till five,' she said when she returned. 'But they won't let you see him. Family only.'

I almost issued a heartfelt *phew*, but restrained myself.

'Still, you can see his parents. They're there at the moment. They'll be there all day.'

I was about to protest again, but she didn't let me.

242

'There's no change in his condition,' she said. 'That's good, isn't it? I mean, he hasn't gotten any worse.'

'He can't get any worse,' I sniffed. 'The only way he can get worse is if he dies.'

It wasn't news to me, anyway – I had called the hospital myself when they were out. The terse voice on the other end asked me if I was a relative. I told her I was a friend. 'A close friend,' I added when she hesitated. Boy, *that* felt good.

Mum ignored my bad temper and smiled like her old good-in-a-crisis self.

'So it's settled,' she said. 'Best decision you ever made.'

19

Deirdre drove to the hospital very, very slowly. I said little, thinking of Bruce Willis, and shivering.

The few words I did say were almost all four-lettered. Deirdre did a good job of ignoring me – her mother's daughter. To be honest, I think I expected her to admit at any stage that the whole thing was a bluff, some sort of test that I had passed by going that far. But no. Just as Mum had said, she was absurdly enthusiastic about the venture.

'But what am I going to *tell them*?' I moaned, grabbing her arm as she pulled into the hospital car park.

'For the fourteenth time, just tell them what happened.'

I stared out at the bland, ugly building, feeling like a child being dropped off at the first day of school. An old man with a Zimmer frame was making glacial progress around the front entrance. His dressing-gown flapped about his legs in the stiff breeze.

'I don't see what that's going to achieve. I really don't.'

'It's going to help you and it's going to help them. Less guilt for you, less anguish for them.'

'You got that from your mother,' I said.

'Yeah, so what? We had an interesting conversation this morning. Very interesting. I think she's turned a corner.'

'Phthtp. She's just gone a different kind of mad. I think these people are in enough emotional trouble without me showing up.'

'We disagree. We think –'

'*We?*'

'– we think they'll appreciate the gesture.'

Apparently, there was no point in arguing. I undid my seatbelt and climbed out, in furious silence.

I hate hospitals. No one actually likes them, I suppose, but I utterly despise them, fear them even. It's the smell, partly. Hospitals smell like desperation. Not out in the bright open spaces, among the broken-legged, or the heavily pregnant. In the corners, where they keep the dying. The forced cheeriness gets to me too. I don't know how doctors and nurses do it, how they keep smiling, but frankly I wish they'd stop. When they wheel me into one, and gather the family round, I'm going to give a clear order – 'No fucking smiling, right? I'm *dying* over here.'

What am I saying? I smiled like a loved-up air hostess when my dad went into his corner. He smiled back, most days. But I bet he wanted to give that order.

It took me a good ten minutes to find intensive care. It was tucked away on its own, on the third floor. As I traipsed around, mumbling opening lines to myself, I saw an elderly nun meandering down a lonely corridor. I stopped dead. Hospitals and nuns, together at last. It was like all my Christmases had come at once and I didn't get anything for any of them. She had her head down, consciously forcing one foot in front of the other. She looked up as I approached, and for a fleeting moment,

I thought it was Sister Frances, whose advice I still had filed away, unused. I was shocked to find myself smiling. But no. This nun was older than time. She made Frances look like one of the Spice Girls. I hurried past, wondering what I would have said if it had been her.

The nurse who met me at intensive care looked tired and pissed off. When she spoke, I recognised her voice from the phone.

'Afternoon,' she said, looking up from a ledger of some kind. 'Can I help you?'

'I'm looking for a Brendan Feeny,' I said, as though any Brendan Feeny would do.

'Yes,' the nurse said, as though that was an answer.

'Is he . . . here?'

No, genius, he went out for a walk.

'And you are?'

'A friend.'

'No visitors for Mr Feeny, I'm afraid,' she said, 'except immediate family.'

'Well . . . actually, it's his family I want to see. Are *they* here?'

'His parents, yes.'

'Can I see them?'

The nurse regarded me with suspicion. 'Yeeess. They're having a break and a cup of tea.'

Fucking tea again.

'In the canteen?'

The nurse pointed past me down the hallway. 'They're in a small private room. Third on the left. Please make sure you *knock*.'

'Yeah. Thanks.'

I half turned to go, then cleared my throat and asked how the patient was, even though I knew.

'He's stable,' the nurse said, nodding, and looking sympathetic for the first time. If only she knew that I was the one who put him there.

'Do you know . . .' I began, and faltered. 'Do you know how long he'll be . . .'

I tore through my memory for the word. Comified? Comulous? '. . . comatose?' I said, finally.

She shook her head, biting her lower lip. 'There's no way to tell. Could be hours. Could be days.'

'Could be permanent?'

'There's no way to tell,' she repeated. I took that as a yes, and was overcome again with the feeling that I was in some cheap soap opera. If I slammed a door, would the walls shake? If I looked up suddenly, would I see a boom mike intruding on the shot?

'OK. OK. Thanks.'

'He's getting very good care,' she said, and touched my arm. I recoiled, and she withdrew her hand immediately, looking shocked. Maybe she thought I had intimacy issues. I almost explained. I almost said, 'Don't worry. It's just *shame*.'

I stood outside the door for maybe a full minute, thoughts whirling, before giving it a timid little rap. Feet shuffled on the other side. It swung open.

'Yes?' a grey-haired man said. I guessed he was in his late fifties. He wore a dark blue polo shirt and black corduroy trousers. He didn't look like the sort of man who owned a pink house.

'Mr Feeny?' I said.

'Yes?'

'Uh . . . hello.'

He looked very tired.

'What can I do for you?' he said, remarkably calm. His face was tanned. Intelligent-looking, I thought for no good reason.

'It's about Brendan.'

He sighed and opened the door wider, stepping aside.

'A friend of his, are you?' he said. 'Come in, come in.'

Somehow, I didn't want to go in while he was under that impression.

'Not really,' I said, glancing beyond him to his wife, who peered out, looking concerned. Mr Feeny waited for elaboration. I took a deep breath. There was no way to lead in to what I had to say.

'I was driving the car,' I told him, flatly.

He stood on the tip of his toes then settled again. Inside, his wife stood up, and ran an anxious hand through her hair. She whispered something to herself that I didn't catch.

'I'd like to talk to you both,' I went on – a blatant lie. It was the last thing I wanted, but I was there now.

'You'd better come in.' He stepped aside.

The room was dull and in urgent need of decoration. The walls were institutional yellow, the paint peeling. There were two small couches and three of those awful plastic chairs you see at public meetings. A battered coffee table sat in the middle of the room, covered with torn and faded magazines. There was a drinks machine humming violently in the corner.

'Sit down,' Mr Feeny said, returning to his own couch and urging his wife to retake her seat. I crept in, head down.

'I expect you feel terrible,' Mrs Feeny said, as I sat down.

I was startled by her caring tone.

'Yes,' I said, my voice trembling slightly. 'I do. I really do.'

She was what my mother would have called a 'handsome

woman', a phrase that has always sounded more insult than compliment to my ears. Maybe it's supposed to sound that way. She looked a little older than her husband, if anything, although that may have been due to circumstances. She had clearly been crying, and very recently. Her face was still tear-tracked. But it had a certain quality.

'I don't know what to say to you,' I said, sincerely.

'You could start by telling us what happened,' Mr Feeny said, still calm. And calming. He made me feel, instantly, that I could speak frankly and not be afraid.

I blew some air, puffing my cheeks, and began.

'It was an accident,' I said, too loudly. This was a phrase I was now thinking of having printed on a card, so I could just hand it out to everyone and save breath. 'It was a horrible night, last night, the rain and everything, and I came round a corner – I wasn't speeding – and the guy, I mean Brendan, was right there in the middle of the road. I barely had time to see him. The road was slippery and I couldn't stop in time. I just couldn't . . .'

'You're sure you weren't speeding?' Mr Feeny said.

I almost shook my head off. 'Absolutely not. I'm a very careful driver, Mr Feeny. Honestly. I drive like an old woman.'

They gave me a disdainful look. It was an inappropriate remark.

'I'm so sorry,' I said quickly. 'I know it's pointless saying that, but I want to say it anyway. I'm really . . . sorry.'

'The Gardai told us you were sober,' Mr Feeny said. 'Lucky for you.'

I could think of no response other than a slow nod. 'I would never drink and drive. Ever. Look . . . I don't know what to say to you. I mean, if you want the absolute truth, I didn't want to come here. Not because I don't care that I ran someone over. I didn't want to come because . . .'

'Because it's hard,' Mrs Feeny said. 'It must be hard for you.'

My face begin to make movements I wasn't telling it to make. Tears were imminent.

'I'm sorry,' I croaked, yet again.

There was another unpleasant silence, filled only by the hum of the drinks machine, and my hitching breaths.

Mr Feeny ended it by asking my name.

'Joe Flood,' I whispered.

The Feenys froze in tandem.

'Anything to Deirdre Flood?' Mrs Feeny said.

My throat clenched shut for a moment. 'Uh . . . yes.'

'Deirdre Flood? The Deirdre Flood who's been accusing my son of fathering a baby?'

My stomach turned over.

'Oh. You know about that,' I said.

They both gave slow nods.

'Would you like a cup of tea?' Mr Feeny said. 'We've got a lot to talk about.'

What followed had an air of unreality, like so much of my recent experience. The Feenys were politeness itself, treating me like a guest in their home. They even sprang for the tea, when it emerged that I hadn't got the correct change. The name Deirdre Flood was 'burned on their brains', in Mr Feeny's phrase. It was all they had heard about from Brendan for weeks – this girl, this pleasant but slightly batty girl who had convinced herself that she was carrying his child. Apparently, Brendan had told them the whole story – the *whole* story, mind, including the rows. He had even admitted to saying 'horrible things, things he regretted'. I presumed that this was reference to the 'money-grabbing slut' comments, but didn't ask for details. As they told me what they knew, interrupting each other, correcting the chronology or what was actually said, I sat perfectly still, mouth agape. Brendan was 'badly cut up' about the accusation, was off his food, wasn't sleeping. Going for long bike rides alone. They said their piece quietly, with no trace of anger. Right until the end. Then Mr Feeny fixed me with a steely glare and said, 'Now. You must admit. This is some coincidence.' He showed his teeth when he said 'coincidence'.

'I . . . yes, it is,' I said.

'Your sister and my son have this . . . misunderstanding, and then, next thing you know, he's in hospital. In a coma.'

I could feel my heart race, and broke cold sweat.

'It's not what you think,' I said. 'It's not what you think. It was a terrible, stupid accident. I was on my way to a friend's house, it's just awful, stupid chance that I met Brendan on the road.'

They looked at me with an intensity I have rarely felt. I knew, could see as plain as day, that they were good people (whatever that means) who didn't want to think badly of anyone. I bit my lip as they stared, trying to communicate my innocence without words. Attempting further speech would surely lead to tears, I felt.

'On your way to see a friend,' Mr Feeny said, finally.

I thought of Mum and Deirdre and their new-found enthusiasm for clarity and honesty.

'No,' I told him, swallowing hard. 'No. That's a lie. I was on my way to your house. To see Brendan, just to *talk* to him, I swear.'

'Go on.'

'Deirdre told me that they'd had terrible rows, in public. She was very upset. I wanted to hear Brendan's side of the story.'

'Play big brother?' Mrs Feeny said.

'No! Well. Yes. Yes, but not in the way you mean. There was nothing threatening about it, all I wanted to do was talk. I'm not the violent type, Mrs Feeny. Really. That's what makes this so awful. The . . . irony of it.'

For the first time, she looked properly angry. She pulled the face I had expected her to wear for the whole conversation – bitter, vengeful.

'You think this is "ironic"?' she hissed.

I rubbed my forehead and tried to straighten my thoughts. 'I'm sorry. That came out wrong. That was a stupid thing to say. Look, I shouldn't have come . . .'

'Ah, sit down,' Mr Feeny said, as I started to get up. 'You don't strike me as a tough guy. If you don't mind me saying so.'

He looked to his wife.

'No,' she agreed. 'I'm sorry I snapped at you.'

'Sorry?' I bleated, incredulous. 'You're apologising to *me*? Please. You're making me feel worse. I'd rather you shouted at me.'

She shrugged. 'What good would that do?'

I nodded, seeing her point, but failing to understand how they could both cope so well.

'I appreciate your being so understanding,' I said, a little stiffly. 'I don't think I would be, in your shoes.'

'Well. You don't solve problems by getting annoyed about them,' she said in a clear and steady voice. 'There are only two types of problem, really – the ones you can do something about, and the ones you can't. If you can do something, you shut up and do it. If you can't . . . you just wade through it to the other side, as best you can.'

'Yes,' I said, dreamily. 'Yes. Wade.'

'Now,' Mr Feeny said. 'About this baby.'

'Yes,' I said, once again.

'What makes your sister so sure it's Brendan's?'

'Well . . .'

'It's just that I find her story a little hard to believe . . .'

I paused, biting my tongue to stop myself saying something unpleasant about their son.

'. . . because . . . well . . . Brendan can't have children.'

My jaw dropped.

'*What?*'

'Brendan can't have children,' his wife repeated. 'Ever.'

Mr Feeny nodded that I should believe my ears.

'He was very ill a few years ago, before we moved here. He had . . . well, he had testicular cancer, Joe. It's quite common in young men, you know.' He lowered his head, and his voice faltered. 'Mind you. Brendan was unusually unlucky. It's very, very rare to have it in . . . both. Very rare indeed. He, eh, he had an operation.'

'Operation?' I said, keeping up the parrot act.

'Yes. A double orchiectomy.'

Mrs Feeny couldn't look at me. Her husband, however, glared right at me, challenging me to make some awful joke. But I never felt less like cracking wise. To be honest, I felt afraid, because I thought maybe I was going mad. Hearing things.

'But then . . . how can he . . . if he . . .'

'Sexual performance is not impaired,' Mr Feeny said quickly. 'He takes hormones. And he has prostheses.'

This was almost too much for me. For a brief moment, I heard the *Dynasty* theme. *Deh-de-deh, deh-dehhh-de-deh.* What was next? Was he about to reveal that he was my real father? I glanced up for the intruding microphone. Nothing.

'I don't know what to say,' I whispered, quite honestly. My mind whirled. I couldn't work out if it was bad news or terrible news. 'Why didn't Brendan tell Deirdre about this?'

Mr Feeny looked at me like I was an idiot. I was beginning to get the feeling he was enjoying this. I couldn't blame him. He deserved to see me squirm.

'Why do you think? Would you go around telling everyone? And, of course, he was hoping he wouldn't have to. He was hoping she would admit that there was someone else. There was someone else, wasn't there? Because if there wasn't, she should get on the phone to the Vatican. They'd be very interested in this, I'm sure.'

'I don't know,' I said. 'But I'm going to find out.'

'That might be a good idea.'

I held my head, the shock of it starting to sink in. 'I'm—'

'Sorry?' the Feenys said.

There wasn't much else for us to say to each other after that. I wanted to run, but made myself sit there for another few minutes. We discussed Brendan's condition, or rather they did, and I listened, still dumbstruck. They said something about the power of prayer and I told them my mother felt the same way. Mrs Feeny talked briefly about Brendan's love of cycling and how strange it was, for someone surrounded by cars his whole life. I smiled when I thought it was expected of me. Eventually, I said I had intruded on them for too long and rose to leave.

'We appreciate your coming,' Mr Feeny said and offered his hand.

I shook it and then his wife's.

'I hope . . .' I began, but couldn't finish the sentence.

'So do we,' Mrs Feeny said.

20

The kind thing to do, on reflection, would have been to confront
Deirdre in the car. Give her a chance to explain herself to me in
private. But I didn't do that. I didn't want to deal with it alone.
So I sold her down the river.

'Well?' she asked as I got into the car.

'It went fine,' I told her.

She didn't notice my monotone.

'Told you!' she said happily. 'I bet you feel much better
now.'

She spent the journey home wittering about how important it
was to face up to difficult situations.

Even after we arrived home, I said nothing for a while. It was
as if, having started out concealing what I knew, I found it hard
to come out with it at all.

'And they were glad you went along?' Mum said, looking
distinctly pleased with herself.

I nodded dumbly. They probably put my relative silence
down to ongoing guilt. Which was partly true, of course. I

didn't think I could possibly feel worse about hitting Feeny. I was wrong.

'I knew it. Didn't I tell you? People know what an accident is. God help them, though. Were they very upset?'

'They seemed OK,' I said. 'Very calm. Very centred.'

Mum had laid on cake and biscuits. We were sitting around the kitchen table.

'Centred?' Deirdre said.

I didn't look at her as I answered. I looked at a chocolate sponge. 'Centred. Sensible. Reasonable.'

'And there's no change in his condition?' Mum said, pouring tea.

I shook my head. 'There's no way to tell how long he'll be unconscious.'

'He'll be OK,' she said. 'I can feel it. He'll be grand.'

'Maybe,' I said.

'I've got a good feeling about it today, too,' Deirdre said, popping a piece of cake into her mouth. 'I woke up sure he'd be OK.'

She was so cheery. So unconcerned.

'They do wonderful things in hospitals these days,' Mum said. 'Even in *our* hospital. Sure even a few years ago, he would have had to go to Dublin straight away. I remember when—'

'Is it the money?' I said, looking right at Deirdre.

I could feel Mum staring at the side of my face.

'Sorry?' Deirdre said.

'The money. Is it all about money? You and Feeny? Tell me that isn't it.'

'What are you talking about?' Mum said. 'We're not getting into this again, are we?'

'Brendan Feeny can't have children,' I said, still fixed on

Deirdre's face, which crumbled as I spoke. 'He had testicular cancer. He's sterile.'

I didn't go into the details, but I had said enough. Deirdre dropped her fork, and closed her eyes.

'His dad told me,' I went on. 'They know all about you, and your . . . claim.'

Mum said, 'Testic . . .'

'So who's the other guy, Deirdre? Someone poor, was it? Tell me I'm wrong. Please.'

'What are you talking about?' Mum said, her voice rising in confusion and panic.

'You're wrong,' Deirdre said, eyes still closed. She suddenly looked very young.

'Who was it?' I said.

'You don't know him.'

'*Who?*'

'You don't know him, he was a tourist.' She paused. 'Brendan's *sterile?*'

Mum said, 'A tourist?' like she'd never heard the word.

Deirdre nodded pathetically. 'A German tourist. Oh my God . . . I feel sick.'

'Where is he now?' I asked.

'I've no idea. I only . . . met him once. Right before I met Brendan Feeny.'

'I don't understand, you, you, you had *intercourse* with him?' Mum said, pale with shock.

Deirdre nodded, and finally started to cry. 'Once. *Once.* Like it was just once with Brendan.'

Mum said, 'I . . . I . . . I . . .'

'Why didn't you tell us?' I asked. 'We would have understood. I would, anyway.'

'I didn't want to sound like a slut,' Deirdre said, shouted really. 'Because I'm not. If you want to know the truth, they were the only two ever. Adolf was the first ever.'

'ADOLF!' Mum and I screamed together.

Deirdre bawled. 'Yes, Adolf! Get it over with! Make your little jokes! I don't care any more!'

The room was quiet then, briefly, save for Deirdre's sobbing and Mum's hyperventilation. I used the time to scramble a theory together.

'You didn't tell us because you didn't want to sound like a slut, having to say you didn't even know who the father was,' I surmised, in a hopeful tone. 'You didn't want to cause any more trouble. There's been enough trouble in this house, you thought.'

Deirdre nodded through the sobs.

'And this Adolf character was gone before you knew you were pregnant. So you pointed the finger at Feeny. You thought that was best. You thought we'd approve. Or not disapprove, at any rate. Because at least he's here. His money was . . . a bonus?'

Deirdre nodded sadly. Mum blessed herself again.

'And now I've killed him,' I concluded.

'Injured him,' Mum said.

'What a mess,' I said.

'I'm sorry,' Deirdre said.

'Your father . . .' Mum began.

'. . . would turn in his grave,' we all said.

I'm not sure why I hung around for the rest of the weekend. On the face of it, I had solid reasons for wanting to hightail it back to the flatlet for a good old-fashioned wallow. But I stayed put. The only serious consideration I gave Dublin was to curse myself for not knowing Catherine's home phone number. I felt sure that she would want to talk to me, for no better reason than I wanted to talk to her, to hear about Other Things. Stupid, really.

We were all understandably quiet for the rest of Saturday. Deirdre and I stayed in our rooms, mostly, while Mum took The Dog for the longest walk of his life. When they arrived back, nearly three hours after they left, Mum looked quite peaceful, rested almost. The Dog looked knackered. His tongue lolled halfway to the floor and his eyes swivelled wildly in his head. I met them when I crept down to the kitchen for a much-needed sandwich. I said more to The Dog than I did to Mum (I sympathised with his physical exhaustion; he whined and then lay down in the hall for a snooze). I left Mum to her own devices because I knew that, like me, like Deirdre, she just wanted to be left alone to digest all of this.

Sunday was a less private affair. We drifted around separately in the morning, going out for the papers (me), attending mass (Mum), and taking The Dog for a walk he could do without (Deirdre). I watched her physically drag him down the road, his little legs digging in, and had to smile.

Later, we had lunch together as usual. Mum talked about how pleasant mass had been, to raised eyebrows from her children. Deirdre gave us the latest scandal from her job. Her boss, a whip-thin bachelor called Tony Hickey, had lost his temper with her when she made some minor change to the way they handled old customer records. He got really mad and told her, in front of two other staff, that he'd been in the business a lot longer than she had and knew what he was doing, thank you very much. 'I was feeling small and embarrassed,' she reported.

261

'And then he looked me right in the eye and said, "Listen, *girlie*. Don't teach your grandmother to fuck eggs." I mean, hello? A Freudian would have a field day with that man.' This raised a giggle even from Mum, who then grew serious and told Deirdre to 'watch herself' around him.

We all paid great attention to our carrots for a while after that comment.

There wasn't much to do in the afternoon but hang around, pass bits of the paper to each other, and try to ignore the Norman Wisdom film on TV. I considered taking The Dog for another hike, just to get out of the house, but he scampered away – limped, really – every time I approached. As the clock ticked ever on, I began to wonder if anyone was going to say anything about . . . everything. Not a word, all day. It was weird. But then, around four o'clock, Mum announced that she was going to the cemetery to tend to the grave. Traditionally, the grave had been a bone of contention between my mother and me. I visited it, of course, but never with any enthusiasm. It didn't depress me or fatigue me. It left me completely cold, which she mistook, I think, for indifference to the fact of his death. Still, Deirdre and I both offered to help (and Deirdre probably meant it). Mum insisted on going alone though, to my twitching discomfort. I couldn't tell if Deirdre was angry with me – couldn't even tell if she should be – and I wasn't really keen to find out. I knew she'd say nothing until Mum left.

'So,' she said, before Mum had even made it to the car. 'What do you think?'

I looked up from the movie page. She would have to be more specific. 'About what?'

'About what,' she mocked. 'About your *mother*.'

I pondered for a moment. What was I missing? 'What about her?'

'Oh, for fuck's sake. Have you not even noticed the change?'

'There's been a change?'

'Yes. She isn't mad.'

I still wasn't following. 'That I didn't go to the grave?'

'No, asshole, not mad-angry, mad-*insane*.'

I put the paper down. 'Isn't she?'

'No. She isn't. I mean . . . considering. Come on, Joe, you know what she's like. Any other weekend, she's picking on us and bitching and moaning about, I don't know, how we treat the place like a hotel or some shit, some silly made-up crap that she would never have complained about when Dad was around. Fuck, you know it better than me, even. She picks on you more because you're not here most of the time and she has to make the most of it when you are. But this weekend, when –'

She paused and pursed her lips.

'– when she finds out that you've ACCIDENTALLY run over the bloke who was supposed to be the father of my baby and then turns out not to be, and then I reveal that I had a stupid fling with some unshaven backpacker and got frigging knocked up, fuck my luck . . . *this* weekend, she's fine.'

I didn't point out that Deirdre didn't 'reveal' anything, Feeny's poor father did, partly because I didn't want to argue, but mostly because I was surprised and touched by her emphasising the word 'accidentally'. She was her mother's daughter in more ways than one. She could say the right thing when it counted.

'Maybe . . .' I said cautiously.

'There's no maybe about it. She's turned a corner, I'm telling you. All she needed was for her children to feel worse about something than she does about Dad.'

I gave her theory some silent thought. It wasn't bad.

'This backpacker . . .' I began, trying to take advantage of her philosophical mood.

'Forget about him, he's gone. I don't . . .'

She looked acutely embarrassed.

'I don't even know his second name. I was rotten pissed, I'm ashamed to say. I only remember his first name because, well . . . you're not going to forget it, are you?'

I gave her the most sympathetic look I could muster. 'Where did it . . . happen?'

'He was in a B & B in town. He snuck me in.'

'How romantic.'

'Fuck off.'

I whistled through my teeth. 'I suppose there's no point in worrying about him, then. If he's gone.'

'Correct.'

'There's plenty of point in worrying about Feeny though. He's still here. Just.'

She shook her head. 'He'll be fine.'

'Yeah? How do you know?'

'I know.'

'How?'

'I just know, all right? For one thing, he's a Feeny. They always do all right.'

That sounded a bit cold to my ears. 'He hasn't been too lucky so far, has he? Life-threatening illness, infertility, road accidents. And he had to have sex with you.'

'Har fucking har. I'm telling you. He'll be grand.'

'He better be. Or I don't know what I'll do. Things are falling down around me, without that.'

'What things?'

'Everything. Work's slowly killing me, home's getting more . . . complicated by the day. And there's this girl.'

'Home, dingbat, is getting *better*. But never mind that – girl, you say? Spill.'

'There's nothing to spill. I've only met her a couple of times. And never in ideal circumstances. Nothing's happened. Nor will it, by the looks of things.'

A brief montage flickered through my mind – Norm holding his broken nose, Brian giving me the thumbs-up in Langley's canteen, the floor girl shaking her head and tutting in Finlay's. Catherine in the background on each occasion, looking at me from under a furrowed brow, shocked or embarrassed or both.

'Has she got a name?'

'Catherine. Dillon.'

'From?'

'Dunno. Dublin, somewhere.'

'Well, why don't you ask her out?'

'I did.'

'Oh.'

'She said no.'

'Oh. That's that then.'

'No it isn't.'

She pretended to glance nervously around the room. 'No means no, Joe. Remember? The judge was very clear on that point.'

'I know that, I'm not *dangerous*, for Christ's sake. But we have banter. I've got a feeling about her. The way you've got a feeling that Feeny will be OK. For no reason whatsoever.'

'Yeah, but you've popped the question and got shot down, banter or no banter. Where can you go from there?'

'Nowhere. Fine. Nowhere. Forget I brought it up.'

'Well, don't blame *me*. I'm only saying. If she's said no, that's it.'

'Fine.'

'Joe—'

'*Fine*.'

Deirdre rolled her eyes. 'OK, Jesus. So, what's wrong with work then?' She pressed a limp wrist to her brow. 'Draining your creative spirit, is it?'

'You're *funny*. So very, very funny.'

'All right, sorry. That electronics place still closing, then?'

'We still dunno. Probably, the way things are going. Catherine works there, you know.'

'Well, that's good, that's your in, isn't it? Slip her the word, warn her about it. She'll think you're the bollocks of the dog.'

'Pah. Already did. By accident. Stuart would fucking kill me if he knew.'

'And?'

'And nothing.'

'Forget about her, so.'

I frowned a teenage frown. 'It's not that easy.'

'Of course it is. Throw yourself into your script, luvvie.'

'You're full of advice I'm already following. It's my life jacket, that bloody script.'

'You're so poetic.'

'Fuck off.'

'Must be nearly finished now.'

'All but. Anyway. What about you? You're going to be a single mother, for sure.'

'Yeah. I know. Well, whaddaya gonna do?'

'Flip out? I would.'

'I'm not you, though. No one is.'

It wasn't a compliment.

I was packed and ready to go by the time Mum returned. I met her in the hall.

'Everything all right at the grave?' I asked, immediately wincing at the stupidity of the question. But she took it in the way I meant it.

'Yes, I tidied up a bit, you know. Said a few prayers.'

'Right. Listen, I have to go. Six o'clock bus.' I said it too quickly. It sounded like I didn't care. I waited for her rebuke.

'OK. How do you feel now?'

I blinked in surprise. 'Dunno. The same, I suppose. Only more confused. Since . . . you know. The new information.'

'He'll be OK, Joseph. I'll keep in touch with the hospital and let you know.'

'Don't worry, I'll be ringing them myself.'

'Good man. Try not to worry. Are you going to work tomorrow then?'

'Yeah, course.'

'You could call in sick, stay here another night. Take it easy.'

I was shocked to find myself thinking about it. 'Nah. There's too much on. Better to keep busy, anyway.'

'No time for a quick cup of tea?' Mum asked.

'Better not. If I miss this one, I have to wait until seven thirty, which doesn't get me in until at least ten thirty and then I have to get a city bus up to the flat and—'

'All right, all right. Go on then.'

'I better.'

She took a step towards me, then a half-step back, and then

rushed me. My second hug in one weekend. It was almost unsettling. But I hugged back.

'Take care,' she said. 'You'll be all right. So will young Feeny.'

'So will Deirdre,' I added, testing the water.

Mum raised her eyes to heaven, in the form of our hall light.

'That one's always all right,' she sighed.

21

'You are, I presume,' Go-go said, 'taking the wholesale piss.'

'Nope.'

'Adolf?'

'Yes.'

'As in Hitler?'

'Or Eichmann. Take your pick.'

'Fuck me.'

'I know.'

'You'd think they'd have gone off that name. As a nation, like.'

'Evidently not.'

'And he's gone?'

'As the age of steam.'

'Jesus. I can't take it all in.'

'*You* can't take it in? How do you think I feel?'

'I don't know. How do you feel?'

I pushed my plate of toast away. 'I don't know either. I can't get it straight in my head. There's too much going on at once. It's . . . overload. I need time to think it through. The last place I want to be is *this* hole, doing this shit.'

Go-go nodded in sympathy. 'And what, she did this German at the same time as Feeny?'

'More or less. And please don't refer to it as "did".'

'Sorry. Jesus, though. I didn't think she was so . . .'

I cocked an eyebrow.

'Choose your words carefully,' I warned him.

'. . . so . . . reckless.'

'Good choice. Well, neither did I. Neither did she, by the sounds of things. But there you go. She made a mistake. Two mistakes.'

'I suppose. And, what, they can't tell you when Feeny's going to pull out of it?'

'Go-go, they can't tell me *if* he's going to pull out of it.'

He stared hard at his own plate for a moment. 'Sterile! I can't get over it. Did they say how? Why?'

'No,' I lied. 'And I didn't ask.'

'Maybe it's a genetic thing.'

'And, remind me, how exactly do you pass on genes for sterility?'

'Good point. I suppose your mother had a fit.'

'That's the thing. That's the amazing thing. She's been fine. Better than fine, she's been great. Saying the right things, being supportive, all that mother shit she stopped doing when my dad died.'

'To you, maybe. She'd feel bad for you. I bet she went through Deirdre for a short cut.'

'Nope. I think she's blaming herself for everything now. Which is not much better than blaming herself for nothing. No, I take that back. It's miles better.'

'How's Deirdre anyway?'

'Ah, you know what she's like. Bounces back. Made of rubber, that one.'

A grin started to form on Go-go's face.

'Don't even try to find a rubber joke, Go-go. It's not there. And I'm not in the humour.'

'Fair enough.'

Geraldine walked in then, cocking an ear in our direction as she made herself a cup of coffee. Go-go tipped his head in her direction and rolled his eyes.

'Better get to work,' he said.

Geraldine nodded with satisfaction as we got up to leave.

I had the first twenty minutes of the day to myself, which I spent staring in silent despondency at 'Live Wire,' before the phone beeped.

'Down here, now,' Mary said.

'Fine, thanks. How was your weekend?' I replied.

There was silence on the line. Did I imagine she'd laugh along? Probably not, no. If I'd given it even half a second's thought, I'd have remembered that Mary didn't have a sense of humour. It wasn't that she didn't have a well-developed sense of humour, or that she had a particularly weird one. She didn't have one at all. She lacked a sense of humour the way Stevie Wonder lacks a sense of vision. But Stevie Wonder makes up for it by being musical. Mary had no such redeeming quality.

'NOW,' she seethed (atonally), and slammed the phone down. In fact, she slammed the phone against the cradle and mashed it around a bit first, before jamming it home.

Now that I think about it, of course, I was deliberately provoking her. Not consciously, but not accidentally either. Like when you're coming to the end of a relationship with someone and you start picking on them, trying to start a fight. They haven't changed, probably, they haven't done anything in particular to annoy you, but still. You go for them, taking every opportunity to snipe and complain, hoping to goad them into a full-on row, so you can pour out all the bile you've been storing up and, ideally, blame the whole thing on them. If no opportunity presents itself, you make one up. That's why I said it. I was trying it on.

Anyway, I didn't go down NOW. I spent a few minutes staring out the window at nothing in particular. Then I spun around in my chair and asked Marian how her weekend had been. Barry was missing, already trapped in Mary's office, I guessed.

Marian looked surprised that I was showing interest. I barely said good morning when I first came in. Like everyone else, she was well used to my periodically grumpy Monday mornings and kept her distance.

'It was pretty good,' she told me. 'My friend Gareth was home from London for the weekend. So I spent most of it in one pub or another, you know how it goes. I've still got the shakes, look.'

She held up her right hand, which was rock steady.

'You crazy bitch,' I said.

'Yeah, well, you're only young once.'

Marian was thirty-one or -two. I couldn't tell if she really thought this was the full bloom of youth or was just taking the piss. I didn't get to ask her. The phone beeped again. I used to imagine that my phone had a variety of beeps at its disposal. Upbeat and friendly for Go-go, plain and businesslike for Stuart. Ugly and ill-tempered for Mary. This was definitely one of the latter.

'Excuse me, Marian,' I said, trying to be cool, picking the phone up as casually as I could. 'Yep?'

Heavy breathing on the line. And not the good kind.

'Get . . . down . . . here . . . now.'

'OK,' I said and put the phone down gently before she had a chance to slam it.

Barry and Lisa were already in Mary's office when I arrived. They whispered hellos as I joined them on the pleb side of the desk. Mary didn't look up for a few seconds. Then she barely glanced at me and said, 'I'd like few minutes of your precious time when this meeting is over.'

'Anything for you, Mary,' I smiled. 'You know that.'

There was an audible *hoo* as Barry and Lisa sucked in some air. Mary pretended not to have heard me and carried on shuffling papers. *We've got a lot to get through*, I said to myself.

'We've got a lot to get through,' Mary said.

And off she went.

The meeting lasted about an hour, which was an eyeblink for one of hers. I think she rushed through it because she couldn't wait to get me alone. It was the usual – have I been talking to myself, this is awful, that's terrible, why don't I just handle all this myself so you three can take a little holiday, and so on. Lisa had no particular terror of Mary – that honour was reserved for Stuart – but she shrank further into her chair as the abuse continued. Even Barry, who was older (and wiser) than Mary, looked cowed and childlike. I, however, smiled and giggled throughout. I felt drunk. In the light of the weekend's events, work suddenly seemed like something I could waltz through. We wound up shortly after eleven. Barry and Lisa left with sagging shoulders and maybe

273

two dozen pages of scribbled notes between them, the majority belonging to Barry. I even saw him write something down when Mary called a draft speech he was working on 'hopeless'. What could that have been? *Make speech less hopeless?*

And so, eventually, we were alone. After the door had closed and the only sound came from the carriage clock – which was inscribed, I noticed for the first time, to Stuart rather than Mary – she did more paper shuffling. This was supposed to make me feel nervous. It would have too, on any other day. But not today. Today I was invulnerable. Or so I thought.

'I'm going to make this quick,' Mary said, looking up. 'In my opinion, your work here has never been first-rate or even second-rate. You've shown almost no interest in this business since day one. You spend more time giggling with Eamonn like a couple of schoolgirls than doing your job. And since we started working on the Langley's closure, you have failed even to live up to your own mediocre standards. You've been sloppy, careless, lackadaisical . . . and you've wandered around with a gob on you like the world was ending. Stuart's noticed too. If you want to know the truth, I asked him to take you off this account, give you something easier. Filing, maybe. It makes no sense to me that I should be lumbered with a surly layabout like you, when someone like Eoghan, someone with real ability and enthusiasm, is stuck upstairs handling some silly sponsorship. Now. I want you to give me some reassurances that you're going to pitch in and do your bit on this job, or I want you to go to Stuart and tell him you want to work on another account. Or in another company, I don't care either way.'

My first impulse was to tell her to go fuck herself. Her and her account and her company and her whole fucking business. It would have tasted so sweet. But I didn't. For one thing, Stuart obviously didn't agree with her assessment. If he did, I'd be gone already. I wasn't his favourite employee, by any stretch of the imagination, but he never gave me the impression that he considered me a lost cause. And he had shown some understanding and subtlety when I almost slept through his meeting the previous week. She claimed she wanted me to go to him and ask to be moved, so she was exaggerating the precariousness of my position. Besides, I told myself, the script is almost done. I could be gone for good anyway, in a matter of months. Plus, of course, I had no other job to go to. There was no question of my being transferred to another account. She may have thought I was doing a terrible job, but the fact was, I was up to my neck in it. Eoghan was a better bet than I was, in every conceivable way, but he knew nothing about Langley's, and this was no time to start learning. Despite the ferocity of her assault, Mary was simply telling me to pull my socks up. It said a lot about her style that this was how she chose to do it. Anyway – I buckled.

'I've been having some personal problems, Mary,' I mumbled. 'Nothing to do with work. And I may have been allowing my work to suffer. I'll do better.'

She nodded and drew breath to speak. For a moment, I feared she was about to ask what these personal problems were. God knows, I might have told her. But I must have had her confused with someone else.

'Just go and do some bloody work,' she said.

22

I tried to do some bloody work. I really did. But it was impossible. There was too much noise in my head. 'Live Wire' was supposed to be a bit of fluff that I was knocking out in between my real jobs, just to keep up the pretence that all was well in Langley's. But it took me twenty minutes to write a single headline ('BABY BOOM!'), let alone any copy. I was reminded of the *Far Side* cartoon that shows a kid with his hand up in class, asking to be excused because his brain is full.

I told myself that I might be able to concentrate harder on a more significant task, and turned to the brief history of the company I'd been writing for the press pack. As I opened the document, it suddenly occurred to me – for the first time, unbelievably – that this was more fluff. In fact, all the really important tasks went to Barry and Lisa, or were handled by Mary herself. And there were a lot of them. Barry was writing the crucial press release that would be issued in the event of a Dublin closure. Lisa was writing the release that would be issued in the event of an Edinburgh closure. Mary was doing most of the liaison with the Department of Enterprise and Employment. She was looking after Andrew Holland's media training too, making sure that he knew how to look good on TV. Barry was working on Andrew's speech (one for either eventuality). Lisa was drafting what we called the Bad News speech that Andrew might have to give to his employees. And on it went. I had input into all of these things, sure, was allowed to dot Is and cross Ts, but none of them was *mine*. I got 'Live Wire' and minor letters and company histories and other frippery. Clearly, I couldn't be trusted. It hit me like a bullet in the brain that I really was bad at the job, and that everyone knew it. Not just unsuited, or unmotivated, or any of the other things I told myself. I was simply no good at it. All along, I'd been pretending that I *could* do it, if I really wanted to lower myself to engage in crass commercial activity. But no. That was a lie. Another one. Maybe I was even kidding myself to think that Stuart would never fire me.

Suddenly, I wanted to be back in the flatlet, working on my script. At least I had control over that.

Go-go was out with a client all day, so I had no chance to vent. The afternoon was a total wash-out, a drawn-out wasteland of teeth-grinding and slow, gentle chair-rocking. As the hours slipped by, it became ever clearer that I wasn't going to do any work, even on 'Live Wire.' My only consolation was that Stuart and Mary stayed away from me, deliberately perhaps. Marian and Barry were missing most of the time too, stuck in various meetings.

When the time came, I literally ran home. Or rather, I ran for brief periods, and then goose-stepped, huffing and puffing for all I was worth. This rare burst of physical activity made my heart pound and my hands shake – I'd be all for getting fit if you could do it by eating something (something tasty). When I opened the front door and saw yet another Post-it note stuck to the phone in the hall, my bouncing heart nearly stopped altogether. I stood stock-still in the open doorway, afraid to approach the note and read it. I thought of all the things it might say, if it was for me. Maybe it was from my mother saying Brendan Feeny had died. I had called the hospital at lunchtime and was told there was no change, but it was certainly possible. Or maybe it was my mother reporting that Deirdre had cracked after all and attempted suicide – or run off with an Albanian trucker she met in the corner shop. Perhaps Stuart had called while I was on my way home to say he'd thought it over, and really, it would be better if I didn't come in tomorrow. I swallowed hard and took a step towards the note. Its text swam into view. JOE: NORM CALLED, it said. RING HIM BACK AT HOME.

Oh. Right. Norm. I'd completely forgotten that he called on Friday evening. Technically, I was still mad at him for urging violence towards Feeny. But that issue was now so clouded in confusion, I was no longer sure that my anger was justified. Just as I snatched the note from the hand set, Julie opened her door and peeked out into the hallway.

'Oh, it's yourself. I thought I heard shuffling.'

'Yeah, hi.'

'You had a phone call, about five minutes ago. Norm. He wants you to ring him back at home.'

I waved the Post-it. 'Got it, thanks.'

'OK. Listen, why don't you pop in tonight? If you're not doing anything. We haven't had a natter in ages. You could bring some Jaffa Cakes.'

I knew this was Julie-code for 'We could get stoned to within an inch of our lives.' It was tempting, but I really wanted to get my teeth into the script. It was so nearly finished. Besides, it seemed to help me to think straight. Which was more than could be said for smoking.

'We'll see, Julie,' I said. 'I better make this phone call.'

'Suit yourself,' she shrugged, and disappeared inside again.

Norm answered on the third ring. 'H'lo?'

'Norm. Joe.'

'Oh, yeah. Howiye.'

'I forgot you rang on Friday. I meant to ring you back.'

'Yeah. Anyway. Listen – what are you doing tonight?'

Jesus. Suddenly I was Mr Popular.

'Ah, I'm busy, Norm. Things are a bit messy these days, I want to just sit in and take it easy.'

'Messy?' he asked. 'What way messy?'

I scratched my head and sighed. There didn't seem to be any easy way to explain it all on the phone. 'I'll tell you in the pub some of these nights. I don't feel like going into it now, to be honest.'

'Is it anything to do with Go-go?' he asked.

'Go-go? What about him?'

'He didn't tell you then?'

'Tell me what?'

'I thought he wouldn't. That's why I was looking for you.'

'*What?*'

'About, eh, Sheila.'

My breathing stopped momentarily. 'Go on.'

'Well, I, eh, I bumped into her in town last weekend . . .'

'Oh, *shit*,' I said.

'And eh . . .'

'Ah, *shit* . . .'

'. . . well, you know, there was drink taken, and she got all confessional . . .'

'Oh, fuck me.'

'. . . and told me she's emigrating. Next month.'

I thought I'd misheard him. 'What?'

'Emigrating. Australia. Next month.'

'Oh. Oh right. I thought you were going to say you shagged her.'

'WHAT? Thanks a fucking million.'

'Well . . .'

'You *cunt*. That's the most insulting thing I—'

'I'm sorry! It's just, well, I always got the impression she might fancy you, and—'

'And what? I'm such an arsehole that I'd fuck Go-go over to get to her? Charming.'

'Well, no, not exactly, but, I mean, she is very attractive and all and—'

'Don't apply your standards to me. Just because you'd do it, doesn't mean I would.'

'I'm sorry! And I would never do that to him, he's mad about her, he—'

'You've got that right. He's going with her.'

'He's *what*?'

'He's going with her. She told me in the pub that she thought they'd make a good couple but he obviously didn't feel the same way, so she was off.'

I blinked in such violent disbelief that Norm probably heard my lashes slap together. 'Is she out of her mind? This is *our* Go-go she's talking about?'

Norm sniggered his filthy snigger – a good sign that he didn't really want to fall out with me.

'Apparently so. I set her straight, anyway. Told her he talked about precious little else. That he only stayed away out of fear.

She was speechless. Only delighted with herself. She left me sitting there in the pub to go see him.'

I felt a huge smile dawn on my face. 'I can't get over it. The jammy *prick*. He's spent all this time ... and she's ... I can't get over it.'

'There you go,' Norm said.

I shook my head in silent wonder. It was like something out of a Frank Capra movie. The question didn't occur to me for several seconds.

'Hang on,' I said. 'Hang on. Why hasn't he told me all this himself? If it all happened last weekend?'

Norm took a deep breath. 'He doesn't want to tell you he's leaving because ... Well, because he says you're having a tough time these days, and he doesn't want to add to your woes.'

I thought I knew everything there was to know about guilt. I thought that someone who had dealt with my mother for the past two years could give fucking lectures on guilt and its effects. But I never felt anything like the skewer of shame that went through me when I heard what Go-go had said. I thought of the previous Monday when I gave him the 'My whole life is shite' speech on the steps outside work. That was the day after he got it together with Sheila. And I didn't even give him a chance to tell me. I blustered and flapped and flailed, while he simply stood there, wondering how he could break his good news. No wonder he got irritable with me during the week. Even then, his anger hadn't lasted.

'That's crazy,' I said in a very small voice. 'I couldn't be happier for him.'

'Well, that's what I said,' Norm replied. 'I think he's coming round, anyway, but he's still worried about how he's going to tell you he's going. He thinks you'll "drown" without him to rave at. That's what he said – "drown".'

It was like being physically punched.

'I've been a total shit,' I said.

'Ah, I wouldn't worry about it,' Norm said in his seldom-used reasonable voice. 'Just let him know that you'll be grand without him to moan at. Sure you can moan at me or Stevie if you want to. You do anyway.'

'Right, yeah. Look, I'm sorry I've been whinging so much—'

'Ah, forget about it.'

'Things have been—'

'Oh shut up, you're embarrassing us both. Tell Go-go you're delighted for him and that'll be an end to it. I told him you would be, but he wouldn't believe me.'

'Yeah. Yeah. Course.'

'Right. I'm off.'

'OK. See you then.'

'Bye.'

It took me three attempts to drop the phone into its cradle, my hands were shaking so badly. I looked at my watch – 6.25 p.m. Go-go wouldn't be home yet. I stood there trying to decide what to do. As I stared at the phone, lost in thought, whispering to myself, I gradually became aware of a distinctive aroma wafting out from under Julie's door.

Hmmm.

'You changed your mind damn quick,' Julie smiled when I knocked on her door.

'Yeah,' I said. 'I'm suddenly in urgent need of . . . relaxation.'

She poked her tongue out, accidentally perhaps.

'You've come to the right woman,' she said.

Julie's flat never failed to surprise me. It was the very antithesis of the lazy stoner's den. Where the casual visitor might expect lava lamps and beanbags, there were ornate wood carvings and original oils. Her coffee table, which might have been covered with Chinese takeaway remains and battered copies of *2000 AD*, was bare save for a vase of fresh flowers. Her extensive bookshelf had no Tom Robbins, no William Burroughs, as far as I could see. But it had any number of Graham Greenes and more than one Henry James. It wasn't *palatial*. But it made my place look like . . . my place.

'Bad news on the phone?' Julie asked, passing the World's Biggest Joint as we sat on her springy sofa.

'Yeah. Well . . . no. Significant news.'

'Intriguing. Tell your Auntie Julie all about it.'

I took a huge hit and immediately felt my eyes close, without my express order to do so.

'Jesus *Christ*,' I said. 'What the fuck did you put in that? Holy shit.'

Julie shrugged and didn't reply.

'Holy *shit*,' I said again, passing it right back. She waited for me to tell her what was wrong. It took me a moment to get my bearings.

'Right,' I said with a small cough, wondering if the coffee table was that far away when I sat down. 'Right. Right. Where do I start?'

An hour later, and we're halfway through number three.

'I'm so fucking sorry, Julie. Sorry. You know? I *mean* it.'

'Forget about it.' She says it Donnie Brasco-style – *fuggedabahdit*.

'No. No. It's not on. It's not fucking on. I stroll in here like I own the place . . .'

'Forget it.'

'. . . and you welcome me like an old friend . . .'

'For*get* it.'

'. . . and not a Jaffa Cake to my name. One arm as long as the other. It's not on.'

'We can get some later on.'

'But fuck me, that's not manners. There's no manners there. I am *sans* manners on this one. You don't have to be nice, I know they're not good. The manners.'

'Get back to what you were saying.'

'I'll get a family-pack. You'll never want for Jaffa Cakes again. It'll be Jaffa Cake city in here. People will come from all around. They'll hear about it on the—'

'Joe!'

'Right, right, you're right. Where was I?'

'You were wrong.'

'When?'

'That's what you were *saying*. You were saying you were wrong.'

'Yes! That's right! Wrong!'

Short break for giggling.

'I've been so wrong. So many times. About everything. About people. About how to solve problems. I . . . I lost perspective. We all did, in my family.'

One of her eyes closes, then snaps open again.

'You lost perspective,' she says.

'Yes. Yes. I've had the answers in front of me, I've had all the *advice*, I've sought it out, and I've still fucked it all up.'

'So . . . how do you solve problems?'

She passes the doob. For me? Why, thank you.

'You solve them . . . ah, fuck it, I had it a minute ago.'

Silence for thirty seconds, or maybe thirty minutes.

'Oh! You take steps. That was it. If there's something you

285

can do about a situation, you do that thing. That you can do. If there isn't, you wade through it. The answers are usually simple. Positive action. That ... sort of thing. I can see it now.'

'It's a beautiful philosophy.'

'You're laughing at me.'

'Only a wee bit.'

'That's OK, 'cos I owe you biscuits. But, Julie, I'm right. Now. I was wrong all along, but I'm right now.'

'So you're going to do what?'

'Yes. I am.'

'What?'

'What?'

'What are you going to do?'

'I'm going to sort it all out. I'm going to take *steps*. When my script—'

'Hang on, hang on. What script?'

'I'm writing a screenplay. A movie. Film. Thing.'

'Get fucked!'

'Yup.'

'You never told me before.'

'Ah, you know. Who the hell's going to even read it, let alone movie it? Film it.'

'I'd read it. If you wanted me to.'

'Aw. Would you?'

'I might have advice.'

'Yeah?'

'I mean ... that's what I do. Writing.'

'Eh?'

'Yeah. Since I stopped teaching. That's *why* I stopped teaching. Children's books.'

'You're fucking joking.'

'Hang on.' She goes to the book wall, comes back. 'There's the proof. Proofs. Four of the bastards. Where do you think I get money from?'

'Belinda Waters?'

'In person. That's my *nom de plume*. It's better than Julie fucking McGlone.'

'That's the coolest fucking thing I ever saw in my life.'

A happy hour then, silently sharing the adventures of Barnaby Finn and his magic cat, Misty.

Julie's books were broadly aimed at seven- to eight-year-olds and were very brief. When I finished the last – *Barnaby Finn and the Haunted Ship* (quite scary, to someone in my condition) – I was lost for words.

'It's . . . amazing,' I said, when I found some. Talking was becoming slightly easier again. 'I had no idea you did this.'

They say modesty is simply the hope that people will find out how great you are on their own. I didn't quite find out about Julie's talent on my own, but I could see that she was still really pleased by my reaction.

'Did you never wonder where I got money from?'

'I assumed you had some inheritance or something.'

'Are you joking? My family are penniless. *I'm* the rich one in our family. Relatively speaking. I mean, I make peanuts, obviously.'

I smiled and examined the book's cover again. 'You must be so proud of yourself.'

She smiled back, a real smile, not a stoned leer. 'Yeah. I am. I hated teaching. And I was no good at it. Little bastards gave me dog's abuse.'

I was shocked. This didn't sound good coming from a children's author. 'Little bastards?'

'Oh, in a classroom, yeah. Awful shits. When they're quietly reading a book, though – especially one of mine – I'm mad about them.'

We sat smiling in silence for a few minutes then. I was still badly baked, but at least I wasn't getting any worse. I could even feel my feet again.

Out in the hall, the phone rang. Julie and I exchanged glances.

'Not for me,' she said.

'How do you know?'

'Because it never is. I've got my own line. I need one, for the computer.'

'What computer?'

'In the bedroom. Just answer the phone.'

'I didn't know you had your own line. Why do you answer that one all the time?'

'It's called being nice. And what you don't know about me, pal, is a lot. Answer the phone.'

I got to my feet with some difficulty and walked out into the hall with my arms outstretched for balance. It genuinely didn't occur to me that it might be bad news.

'Hel-lo?'

'Joseph, it's your mother.'

'Mum! I was just thinking about you. Well. A while ago. I was—'

'Listen, Joseph, I've got some news.'

'Oh?'

'Yes. It's about Brendan Feeny.'

The temperature seemed to drop.

He's dead, I thought.

'He's come round,' said my mother.

I went blind with shock.

'Say that again,' I said.

'Tonight, just after tea. I'm only off the phone to the hospital. He's fully conscious. Like that.'

I heard her snap her fingers.

'He's . . . all right? Already?'

'I wouldn't call it all right. But he's going to be, it seems.'

A lump grew in my throat.

'It's wonderful,' I said. 'It's a sign.'

Mum's alarm bells rang. She knew I didn't believe in signs.

'Joseph, are you drunk?'

It was a pleasure to lie. 'Maybe a little bit.'

'Hmmm. I suppose you're entitled, given recent events. But take it easy, for God's sake.'

'It was only a few glasses of wine,' I had the nerve to say. 'I might have a few more, too. To celebrate.'

'Take it easy, now. And I told you he'd be all right, didn't I? So did Deirdre.'

'You were right. I never listen to anyone. But I'm going to start,' I said.

'Holy Mother, you *are* drunk. Anyway. I better go. I just thought I'd let you know.'

A thought fluttered into my spinning head and demanded expression.

'Thanks. Listen: before you go. I want to tell you something. About . . .'

I blew the cobwebs off my 'Nuns – Advice From' folder.

'. . . about the baby.'

'Oh?'

289

'Yeah ... it's ... nothing you haven't thought of yourself, I'm sure, but I want to say it anyway.'

'Go on then.'

I drew breath.

'The baby's a ... vague notion now, abstract, so it can seem like a problem, but it's going to be a whole new person running around. It will be a, eh ... it will be a ... joy.'

Momentary silence.

'A *joy*? Is that a noun?'

'It is now.'

'Are you reading this from a book, Joseph? Did you get this from some weirdo cult?'

Drum roll, please.

'Book – no, weirdo cult – yes. I got it from a nun.'

Stunned silence.

'You've never spoken to a nun in your life.'

'Think again.'

'You're delirious,' she said, but I could almost hear the cogs turning.

'Nope. Anyway, I'll let you go,' I said, wanting to quit while I was ahead. 'I just thought I'd tell you.' I tried to start a meaningful silence, turning her own weapon on her, but she was having none of it.

'Right then, consider me told. I suppose we won't see you now for months.'

'Ah, you never know. I might drop by at the weekend. Maybe visit the hospital.'

'I'm speechless.'

'There's a first time for everything.'

'Goodbye, Joseph.'

For a change, neither of us slammed the phone down.

*   *   *

Back in Julie's, I bounced on my toes, rubbing my hands together.

'I can feel it. I'm on a roll. At last.'

'Good. Speaking of rolls . . .' She reached for her Rizlas.

'Not for me,' I said. 'I'm going to do some work on the script.'

'Ha! Feeling all inspired, are we?'

'You're laughing at me again.'

'Nah. Strike while the iron's hot.'

I stepped towards the door, then turned.

'Jesus, more bad manners,' I said. 'Smoking and running.'

'Ah, fuck off, eejit. All the more for me, sure.'

I should have hugged the woman. It was a hugging moment. But my mind was already upstairs, with the aliens.

I finished the first draft of *Come to Beautiful Earth* at around five the following morning. I took one break, at eleven or so, to ring Go-go. His flatmate told me he was out 'with yer woman'. I skipped back upstairs, feeling all James Stewart.

Come to Beautiful Earth ends with Jonathon and Karen renting a small apartment in West Hollywood where – more biting satire here – no one would notice another couple of extraterrestrials. Ian, the obnoxious fiancé, meets a sticky end, of course. The happy couple turn him over to the feds and a couple of pseudo Mulder and Scullys – or maybe even the real ones (crossover potential) – haul him off for some painful anal probing.

Was I pleased with myself? Does the Pope shit in the woods? I sat beaming at the Mac, watching the pages chug slowly from the printer, and practised my Oscar acceptance speech. *This is for me – who never stopped believing. Thanks, me.*

When it had finished printing, I put the script in a large

brown envelope, then went downstairs and left it outside Julie's door. Back in the flatlet, I got undressed and collapsed into bed, exhausted. I had a small travel alarm clock by my bed. My eyes were more than half closed and I was barely able to see the numbers. Squinting and yawning I set it for 11 a.m.

I figured I might as well have a reasonable snooze.

There was no need to quit first thing.

23

I didn't get to sleep in until eleven, as it turned out. Julie woke me up at nine thirty, thumping on the flatlet door with the script package. She may have been out there for some time – I recall having a dream that involved a lot of drumming. Bleary-eyed, shivering, I tiptoed over and opened the door.

Julie was pyjama-clad, and looked like I felt.

'First thing,' she said, 'thanks for the script. I can't believe you finished it. I'll read it today. When I eventually get up. Second, you're wanted on the phone. Eamonn.'

'Oh. Thanks. What time is it?'

'Half nine, or so. Not going to work today?'

'Later. But only to quit.'

'Jesus. I thought that was smoking talk. No notice even? If I wasn't half asleep. I'd be impressed. Let me know how you get on.'

'Definitely.'

She turned and padded down the stairs. I grabbed a pair of trousers and followed her.

'Go-go?' I said into the phone.

'Yeah, hi. Listen—'

'I was trying to get you last night. I want to talk to you.'

'That'll have to wait. Are you sick or something?'

'No, why?'

'Because it's after nine thirty and you're still at home, fuckwit.'

'Oh, that. Yeah. Yeah. Well ... I'll be in shortly. It's a long st—'

'Stuart's going fucking apeshit over here, he told me to ring you. I couldn't pretend I didn't know your number. Langley's have called it. It's Dublin.'

I swayed about on my feet for a second or two, not quite believing my ears. I read somewhere that time is simply a device that stops everything from happening at once. Apparently, it was no longer working.

'Since when?'

'Since this morning. Ahead of schedule. It's bedlam here, all the Langley's people are running around like blue-arsed flies. You picked a bad day to lie in. Mary is going to gut you like a fish when she gets ahold of you.'

I mulled it over for a second. Catherine was out of a job. So was Brian. So were all those other smiling nobodies.

'I'll see you in a while,' I told Go-go.

Like everyone else with a job, I had fantasised long and hard about how exactly I would quit when the time came. I pictured myself swivelling coolly in Stuart's office, legs folded nonchalantly as I summarised my script and whispered confidentially about the seven-figure sum it had earned. There had been a bidding war, of course. Ugly and protracted. Several old friends had fallen out. But it was all behind us now. The light was firmly green. Cameron Diaz was attached.

It was mildly disappointing that it wasn't going to happen that way. I would be leaving as a normal employee, presumably off to find similar work in another company. Oh well. No doubt they'd read about my triumph in the papers when it happened.

I didn't bother with a suit – what was the point? – but didn't stoop to jeans, either. I opted for a reasonably tidy-looking grey shirt and a pair of neatish black bags. I wanted to look casual, but not, you know, *disturbed*. I didn't want them to think I'd had some sort of breakdown. Having said that, I didn't shave. Fuck it.

The weather was starting to turn chilly and I walked briskly to work, chewing over what I might say. I wish I could pretend that I never had a moment's doubt as I edged ever closer, but the fact is, I stopped dead in my tracks after about fifteen minutes. Hang on, I thought. What the fuck is going on? What's changed? Why now, all of a sudden? Maybe I wasn't on a roll at all. Maybe it was my imagination.

Then I started to imagine the scene ahead of me at work. Stuart running around, clapping backs, spouting about 'getting to the end-zone' or 'going the distance'. Mary, snarling orders, and sharpening her gutting knife. Jesus. The question was not why was I doing it now, but why had it taken so long.

I pressed on.

The office didn't look any different from outside. Same imposing Georgian façade, same brass plaque with Stuart Kennedy Public Relations in neat black lettering. But inside, something was clearly up. According to Go-go, it had been a whirl of activity, ringing phones, scurrying employees. It was dead quiet now. Not ordinary common or garden quiet, but crypt-like *silent*. Bernie looked up when I walked in, then looked down again immediately.

'Good afternoon, Mr Casual Attire,' she said. It was ten forty-five.

'Morning, Bernie. So. Where is everyone?'

'Everyone who?'

She knew what I meant.

'Stuart, Mary . . . everyone.'

'Stuart's gone to Langley-Foster Electronics. Mary is in her office with Lisa and Barry. Perhaps you should join them.'

'We'll see.'

She looked up. 'We'll see?'

I shrugged, trying to look casual. 'Might. Might not.'

She narrowed her eyes, trying to figure me out. I sailed past her to the stairs. On a whim, I started to whistle.

How about this? After almost a year working there, I had nothing personal at my desk in Stuart Kennedy PR. No pictures, no books, no plants, nothing. Marian's wall was covered with arty postcards in cheap clip-frames (she was missing too, another sickie maybe). Even Barry had some Frederick Forsyth paperbacks on his shelf, in between the media guides and the marketing guru tracts. There was nothing to suggest that I had ever been there. Which was fine by me.

I looked under the desk and behind it, making sure I hadn't dropped anything useful down there. I hadn't, unless you counted chewed biros and a tattered notebook. The latter was months old. I remembered the panic I felt when I lost it. I'd been in a meeting with Mary, trying to come up with a press release for a new Langley's gizmo. Everything we agreed was scribbled down in that notebook. Later, when I began to write up the release and couldn't find my notes, I had to make it up from memory, with predictable results. Mary fumed so hard when she had to repeat herself that she spat a sizeable wad onto the back of my writing hand. Ah, memories.

There was nothing worth taking in my desk drawers either, except Go-go's gun. I ripped its packing off and stuck it into my pocket, cringing at the memory. I took a draft of the Bad News press release too. I had plans for it.

The office door opened then and Barry walked in, ran in, really. He did a perfect double-take when he saw me.

'Langley's—' he began, but I held up a hand to stop him.

'I know. So. When is it going to happen?'

'They want to announce on Friday. *This* Friday. We're up to our fucking necks in it now, boyo.'

'I don't know about "we",' I said.

Barry dropped his copious notes on his desk and looked at me with a concerned expression. 'Where have you been?' he asked. 'What's up?'

'I'm quitting. Now. I'll be gone as soon as I talk to Mary. I can't do this any more.'

He collapsed into his chair moaning softly. 'Quitting? Is this a joke?'

I shook my head slowly. 'I'm sorry to drop you in it. I know there's a lot to do.'

He made an indefinable noise. 'Today is shaping up really well.'

'Sorry.'

'What brought this on?'

'Nothing brought it on, Barry. It's been *on* for ages. I'm not cut for this. What's more, I'm crap at it.'

'Oh come on, you're not *crap* at it, exactly,' he said, trying to be charitable through his anger. 'You're maybe a bit ... unenthusiastic.'

297

'Anyway. I'm off.'

'Just like that? No notice, no nothing?'

'I don't see the point.'

'So what are you going to do? Have you got another job?'

'Nope.'

'Jesus Christ, you're leaving to go on the *dole*?'

'Yeah.'

Temporarily, I thought.

Barry stared at me contemptuously. 'Stuart's not here, you know, he's gone to see Andrew Holland.'

'I know. I'll tell Mary. Maybe I'll ring Stuart later.'

'He'll go nuts. He'll have you killed. No notice, for God's sake. You signed a contract.'

'I don't think he'll care, to be honest. Anyway. Is Mary alone now?'

Barry nodded.

'OK then,' I said, getting up. 'Better give her the good news.'

I stuck my hand out to Barry as I passed his desk. He shook it limply, but said nothing.

There was no reply the first time I knocked on Mary's office door. I rapped again, a little more forcefully.

'Yes, WHAT?' she barked from within.

I swung the door open and stepped inside. Mary dropped her pen and bared her teeth at me.

'You've got some fucking nerve,' she said. 'Today, of all days, to arrive in at this hour. Look at the state of you. I sh—'

'I haven't come in here to argue, Mary,' I said as calmly as I could. 'If Stuart was here, I wouldn't even be talking to you. I only wanted to let you know that I'm leaving. Now. I can't stand this job, and for what it's worth, I'm not crazy about you.'

Mary sat back, and laughed at me.

'My God. Look at you. Mr Cool.'

She looked me up and down, her face twisted with contempt. Her features froze for an instant as she scanned me, then melted into a watery smile.

'Off you go, so,' she said, very quietly.

I was shocked, and momentarily speechless.

'Is that all you have to say?' I asked after a pause.

She didn't reply, but nodded briskly. This was all wrong. It was almost disappointing. I had imagined I'd be quitting to Stuart, so I was steeled for a fight, and in a strange kind of way, even looking forward to it.

'I might call back later for a reference,' I said, marvelling at my own cheek. Surely that would get a rise out of her?

'OK,' she croaked. 'Whatever.'

She's having me on, I thought. She's trying to psych me out.

'That's it, then,' I said, puzzled.

'Goodbye, Joe,' she said quickly. 'You take it easy, now, OK?'

'Yeeess, all right,' I mumbled. 'Goodbye.'

I stood there for a moment, watching her smile at me, waiting for . . . something, anything. Nothing. So I turned and left, still unable to figure it out. What the hell was wrong with her? Where was the shouting, the name-calling, the threats of legal action? It was so anticlimactic.

No matter — it was over now. I no longer worked in PR. I began to bound up the stairs to Go-go's office. That was when I remembered that the butt of a very realistic-looking gun was sticking out of my pocket.

* * *

I'm not going to describe the details of that conversation with Go-go. We stood on the steps outside the office, waving our hands around, having one of those back-and-forths that are normally the preserve of teenage girls who've fallen out over which one of Boyzone or 4's Kin is the cutest. All 'I'm sorry', 'No, *I'm* sorry', 'No I'm the one who's sorry'. Nauseating, I'm sure, to the casual observer.

I told him I was finally on a roll. He said he was glad. He told me that Sheila was fudge-coloured all over. I said I was glad. And so on.

We arranged to meet that night in Jolly's, with Norm and Stevie. Chew the fat. Laugh at Leonard. It sounded good.

When we finally parted, Go-go said he'd explain about the gun – stop her calling the cops, if she hadn't already done so.

24

Another sign – the taxi driver knew exactly where to find Langley-Foster Electronics. This was a first, and it added to my conviction that I was doing the right thing. The effect was ruined when he told me how he knew.

'The nephew works out here,' he said, turning his head around almost completely to do so. 'Don't ask me what he does. Something to do with . . .'

'Gizmos?' I said, looking nervously at the unwatched road ahead.

'Aye, gizmos of some bloody kind.'

'It's a mystery to me too. What they do here.'

I almost added, 'Whatever it is, they won't be doing it for much longer.' But I didn't. Instead, I kept silent until we arrived, then tipped him heavily.

'Give it to your nephew,' I said, and he laughed.

'What a treat. Your boss is here too,' Angela said in place of a hello.

'I'm not looking for him. I'm looking for Catherine Dillon.'

'Catherine Dillon,' she said with a sigh, and punched her phone buttons.

'Thanks,' I said and took a seat.

'Catherine, Joe Flood from the PR company is here for you,' I heard Angela say. 'No ... yes ... I don't think so ... OK.'

I looked over hopefully.

'She's on her way.'

'Thanks.'

I didn't even pretend to read the business magazines in reception. There was no need to fake interest any more. Catherine appeared within minutes.

'Hello, Catherine,' I said, standing. I patted my pocket to make sure the gun was fully hidden this time.

'Hi,' she said, folding her arms. 'What's up?'

I was aware that Angela was doing a Geraldine, listening hard while pretending to read something fascinating.

'Can we talk somewhere?'

Catherine nodded and led the way. More standing around outside.

'How have you been?' I said.

She shrugged unhappily. 'I've been feeling very guilty. You?'

'Likewise. Did you get the snooker cue for your dad?'

I was expecting to catch her in the lie. I thought she'd hesitate, struggle to remember what she'd said.

'Yeah. He didn't even say thanks. I could have left it till the weekend.'

'Oh. Right. So ... did you get your CV out?'

'Yeah. Yeah, I did. Got a couple of interviews lined up. Things are certainly picking up, jobs-wise.'

'Good. Good for you.'

She waved me away. 'I feel . . . despicable. Slinking around. Trying to save my own neck. And for what, a week's head start on the crowd?'

'You shouldn't feel bad. You did the right thing. It's just business. Listen, I've got something to show you.'

She blanched. Maybe she thought I was going to drop my trousers. It would have been par for the course. She looked relieved when I reached into my pocket and produced the folded paper.

'This is a draft press release. It's what we were calling the Bad News version – to be released in the event that Dublin closed, rather than Edinburgh.'

Catherine nodded slowly. She could see where this was going.

'It's complete, pretty much, except for the dates, and a few other details. They were going to be filled in if and when the call came from Phoenix.'

I handed it over.

'Catherine, this is going out on Friday. This Friday. Staff will be told that morning.'

She read it through, chewing on a fingernail. Some of the greasier phrasing made her eyes narrow in contempt.

'That's that then,' she said when she finished. 'You're going to be a busy little boy.'

'Not me. I quit this morning.'

She blinked. 'No!'

'Yes.'

'Why? Because . . . ?'

'Well, basically, because . . . I don't like it. I'm not suited to it. And I'm no good at it. And because I'm on a roll.'

She looked confused.

'Never mind about the roll bit. Look, I just wanted to let you know, so it doesn't come as a total shock. And, to be honest, I wanted you to know that I've walked away from it. I didn't want you standing there in your canteen, listening to Andrew Holland giving the speech, thinking I was still part of this whole plot.'

I got my fishing rod out then.

'I know you think badly enough of me already.'

She said nothing. I counted backwards from five, giving her every chance. Nothing. Oh well. I would have to wade through this one. So be it. It was based on nothing anyway. I took a step backwards.

'Anyway, I'd better—'

'You're not so bad,' she said.

I bounced on my toes. 'No! That's right, I'm not.'

'You don't seem to be entirely without principles. Not like me. Self-serving bitch.'

'Come on. You looked after number one. Exactly like anyone would have done. Exactly like I would have done.'

Catherine bit her lip, looking at the press release again. I played my trump card.

'Highly confidential, that press release,' I said in a serious tone. 'I'd be in real trouble if anyone found out I'd shown it to you. Well, I would if I still had a job.'

She looked up quickly. I smiled a sneaky smile.

'I hope it doesn't fall into the wrong hands. I hope it doesn't get left lying around where anyone could see it. Or, you know, photocopied and distributed in the canteen. On the other hand, if it did, you might feel a little less guilty.'

Catherine began to smile, then stopped.

'No,' she said. 'They'd sue the shit out of you.'

'Probably,' I said, affecting cool. My heart had all but stopped. This could backfire very badly indeed.

'No. No. I'll keep it to myself. But thank you for the idea.'

'OK,' I said, like I didn't care either way, when really my knees were knocking. 'It's up to you. OK, then. I'd better go. Will you ask Angela to call a taxi for me? I really don't want to deal with her ever again. She hates me for some reason.'

'She says you're always staring at her tits,' Catherine said simply. 'That's why.'

I recoiled. It wasn't true. As far as I knew.

'I do NOT!' I yelped. 'I never . . . not in the entire—'

'Oh calm down. Maybe you do it without noticing that you're doing it. You are male, after all.'

I tried to come up with a witty riposte. None occurred to me, so I resorted to smiling inanely, pleased that she had noticed I was male.

'Oh, there you go,' Catherine said, pointing behind me. 'I don't have to bother. You can steal that one.'

A taxi was making its way around the car park to the front entrance.

'Great,' I said. 'Well. Bye then.'

'Yeah. Bye.'

Silence, as the taxi rolled to a halt. Here we go, I thought. Once more, for old times' sake.

'I'm going to be in Jolly's again tonight,' I said. 'With those other morons. About eight o'clock, probably.'

'Really?' Catherine said. 'How fascinating.'

'That's me,' I replied, walking to the car. 'Anyway. See you around. Good luck with the interviews.'

She smiled goodbye.

'Stuart Kennedy?' the taxi driver said, as I got in. 'Am I in

305

the right place? I've been driving around this fecking maze for twenty minutes.'

I looked back to Langley's front door. Stuart was coming through it with Andrew Holland.

'That's me,' I said. 'Let's go. Quickly.'

'All right, James Bond, keep your hair on.'

I turned to look out the back window as we moved away. Stuart, Andrew, and Catherine stood in a row. Stuart was peering at the disappearing car. I saw his face change as he spotted me. He nudged Andrew, who was too miserable to respond. Catherine giggled, waved, and turned to go back in.

25

Back in the flatlet, I made a cup of coffee and switched on the Mac. Returning in the taxi, I had begun to worry that I'd been premature in giving the script to Julie. After all, I was still fairly whacked when I wrote the last few scenes. Maybe they were total guff.

But no. I reread them with mounting glee. OK, there were numerous stoned typos, and some of the spacing was decidedly off, but the substance was fine. I couldn't wait to see what she thought. It was one thirty. Give it another hour or two, I thought. Maybe a quick nap first.

I dozed happily for the entire afternoon. Always very literal-minded about these things, I dreamed that I was drinking in Jolly's with Jim Carrey and Cameron Diaz. Jim was asking me how I was doing, all things considered. Cameron was playing footsie under the table. I said it all seemed to be working out for the best.

I woke at six, had a quick shower, and went downstairs to get the verdict.

*   *   *

'So,' I said, going through Julie's door. 'What do you think?'

She moved to the centre of the room, and turned to face me.

'Did you quit your job?' She looked nervous.

'Yes. I sure did. But never mind that. What—'

'Joe, did you quit your job on the assumption that this script was going to make you a fortune?'

My knees wobbled.

'Why? Is there . . . Do you . . .'

'Come here, for a minute. In the bedroom.'

She strode off. I followed. Julie's bedroom was neat, orderly. Lots and lots of books. She had a desk in the corner, with a PC.

'I'm a bit of a movie buff,' she said. 'You know, I buy all the magazines, read all the reviews. And I visit the websites.'

She sat at the computer and launched the Internet browser. After protracted bleeping and whistling, she was connected.

'Now. There's a site called *Max's Movie Mayhem*. Have you heard of it?'

I shook my head.

'It's very popular with movie geeks,' Julie said, choosing the name from her list of bookmarked sites. 'Lots of background information, gossip, that sort of thing.'

A brightly coloured and badly organised page appeared on the monitor.

'It also has the suss on upcoming movies.'

She sat back in her chair, and I moved closer.

ZEMECKIS SET TO PARTY!! a headline screamed. Julie clicked on it. The page changed. I moved closer and began to read.

Robert Zemeckis, the man behind *Who Framed Roger Rabbit?* and *Forrest Gump,* is set to fuse high comedy and state-of-the-art graphics once again in a new for Paramount. The working title is *Party Planet* and word is this script is HOT! Details are thin on the ground, but we can confirm that the story revolves around a group of rowdy aliens vacationing on our own beloved rock. All hell breaks loose when their keg-party antics attract the attention of the alien cop types paid to keep this planet a safe destination for wholesome ET families . . . Keanu Reeves and Julia Roberts are pencilled in for major roles. More when we hear it!

'Oh,' I said. 'Oh.'

'I'm sorry,' Julie said. 'I read this the other day. Then I read your script, and they're not identical, but if—'

'It doesn't matter. It doesn't matter.'

'You can scream and shout, if you like. I don't mind.'

'No. That's OK, thanks.'

Julie gave me a concerned look. She seemed to think I might crack up at any moment. I thought so too. I only said it didn't matter for the sake of saying something. I stood there waiting for it to sink in.

'It's hard to believe, isn't it?' Julie said. 'It's too weird. Listen, would you like a cup of tea? Or a spliff?'

I shook my head, still waiting for the shock to hit so the howling could begin.

'If it's any consolation,' Julie began, then paused.

'What?'

'Nothing. It wouldn't be any consolation.'

'No, what?'

'Well . . . No, never mind.'

'*What*, for God's sake? Tell me.'

She scratched her head and clapped her hands.

'OK. In my opinion . . . In my opinion, which is probably worth nothing . . . you had no chance anyway.'

I could only nod. I had always known that. Since day one. Unsolicited scripts don't get read, no matter how good they are.

'Yeah. You're right.'

Julie looked emboldened and went on. 'I mean, it's not very good, is it?'

My heart stuttered.

'Don't get me wrong,' she said, 'it's not completely awful. Some of it's quite funny . . .'

Quite funny?

'. . . but it just doesn't work. As a whole. It doesn't hang together. And the end's a bit of a mess, isn't it?'

'Yeah,' I said, maybe a little too quickly. 'You're right. It's hopeless. Anyway, lookit, I have to go. I'm due in the pub soon.'

'I've said too much, oh shit . . .'

'No. Don't worry. I knew. I knew all along.'

'Will you be—'

'Gotta go.'

I exited, apace.

As promised, Go-go had made the necessary phone calls. They were all there when I arrived, at a corner table. I was late. I'd been thinking.

'Hello,' I said, dragging a stool over. 'And how are we all?'

A chorus of fines and grands and not-a-bothers.

'Sheila,' I nodded. 'Keeping well?'

'A-1. And yourself?'

'Never better. Any improvement on the nose, Norm?'

'He adjusted his bandage. 'I may never smell again.'

'You smell *now*,' Stevie said, wafting his hand around.

Laughs all round, even from Norm.

'So – anyone for a pint?' I asked.

'Just got some,' Go-go said. 'Sure, get yourself one.'

'Thanks very much,' I said and went over to the bar.

Leonard ignored me for several minutes, of course. I stood waiting for his attention, taking deep breaths. It wasn't happening. The mental collapse. And it wasn't going to happen. I could feel it. The script debacle didn't matter – a downward blip on an ultimately upward trend. Its *raison d'être* was gone now. I didn't need an artificial escape any more. And if Catherine didn't show, that wouldn't matter either, for the same reason. I don't need her any more, I told myself. She was just a symbol. Nothing more. Now that I'm free, now that the slate is clean, I can start again, I can get a job that suits me, I can—

'Fuck my luck.'

I turned, slowly.

'First I lose my job,' Catherine said. 'And now this. I run into *you* morons in the pub.'

Forget what I said about symbols.

I have been known to get things wrong.